all too well

All Too Well

Here and Now

Against All Odds

Come What May

all too well

NEW YORK TIMES BESTSELLING AUTHOR
CORINNE MICHAELS

All Too Well

Cover Design: Sommer Stein, Perfect Pear Creative
Editing: James Gallagher, Evident Ink
Proofreading: Julia Griffis & Michele Ficht

Dear Reader,

It is always my goal to write a beautiful love story that will capture your heart and leave a lasting impression. However, I want all readers to be comfortable. Therefore, if you want to be aware of any possible CW please click the link below to take you to the book page where there is a link that will dropdown. If you do not need this, please go forth and I hope you love this book filled with all the pieces of my heart.

https://corinnemichaels.com/books/all-too-well/

dedication

To Tyler, thank you for providing me with an accurate look at former college athletes when they reach middle-age and still think they're in their 20s.

one
Ainsley

~Four Years Earlier~

"You should talk to him, Ainsley," my mother urges as we stand in the kitchen of Lachlan's childhood home.

Lachlan West—my brother Caspian's best friend and, if I'm honest, my friend—is outside alone, holding a bottle of alcohol, his head lowered.

Today we buried his mother, who had been a part of my life for as long as I can remember.

My heart is breaking for him.

The house was filled with family and friends, but they've all left. My mother and I stayed to put food away and clean up. I'm standing at the French doors while the man I secretly love grieves.

I turn to her, grabbing the towel off the counter to dry dishes. "And say what?"

My mother gives me a soft smile. "You'll know."

No, I never know with him—that's the issue. Everyone loves to tell me how great I am in difficult situations, that I always know what to say, but most of the time I feel just as awkward as anyone else. I just . . . at least try.

However, in the last three years, things have changed so much between us. I'm no longer the annoying little girl who follows him and Caspian around. I'm a grown woman, in college, and desperately in love with him.

That last part is the real crux of the issue, because he's definitely not in love with me.

She nudges me toward the door, and I sigh because I can't watch him suffer. I open the glass door and walk barefoot onto the cool stone walkway.

He looks over, eyes glazed from the alcohol. "I don't want to talk."

I nod. "Good. I don't either." I grab the bottle from his hand and take a swig. Dear God, is he drinking acid? I cough, because it tastes like burnt wood, and hand it back.

Lachlan laughs and shakes his head. "Amateur."

"Sorry, I've spent my college days actually going to class—not drinking sludge."

"Good. You're too smart to waste your life away."

"Or I'm a dork, like you've said a hundred times." I sway, bumping into his shoulder.

"You're not a dork."

"That's the booze talking."

He looks at me, really looks at me, and shakes his head. "It's not."

Well, there's an improvement.

We both sit on the bench Lachlan bought his mother six years ago so she'd come out to the garden she loved so much. This was truly the one place she felt joy in this house. I grew up next door, and I can remember her little bamboo hat floating around her yard as she trimmed hedges and sang.

This place is like a magazine-worthy arboretum, complete with stone arches.

I rest my head on his shoulder and sigh. "I used to love sneaking over here to read. I always worried your mom would toss me out."

He snorts. "Please, she built you a freaking nook with a swing."

I grin. "She didn't do that for me."

He turns, forcing me to sit up. "She did. I had to install it because she wanted you to have a tranquil spot where you thought you could hide easier."

"That's so sweet."

I wish I could thank her. I wish I could ask her a hundred questions, have another slice of her cake or cookies. So many things that Isabelle will no longer be able to give to this world.

"She thought you were special," he says softly.

"Most people do."

"Most people are right."

"Are you saying *you* think I'm special?" I tease.

"No, I think you're Painsley."

I huff, hating that stupid nickname more than ever. I'm not a pain, I'm . . . unique and completely lovable.

Instead of going at him, like I normally do, I let the jab go and return to resting my head on his shoulder.

He takes another long drink from the bottle, and I can feel the sadness coming off him in waves.

I wish I could fix this. I would take all this hurt and carry it if it meant he wouldn't be in this much pain.

"Lach, you don't have to do this all on your own, you know? We're here for you, we love you."

He scoffs. "I'm always doing it on my own. Always."

"That's not true," I say softly. "You have support."

"You don't get it, Ainsley. I do this on my own. All of it. I'm raising Rose alone. I was alone when my father deployed all the damn time and Mom would shut herself off because he left her."

The order of that statement is a little off, and also very skewed, but he's grieving and drunk.

However, Lachlan's father didn't leave. In fact, their marriage was one that I always admired. Two people who loved each other so deeply that when his father had to deploy with the navy, she felt his loss in her soul.

Where my parents barely tolerate each other and I'm pretty sure my mother is going to leave as soon as I'm done with college.

"Okay, let's say that's true. That doesn't change the fact that you have people who love you and want to be here for you."

He drinks more and then places the bottle on the ground. "I would never abandon the people I love."

"I know."

"You can't know. You can't see it. You can't understand that all I want is to be a good man, better than my father. To give the people in my life stability, and all I do is fuck that up."

He's loyal beyond measure. When Lachlan cares about someone, he does it with his whole heart. It's what made him the incredible father he is. He walked away from a chance at playing professional football and became a firefighter in a small town in Virginia because he wanted to give Rose the life he never had.

One where your father isn't constantly absent because of his naval career.

I reach forward, resting my hand on his arm. "That's not true. You're not fucking anything up. You're an amazing dad to Rose. She adores you."

"She's two."

"And she loves you, Lachlan."

He gets to his feet, pacing in the small space. "Because she doesn't know any better."

He's not making sense. "Well, I know better. I know who you are, and there is nothing but goodness inside of you."

He laughs once and drops his head back, staring up at the sky. "You wouldn't say that if you knew what I thought half the time."

I stand, moving closer to him. "What does that mean?"

Lachlan turns his head to stare at me. "You should go home, Ainsley. Please."

"Why?"

"Because I'm piss drunk, and you shouldn't be out here with me alone."

"You would never hurt me," I say, feeling as though I'm missing something.

"That's not why you should go. It's not hurt I want to cause."

Slowly, as though time is in the process of becoming

suspended, something changes. His eyes aren't full of anger, but something else. Something I've never seen. There's a charge in the air and my stomach drops.

Is he . . . does he . . . want to kiss me?

No. That can't be.

It's me who lives in this wild desire-filled haze around him.

Not Lachlan. I'm that annoying brat he had to have tag along when he was with Caspian.

I step back a little, and that look fades just a bit.

"What do you want then?"

"I want things with you I shouldn't want," he says aloud.

"What things?" I ask, unsure if he meant to say that.

He steps forward. "You."

"You want me?" I move back.

"Every fucking minute, and I hate myself for it." Another step forward.

My stomach tightens a little and I stand my ground. "What if I want you too?"

He shakes his head slightly. "You shouldn't."

I don't know that I'll ever get a moment like this again. If it's a dream or a chance or something else, I need to take it. I step to him, pressing my hand to his cheek. "Lachlan." I say his name with all the love in my heart.

Since I was fourteen, I've dreamed of him, wanted him, and never thought there'd ever be a chance for this.

He leans forward, resting our foreheads together. "It never makes sense."

"What doesn't?" I whisper, not wanting to break this connection.

"That I can't have you."

I suck in a breath, tension rolling through me and settling in my belly.

Instead of pulling away, like I normally would, I shift forward so he has no choice but to look at me. When his dark-brown eyes open, I see the longing there.

I lift my hand and cup his jaw. He doesn't move, allowing

me to touch him in a way I've imagined a million times. I think
. . . I think he wants to kiss me, and heaven knows I want to
kiss him.

"You have me now."

I inch up on my toes, not letting my mind do the talking this
time, allowing my heart to lead, and press my lips to his.

He moves quickly, lifting me in his arms. My legs wrap
around his waist, and then the cold stones are against my back.
He's kissing me, his tongue delving into my mouth, and heat
floods my veins.

Lachlan grips the skin at my waist, his body pushing me into
the wall. We kiss and kiss, and gone are the nerves, now replaced
with bliss.

He's kissing me.

I keep saying it in my head because it doesn't feel real or
possible.

The whiskey taste on his tongue mixed with his cologne is an
aphrodisiac that I could get drunk on.

Lachlan West is kissing me.

He moans, and I let his silky strands slide through my fingers
like sand. Every sensation I commit to memory. The way he
smells, the oak, tobacco, and chocolate scent that is all him. The
feel of his calluses against my skin, slightly scratchy but absolutely
perfect.

"Lachlan," I sigh.

He groans and kisses me quiet again.

I don't know how long this goes for, but I hope it never ends.

"Fuck, Ainsley." His hand moves to my stomach, then lower.
Everything inside me clenches in anticipation, and then, without
warning, he pulls back.

His eyes seem to focus, and it's as though he sees it's me.

My legs fall from his waist, hitting the ground with a slap, and
he takes two large steps back.

"What am I doing?" he asks, running his hands through his
hair.

I open my mouth, but nothing comes out. What happened?

We were having this amazing kiss, and now he looks as though he wants to throw himself in his mother's fountain.

"We can't do this. You . . . I'm . . . Jesus, I'm sorry. I'm drunk and we . . . I'm such a fucking asshole."

He turns his back to me, grabs the bottle on the ground, takes a large sip, and spits it out. Like he can wash the taste of me from his mouth.

I'm standing here now, feeling the tingle of my lips, the smell of him embedded in my nose, and I would love for nothing more than to not see that look on his face.

"Lachlan, I'm sorry."

That causes him to snap his gaze to me. "For what? You didn't do anything."

"I kissed you."

He pinches the bridge of his nose. "I'm drunk."

"I know."

"I never should've kissed you," he says, still not looking at me.

And I never should've come out here. I'm so stupid. I thought he wanted me, that he felt something, but he was just drunk.

God, I can never look at him again. I've ruined everything.

"It's my fault." I choke the words out, fighting back tears of embarrassment and self-loathing.

"No, it's . . ." He looks up to the sky. "Fuck!"

I stand here, my feet feeling as though they've been cemented to the ground. I want to run. To hide in my room and close the blinds so I never have to see this garden again.

"I should go."

I wasn't planning to go back to NYU for another three days. My parents asked me to stay and attend a ceremony for the Admiral, but there's not a chance in hell I'm staying in this town another minute. My father will have to forgive me.

"That never should've . . ."

I lift my hand. "Please give Rose a hug and tell her I said goodbye."

I turn to leave, knowing those tears aren't going to stay away for another second.

As soon as I open the door, he calls my name.

I don't turn. I can't. Already my vision is blurry, and I won't let him see me that way.

He speaks to my back this time. "We'll talk about this tomorrow. When I'm sober."

There won't be a chance to do that, because I won't be here. I kissed him, he rejected me, and now I can never go back to the way things were.

"Goodbye, Lachlan."

Then I close the door and leave my heart in the garden with the boy who it has always belonged to.

two
Ainsley

~*Present*~

"Does anyone else have any stories they'd like to pitch?" my boss, Mr. Krispen, asks.

I've learned if I'm the first one, I'm always shot down, so I bide my time, waiting for the sacrificial lamb to go forth.

I wait.

I wait some more.

I glance around, waiting to see if any of my coworkers are going to say anything, but they don't.

It's like a game of chicken. They're waiting for me, and I'm going to wait them out.

"No one here has a single idea?" he asks again, his eyes finding mine. "I find that hard to believe."

Of course he does, because Mr. Krispen knows me. I mean, he knows I'm a little eager beaver who just wants to do well. However, for the last six months I've been relegated to writing absolutely horrible pieces.

Well, horrible to a girl who is ready to tackle the world.

First, I was assigned a story about whether white really is a faux pas after Labor Day. Spoiler alert, it's not. Then I got to write a piece about the proper steps for skin care in your early thirties. Which might sound great, but I'm twenty-six. Last month I wrote about hats. Yes, hats.

Therefore, this time, I'm going to keep my big mouth shut and wait for the perfect opening.

I give him a tight-lipped smile, hoping he'll move on to Tori, his golden child reporter who does not have to write the crap I do.

The difference between Tori and me is that I don't know how to keep my mouth shut and she does.

It might also be that Tori has been here for five years and has contacts at the Pentagon, but . . . we'll go with option one.

He continues to surf the room and then lands back on me. Shit.

Stay quiet. Stay quiet. Stay . . . quiet . . .

"I have two ideas," I say before I'm able to stop myself.

One day I'll learn. It's not today, though.

He grins like he knew this was exactly what would happen. "All right, let's hear it, Ainsley."

"I'd like to do a story about Senator Erickson and the allegations of his family ties to the terror ring overseas."

That was my second-choice story, and since he always shoots me down, my hope is that he'll follow his usual process, and then I can write what I really want to write about, which is the tension around the newly proposed bill to add term limits to judges and all public officials.

It's not getting a lot of attention, and if we could get it into the public eye, it could gain traction, which is exactly what the politicians do not want.

"No," Mr. Krispen says immediately.

My plan is working.

"I see, and why not?"

He leans back. "Because we are a small-press paper that doesn't have the resources to go overseas. When Carson Knight bought us out, we were lucky we didn't get completely shut down. Not to mention, you've been here six months, and that would be a major piece that would go to someone more senior than you. Instead, I'd like you to take the story about the new dating app."

I would rather shove bamboo splints up my nails. "Mr. Krispen, while I think that story probably is just . . . amazing, I was thinking a little something different this time. You know, freshen things up a bit."

He nods slowly. "Like politics and senators who you want to make a connection to a terrorist ring?"

"I don't want to make a connection that isn't there," I defend. "I just want to make sure he's not *already* tied to it."

Aiden, the golden journalist who has been here for two months longer than me, snorts. "I'd like to take a crack at it."

I fight back the urge to poke him with a pencil. Not the pointy end, the eraser side, right in his ear.

My boss looks as though he'd like to poke me with his pencil —the pointy side, though. "No."

I need to refocus him on the point that writing about shoes, dating apps, and hats is just not what we should be focusing on. It's been months of the worst stories, and I need to break into the upper leagues. No more playing in the lowers—or minors? I can't remember.

I clear my throat. "If Senator Erickson is out, what about a story regarding the bill that was proposed regarding term limits? That would require no budgetary constraints."

Mr. Krispen leans back, steepling his hands in front of him. "That story could be good for our circulation. There are a lot of discussions going around since it was brought forth. A lot of the bigger publications are covering it."

I fight back my excitement, not letting my emotions show. "I agree," I say calmly. Inside, though, I'm doing a freaking jig.

Finally.

I'm going to get to write something other than gossip shit and dumb stories that no one gives a shit about. Last week I had to write about school lunches and whether they are really healthy.

Guess how many people that probably attracted?

One. And it was my dad.

He turns to Aiden. "You'll take the story. I want the first draft on my desk by next Thursday."

My jaw falls open. "But, Mr. Krispen, it was my idea."

"Yes, and I'm giving it to the strongest writer on the team."

The tightness in my chest is making it hard to breathe. "Sir, it was my pitch."

He crosses his arms over his chest. "I'm aware of that, Ainsley. My job is to make sure the best stories are written by the most qualified reporters. You've never handled a story of that magnitude."

Because he won't let me.

Ugh. I could scream.

Instead, I think about the Admiral's advice to always be the consummate professional. No one likes a complainer, as he says.

"I understand that, but it's not for lack of trying. How about Aiden and I both write the story, and you can choose the better version?"

He shakes his head. "Absolutely not. I need an array of options for circulation, and I can't sacrifice two writers on one story."

It's not like my stories are worth a damn, but now that my two ideas were shot down, I'm going to need to come up with something that isn't . . . ChapStick versus lipstick or some other crap.

Tori speaks up. "Ainsley can take my story, Mr. Krispen."

Oh, hell no. I'm sure it's terrible if she's offering it to me. I share a pointed look with my best friend, Caroline.

"I'm sure you don't want to do that, Tori."

She shakes her head. "I truly don't mind. I have several options that were approved already."

Of course she does.

"Which one, Tori?"

"Well, I know that Ainsley is working so hard to really diversify her portfolio. I think the story I could part with is about the

Heisman Trophy winner who became a fireman and saved a little girl in that small town."

Seriously, I will die.

Because that Heisman Trophy–winning fireman is none other than Lachlan West.

For the last two weeks his face has been plastered on the news for his heroic rescue. I've done my best not to drool at the television—and failed.

Four years and zero contact since that disastrous kiss and you'd think my heart would be immune, but no, it's worse.

"I don't think that would be a story I'd be good at," I say with a shake of my head.

Aiden speaks next. "He was amazing. I thought he'd go in the first round of the draft."

Mr. Krispen nods slowly. "I remember him. When his team played in the national championship, I thought for sure he'd go into the draft."

"Isn't he from your hometown, Ainsley?" Tori asks.

"Hmm?" I try to play stupid.

"He's from Virginia Beach. I swear I saw your name in the yearbook when I was doing my research."

I shrug, not saying a word.

"I still can't believe he gave it all up," Aiden adds in. "I wonder why."

Under my breath I whisper, "I know why."

For the first time Mr. Krispen hears something I say. Of course it's when I don't want him to. "You know him, Ainsley?"

I have two choices: I can lie and be caught, or I can just fess up and find a way out of any possibility of writing this story.

"I do. I mean, I know of him."

Caroline's eyes narrow, and I pray she keeps her big mouth shut.

I didn't have to worry about that because Tori's big mouth speaks first. "Really? I saw in there that your brother was next to him in, like, every picture."

I sigh. "Yes, I know. My brother is friends with him."

Mr. Krispen clears his throat. "Then you'll write the article, Ainsley. If you know him, that'll make things easy."

My jaw drops and I sputter. "Mr. Krispen, I really can't."

"Why not?"

Because I'm in love with him and he kissed me four years ago, after which I ran and haven't seen him since.

"Because . . ." I pause, trying to come up with something plausible. "Because . . . I'm sure many other journalists have already written something. We need something fresh and new. He's been on the news all week, so, you know, we'll look behind on our coverage."

None of that is untrue.

"Find a different angle then. You have a Heisman Trophy winner who is now a fireman? I want the story on my desk by the end of the month. Wow me, Ainsley."

Wow him? Right. "I just don't think I . . ."

Caroline cuts me off. "I think Ainsley was worried you would want it to be focused on the fire, but I think she's going to absolutely find the right angle."

He nods once. "Yes, focus on the sports angle."

Aiden scoffs. "Wait, you want Ainsley to write about sports?"

My pride takes a hit, and when I see Tori's grin, I know that no matter what, I'm going to write this damn story.

"I know all about the sportsball, Aiden."

"Sure you do, since you just called it sportsball."

"Whatever. I can totally do it. It'll be the best story you've ever read."

It'll be something, that's for sure. Yeah, I know. I'm not the most likely of journalists for the job, but I will be so good. I'll learn everything, find a new, fresh angle, and I'll slay this story.

I hope.

Tori sighs dramatically. "You know, I'll do it. I don't know that Ainsley can handle it."

I can feel the stinging in the back of my eyes, but I won't let the tears come. No way will I cry in front of the entire team. Not. A. Fucking. Chance.

I get to my feet, once again my mouth running away before my brain can catch up. "Absolutely not. I know that I can write an amazing story. One that this paper will be proud of."

Mr. Krispen brings his hands to his mouth and purses his lips. "You're sure you can do this?"

"I know I can."

"You want to write about sports?"

No, but it's all I have. "Yes, and I'll show you that I can cover a multitude of topics, and hopefully, next time I pitch an idea, you'll consider me for that."

"If I give this to you and you don't deliver, you know you're writing about shoes and scarfs from now on?" Mr. Krispen asks.

If I screw this up, he can fire me. Although I have enough self-preservation to keep that to myself.

"All right, Ainsley. You have the article. Good luck."

I'm going to need it when I show up on Lachlan West's doorstep after four years.

Everyone filters out except for Caroline, who leans against the table, laughter in her eyes. "You're going to write about sports?"

"Apparently. I mean, it can't be that hard to learn about football or whatever."

It's better than having to write about Lachlan the child-saving hero.

"Oh, honey, you thought the baseball team in New York was a football team and that there were innings in the hockey game."

"How was I supposed to know it was quarters?" I ask, confused.

She slaps her forehead. "Periods. They have periods, not quarters."

Right. I swear they explained that at the game the other night. I went because it was free. The paper has tickets or something, and they gave them to Aiden, who gave them to Caroline.

I had no idea how freaking cold it was going to be in the arena. That was an unpleasant surprise. Although it *is* ice hockey.

Still, one would think the part where fans are would be comfortable and I wouldn't need a damn coat.

"At least I learned all about icing."

She rolls her eyes. "Yes, every penalty called you just yelled . . . icing."

I shrug. "Well, they called it a lot."

"And do you even know what it is now?"

She thinks she's so smug. I totally know what it is. "It's when the ball—"

"Puck."

"Goes past that line back by the guy in the cage—"

"Net," Caroline says with a sigh. "For fuck's sake this conversation is painful."

"Right. And the other players are too slow to get to the other line. Was it red? Or blue? Anyway, it's a line and they weren't there."

Caroline lifts her head to the ceiling before looking back at me. "You are the absolute last person in the entire world who should write about sports."

"Not the point. I wanted this assignment. It's finally my chance to prove that I'm a capable and intelligent journalist who can handle any type of story that hits my desk. I graduated summa cum laude from NYU, and I'm going to go to Ember Falls, get what I need, and write a killer article."

When I got this job, I had a plan to get some bylines and then work for a much more reputable publication. It's not that this place is bad, per se, just not exactly respected as a newspaper.

Still, I had bills, and my father refused to give me any assistance after school. So here I am, making a living.

Caroline smiles. "I know you will."

I let out a long sigh and lean against the cubicle wall. "I'm going to do amazing, right?"

"You're going to do better than that. What's your plan?"

"First, I need to research his football career, because all I know about him is as my brother's best friend. Is there, like, a football for dummies?"

"Yes, but even that might be too advanced for you."
I stick my tongue out at her. "Shut up."
"Well, have fun in Ember Falls."
"Yeah, I will have the most fun ever."
And isn't that the understatement of the year?

three
Lachlan

"Daddy, I don't want to go to school today," Rose complains as I'm tying her shoes.

"Why not? You love school."

She purses her lips. "Because Briggs is mean."

"How is he mean?"

"He always takes my crayons and then breaks them. And this time he said you weren't a hero, but you are."

I fight back a smile because I was so that kid growing up. I'm not proud of it, but . . . I was a punk ass. My dad was always deploying, and my mother didn't know what the hell to do with me. I was wild and she was also—checked out.

I got away with too much, and since Caspian was as much of a troublemaker as I was, the two of us were absolute terrors to our classmates, and mostly it was his sister who got the brunt of it.

"Well, I'm not a hero. I just did my job."

Her shoulders rise and fall dramatically. "I hate him."

"Did you tell him to knock it off or you'd punch his lights out?" I ask.

Rose shakes her head. "I can't punch him. He's a boy and I'll get in trouble."

I don't encourage violence, but Briggs has been picking on her since school started, and sometimes it's just the way to get a bully to stop.

"Want me to do it?" I ask, partially joking.

Rose sighs dramatically. At six years old, she already has more attitude than I know what to do with. "No, Daddy, I just want to stay home with you."

I finish her shoes and stay in my squat, both hands on the side of her chair. "What would happen when there was a fire? Who would watch you?"

"I'm a big girl. I can stay home all by myself."

"You are a big girl, but not that big. Plus, I'm not a very good teacher."

Rose leans forward, taking my face in her hands. "Please?"

God, this kid has me wrapped around her finger. Still, home-schooling is a bit out of my realm of possibilities. "Sorry, kid, that's not happening. School for you."

Her lower lip juts out, and a part of me, a very small part, debates giving in. She looks so damn cute like that.

Then I remember that I can't do math at all, and don't ask me what a dangling participle or any of that shit is. I can tell you the internal temperature of a house fire and what back draft actually looks like.

However, none of that is applicable to Rose as a six-year-old.

I let out a heavy sigh and wait for her to look at me. "Rose, you are a smart, beautiful, and strong girl. Don't let anyone ever make you feel like you don't belong. If Briggs takes your crayon, take it back and tell the teacher."

"He said I'm a tattletale if I do that."

"And tell him he's a bully."

"What's a bully, Daddy?"

I smile at her and tap her nose. "Someone who is mean because they can be. I'd rather be a tattletale than a bully."

She nods once, and I get up and extend my hand. Rose takes it and hops off the chair, and then we head out to my truck. Once she's all buckled up, we head into town.

"Look at the big horse!" She points to the stables that are

about halfway to her school. They just got two Clydesdale horses after a barn fire a few towns over. We went to assist and asked Bill and Sandy, who operate the stables, whether they could take them until the owners come up with another plan.

The people in Ember Falls never hesitate to help someone in need.

It's why I love it here so much.

"I see. Maybe after school we can go see them?"

She claps her hands. "Yay!"

It's so easy to make this kid happy. I drop her off at school and pull her teacher aside, letting her know about the issue between Rose and Briggs.

"I'll keep an eye out, Lachlan," Ms. Moss assures me, standing a bit too close. Not that it's abnormal, since Pam has been incredibly obvious about what she hopes for out of our relationship. It's definitely not a parent-teacher thing. "I didn't see you at the fire hall for the party last night. I was really hoping you'd be there . . ."

"Sorry, I was busy with Rose."

She purses her lips. "Aww, maybe next time."

"Maybe," I lie.

"We could always make plans for just the two of us."

I don't know how many times I have to explain that's not going to happen.

Dating for me is not a priority. I'm completely fine being single and having my sole focus on Rose. She's probably the only kid I'm ever going to have, and that's perfectly fine by me.

Her mother and I were a one-night thing, and she gave me the option to either take Rose and raise her or put her up for adoption. I didn't hesitate in taking my daughter.

"I'm not sure that's a good idea. I work crazy hours, and you're Rose's teacher. It's better we keep things as they are." Her face falls and I quickly try to smooth things over. "You know how people talk. I wouldn't want to make things awkward for either of us."

She forces a smile. "I get it."

I don't think she does, but it's fine.

"I need to get to the station. Thank you for monitoring the Briggs-and-Rose thing."

"Of course."

I quickly get out of Dodge and make the fifteen-minute drive to the station. When I get there, my three night guys are heading out of the building.

"Hey, guys, quiet night?"

Lopez lifts his chin. "Sure was, Chief."

"Quiet is good."

Davidson huffs. "It would be nice to do something other than clean up after these two asshats."

Jones flips him off. "Yeah, right, motherfucker. It's you who leaves your shit everywhere."

"Now, ladies, let's not fight." I do my best to stop the argument before it gets heated.

They laugh and Lopez speaks again. "I get what he's saying, but I'm happy with quiet as well."

"Good man." I clasp his shoulder. "I'll be switching you guys to days as of next week, unless you'd prefer to stay on nights."

We're a small department, and the one thing I hated when I started here was the rigid schedule. The former chief didn't rotate any of us and that was my first change as the new chief. A lot of them are way overdue for doctor's appointments, and God only knows what else that working nights makes even harder to take care of.

"I'm good with nights, boss. It's with the kids," Jones explains.

"Okay. What about you guys?"

"Who would clean up after Jones if we switched?" Davidson jokes.

I laugh because I should've known better. These three never take the option to switch and work well together.

"All right then. Nights for another month."

They head to their cars, and I enter the station. I check in on the day shift crew, making sure everyone is doing well before going to my office.

There isn't a lot of work to do in a town this size, but as the newly appointed chief, it's my responsibility to make sure everything is ready in case of an emergency. My firefighters are always on the ready, and this month I'm instituting a new set of weekly drills to be run by the captains of each shift.

Today I get to tell them about it and hear the grumbling.

I grab the paperwork and schedule, then head to the bunk room and find them doing what they're always doing—gossiping.

"Did you hear about the girl staying at Brickman's lodge?" one of them asks.

"The lodge? For what?"

"The asshole put it up as a short-term rental. He was in the coffee shop talking about how much he got for it."

I shiver at that thought. The cabin is old, dingy, and there's not a chance in hell it's up to code.

I go inside and see my day guys sitting around. "What's up, fellas?" I say.

"Chief." They stand as I enter.

I really hate this. I was a captain as of two weeks ago, but since the fire and additional press coverage, the mayor decided I should get the vacant chief spot.

Which is ridiculous because I'm one of the youngest officers on the squad, and I'm definitely not the most qualified. However, publicity dictated it.

"Who is renting the Brickman cabin?" I ask.

"Oh, he's calling it a lodge now, as though that'll class it up. Anyway, some girl from New York or something. She saw the listing, and I can only imagine what her face looked like when she actually saw the place," one of my captains says with a laugh.

"Did he get approval to rent it out?"

Considering it would have to go through the fire department, I can't imagine anyone would've signed off on it.

He shrugs. "No clue. Either way, the girl showed up late last night. He was talking about it at the coffee shop this morning."

I sigh. "If he doesn't have it permitted, he can't do that."

"Are you going to tell the mayor's son that?" Don, my other captain, counters.

If it's between someone getting injured in that shithole or pissing off the mayor, I'll battle the old guy any day.

"That's not the point. Who signed off on the certificate of occupancy?"

All of them look to one another, and either they've never seen a permit request or one of them knows I'm about to chew their asses and make them do a whole host of chores until I feel less murderous.

Don speaks. "We can find out if it was submitted and if anyone from the station approved it."

I nod. "Let's do that. I'll head down there and make sure whoever is there is at least safe."

Without another word, I leave, get in my truck, and make my way to the cabin. It's about two miles from my house, but back in the woods. Last time I was there was because a bunch of high school kids were drinking and lit a bonfire. We headed out because we got the reports of smoke and thought for sure the place finally had gone up in flames.

Too bad that didn't happen if he's got someone paying to live there.

When I pull up, there's a newer luxury car with New York plates parked out front, and I can see the smoke coming out of the wood-burning stove because . . . there's no heat and the only electricity is off the generator out back.

We're still in that weird time of year where it's cold in the morning and then it warms up out of nowhere. I swear, Mother Nature is a moody bitch lately.

I walk up to the door and knock.

I can't imagine anyone actually paying to stay in this place, especially driving a new car.

"Who's there?" a vaguely familiar feminine voice calls from the other side.

"This is the fire department. Can you please open the door?"

"No, thank you. I'm fine."

I jerk my head back. Well, okay. "Ma'am, I need to check on the safety of the electrical panel as well as any fire alarms installed."

"I see them. We're good."

Is this woman for real? I knock again. "Please don't make me call the police department and have them come."

I hear a grunt, and then the door flies open only to have me rock back on my heels. It's been four years since I've seen Ainsley MacKinley. The woman I've loved for far too long. The woman whose heart I broke, breaking my own at the same time.

For four years I've kept away from her, pretending she was still the girl next door who was much too young.

This girl—this *woman*—is nothing like that image, and it knocks me on my ass.

Instead, Ainsley is slender with curves in every place a woman should have them. Her hair is long, pulled to the side in a braid, and she's wearing leggings and a crop top with glasses perched on her nose.

Only they don't make her look dorky. She looks smart and fucking stunning.

"Hi, Lach. Good to see you. Sorry, I'm working and I didn't know that you were stopping by. As you can see, the place is perfectly lovely and safe. I'm sure I'll see you around."

Before the most beautiful pain in my ass can shut the door, I push my hand out to stop it from closing. "Why in the hell are you in Ember Falls, and what in God's name are you doing staying in this shithole of a cabin, Ainsley?"

four
Ainsley

The nerve.

The freaking balls on this guy. Not that I'm looking at that region. No, I'm smiling and imagining that I can shoot fire out of my eyeballs as I come face-to-face with Lachlan and all his . . . deliciousness.

Seriously, he's so damn hot. More than my mind let me remember. He's tall and broad shouldered. Every part of him is better than the stupid dreams that have haunted me. His jaw tics as he waits for an answer.

I force the brightest smile I can muster. "I'm here for work."

"And staying *here*?"

"It's the only accommodations I could find on short notice."

I mean, there was that seedy motel. In hindsight, I should've done the hourly place, maybe that would've had hot water. Instead, I'm in this . . . cabin, if you can even call it that. It's definitely not the lodge it was described as online.

But I'm a grown woman. The Admiral used to take us camping every summer, and I can hack it. I'm strong.

Even though I want to pack my bags and run.

"Why wouldn't you call me?"

I blink. "I was going to once I was settled in."

I don't really have a choice since I'm writing an article on him, but that's beside the point.

The real reason is that I didn't want to face him. I've done my absolute best to forget him, and I've done a good job of it.

I've been able to avoid the man, my mistakes, and my absolute embarrassment of the fact that I misread the night of his mother's funeral so freaking much.

That night is burned into my brain, and I would've given anything for a touch of selective amnesia.

He was sad, hurt, and drunk, but I kissed him. I lifted up on my toes, thinking he really wanted me. I have never felt that level of mortification.

Lachlan runs his hands through his thick brown hair. "It's been a long time."

"Yes, but, like I said, I was going to call or come by later. I just needed to unpack."

Which honestly wasn't even my thought, because I cannot stay here. However, now I sort of need to do it, because I don't have another option.

"Ainsley . . . we should talk."

"Yes, we definitely should. I'm not ready for an interview yet, but I'd love to set up a time we can meet."

At that he jerks his head back. "Interview?"

"Yes, I'm here for you." *Yeah, that doesn't sound stupid at all. Way to go, Ainsley.* I clear my throat. "I mean that I'm here for my paper."

"I'm not following," Lachlan says slowly.

I'm just screwing this up at every turn. "I work for a small press out of New York, and I'm here because we'd love to do a piece about you."

"No."

That went just about the way I expected, but it still stings. Lachlan always hated attention, which was ironic since he was so amazing at football. He spent many of his high school days talking to scouts, the school newspaper, and the local town jotter, and he loathed it.

Well, now I'm here to change the narrative. I'm going to make this a better experience so I can stop writing about hats and makeup.

"Listen, I know there's some resistance to this, but it'll be painless. I can just follow you around, take notes—you won't even know I'm here."

He huffs at that. "I don't think that's going to happen. We haven't seen each other or talked in four years, and you just want to show up and follow me around?"

I don't want any of this. I would've been perfectly fine carrying on with my life for the next four years pretending Lachlan West was a figment of my imagination. However, thanks to my asshole coworkers, I can't do that.

"I mean, I think it's the best plan."

"We should talk about that night," he suggests again, and I lift my hand.

"That's all in the past, Lach. I'm really fine. I'm just here to work."

I just dream about it daily.

Hurt flashes in his eyes, and God, this stupid girl in me wants to soothe it. To be the girl he used to come to when he was sad. "Ainsley, you've avoided me for years. I miss . . . I want to talk and . . . Jesus, why is this so hard with you? You were my friend too. I tried to talk to you and you ghosted me."

He missed me?

No. Do not go there.

Lachlan West is that guy who I was never allowed to like but did anyway, and I am way too weak when it comes to him.

When I started high school, I thought maybe, just maybe, he would stop seeing me as Caspian's sister. The annoying girl who followed the two of them around like a rabbit on a string. I wanted that so damn much, but it didn't happen.

Instead, I became a new kind of annoying. The one who was caught staring at him just a little too long. The girl who wanted to comfort him when his mom died and found him alone in the garden, holding a bottle of whiskey, and he kissed me—no, no, I kissed him.

I must keep the facts straight.

Also, I don't want to talk about that night. I want him to pull me into his arms, look into my eyes, and tell me it's always been me for him. That he loves me and the last four years have been the worst of his life.

However, we're not living in a fantasy world.

"Can we just *not* talk about it? Please? After we finish with this article, we can hash it all out." Or I'll just get in my car and disappear again.

It's for the best.

He leans against the doorjamb and sighs. "Caspian mentioned you were a journalist, but I never thought you'd be standing here because of work."

You and me both.

However, the Fates are not on my side.

"I am. I love it there and I have a great job."

Lachlan grins. "Good, I'm happy for you."

"Thanks."

"So, you're writing an article on me?"

Ugh. I guess this is as good of a time as any. "I am, and I'd like to talk to you regarding the piece."

"What exactly is this article about? Because the fire was weeks ago, and I promise, there's nothing new there."

I smile. "I saw that. You were amazing to run in there and get her."

"It's my job. I could never live with myself, knowing I didn't do everything I could to save that child. I just . . . I saw Rose in that window, and . . ."

I step closer on instinct and then force myself to stop. Touching him is an absolute no go. I will not be that stupid again. No way.

"You saved her, though."

His brown eyes meet mine. "I did, but there were twenty

other firefighters there who would've done the same. I didn't do anything special."

"I disagree, as do most of the public. Which is what brings me here. I don't want to write about the fire. I want to write about you. Your life. What made you come here, to Ember Falls. The man behind the heroic savior."

He rolls his eyes. "You know who I am."

I bristle. "Not really. We've changed a lot. Like, I didn't know you were still playing sports."

When I asked my temporary landlord about Lachlan, he sort of laughed and mentioned that he and his friends are in a league of some sort. If he's still playing sports, this will be great. I can talk about the rise of the great quarterback and how he's still involved in the game.

I can show the human side of sports.

Not that I know a damn thing about that side, but this is what good journalists do—they lie.

His eyes narrow and he pushes off the door. "I'm not sure I know what you're talking about."

I fight back a laugh and keep my face passive. "Really? Because my new friend, Harold Brickman, said you play."

And you're apparently the team captain.

"Nope. I'm not on any sports teams."

I nod. "Okay, I'm sure someone around here knows something."

Lachlan steps back, his lips in a tight line. "Whatever. I need access into the cabin so I can check on things."

I lean against the door. "No, thank you. I'm completely fine here. The owner walked me through things. I saw a fire extinguisher and all is well."

"I really insist."

"I really deny your insistence. How about we make a deal? I'll let you in and you let me interview you."

"No."

I shrug. "Then, I'm sorry, Chief West, now is not a good time for your fire inspection."

He huffs. "Fine. I'll have someone come by in a day or two. Do either of those days work?"

"Any time after today would be perfect. I can't wait to meet some of your firemen."

"I'll be here—not them."

"Even better."

He starts to walk away, muttering under his breath, and I realize I might have overplayed my hand a bit. This story doesn't exist if I can't get him to participate in this interview, so I have to try to get things back to the way they used to be, even if they can never really be the same. "Lach?"

"Yeah?"

"It was good to see you," I say, my voice even and calm. "I hope Rose is good?"

The last time I saw her she was just two years old, but I think about her all the time, and my brother shows me photos.

He smiles at the mention of his daughter. "She's great. She's in school now and is discovering all the fun things that go with that."

It's hard to picture what she must be like now. She was just learning how to talk and was seriously the cutest kid, who loved everyone.

"So she's dealing with the horrors of boys?" I ask with a grin.

"Ironically, yes. A boy is stealing her crayons."

"And you haven't beat him up yet? Wow. You really have matured."

He laughs. "I did tell her to punch him and offered to do it if she wasn't up for it."

Of course he did. "Hopefully she can punch better than you could."

His head jerks back. "I punched just fine, thank you very much."

"Not what I remember. You tried to beat up that one kid in middle school, and he totally kicked your ass," I remind him.

I'm not sure it really went that way, but it's still fun to be the annoying girl I've always been to him.

"If I remember, he had to go to the hospital because I broke his nose," Lachlan counters.

I shrug, not caring about the details. "Maybe have Caspian do the instructing either way. He packs a really mean right hook."

My brother was the best at landing a punch. One too many times I got in the middle of the two of them fighting, and one time I took the end of the punch. I thought my dad was going to murder my brother for hitting me, which was totally an accident. I did my best to hide it, but it was impossible when the black eye came. Caspian was beside himself, and the Admiral thought the punishment of him having to look at the bruise was enough since he would practically break down and cry each time he saw it.

"Does your brother know you're here and staying in this shithole?"

I cross my arms over my chest. "I'm a grown-ass woman who doesn't need to tell my brother where I'm going."

"So that's a no. I doubt he'll be happy when he finds out."

"I doubt I care."

That sounded so much better in my head.

"Some things never change, Berry. I'm sure I'll see you around."

He turns and leaves, and I stand here, seething at the nickname that I never wanted to hear again. I am not a stupid strawberry.

"Yeah, I'm sure you will."

———

After the worst night's sleep ever, I'm ready to tackle my story.

I wanted to go straight to the firehouse, but instead I go to the cute little coffee shop, Prose & Perk, in the center of town. While the ad for the lodge said it had a coffee maker, it is probably from 1997, and I'd rather drink sludge, which is what I'm sure that would be anyway.

I park the car and see a text from Caroline.

· · ·

CAROLINE

So, did you talk to him yet?

I sure did.

CAROLINE

And?

And he's still hot and I love him.

He's not all that interested in the article,
buuuuuut . . . I found out he's still playing
sports!

CAROLINE

Really? That's great! You have the perfect
angle then.

Right! I'm totally going to get to write what I
want after this. I'll wear him down so I can get
the interview, but this is perfect.

CAROLINE

I'm excited for you. You got this.

Thanks! I'm heading in for coffee now and
then to get started on this story so I can get
home.

CAROLINE

Happy writing.

The Main Street area of Ember Falls is picturesque, and I found a spot right outside the coffee shop. The street is lined with old brick buildings with storefront windows and what look like apartments above them. A few stores have more ornate facades to mirror the older look of a more Victorian-style home. There's a pizza place, a printing store, a small handbag boutique, and . . . coffee.

The bell above the door chimes, and I'm taken back in time as soon as I enter.

The tables are all mismatched with random chairs, and the walls are decorated in pages from thousands of books, all layering over each other to create a beautiful wallpaper. At a long counter in the back, it's nothing but shelves of books with bent spines and old leather that create the most comforting scent.

Coffee, books, and happiness.

"Good morning!" a girl calls out from the back.

"Good morning. Where do I go to place an order?" I ask, trying to move toward where I think she is.

She lifts up part of the counter and peeks out. "Sorry, we're a bit hidden back here. Oh, you're new in town!"

I smile. "I am. This place is amazing. I'm so glad I stopped to get some coffee."

"We have plenty of that here. I'm Hazel. It's nice to meet you, and welcome to Prose & Perk."

I get closer and extend my hand. "I'm Ainsley, and it's great to meet you too. Seriously, this place is a booklover's dream."

Hazel glances around with a dreamy look on her face. "It is. It's my happy place."

"Do you own it?"

She nods. "I bought it a year ago. It used to be a bait and tackle shop, but I thought the town needed some sophistication."

"Bait and tackle, huh?" I try not to think too hard about the dead-fish smell that once was emanating here instead of old books and coffee.

Hazel grins. "Trying to imagine the before?"

"More like trying not to," I admit.

She laughs and jerks her head toward the back of the building. "Come on, I make a mean cappuccino and I'm pretty sure that's your drink of choice, right?"

"Good guess."

"It's the shoes," she says with a giggle.

I follow her, leaning against the counter where there are two machines, a grinder, and a row of syrups that would make any flavored-coffee lover squeal. As Hazel starts on the coffee, I continue trying to look at everything.

"So where are you from?"

"New York City."

"You're a long way from home."

I smile and peruse the store. "I am."

Over in the corner is a cute little alcove that seems sort of shielded from the store. It has a partition, but it blends so well it took me a minute to really see it.

She must notice where my gaze has landed, because she speaks. "That's the writer's nook."

"It's adorably hidden."

Hazel smiles. "I always wanted to publish a book, but . . . I can't write for shit. I imagined a place that I'd want to try in. I hate being alone, so it has to be a public space, but libraries sometimes feel stuffy—at least, ours here is a joke. I tried to put everything a writer could want in there, privacy if they want it, people watching if they need it, and just a comfy place to create."

"Do you take reservations?" I ask. It seems like the absolute perfect place for me to work.

"Are you a writer?"

"Journalist, not novels, although I've thought about it."

Hazel hands me the cappuccino. "A journalist in Ember Falls? You must be here about our hero fire chief."

"Yes and no. I am here for Lachlan, but it's not about the fire. We just haven't come to an agreement on how this is going to happen yet."

"Do you know him?"

I smile. "I do. We're old friends. We grew up together in

Virginia Beach when our dads were in the navy."

"Well, color me intrigued."

I glance around the room, admiring everything about this place. "I'm more interested in your shop."

"You're welcome to look around."

"Thank you."

"So, how amazing is it to be a journalist?"

"It's not all that glamorous. Especially when your boss makes you write about hats and colors for the last six months, but this article is my big break, or at least I'm going to make it be one."

"You said you're writing about Lachlan but not the fire?"

I nod. "Yes, about his life and how he's still involved in sports. I'm hoping to find out more regarding the team he's with now."

Hazel's brows shoot up. "Wait, you're writing about the team he plays on now?"

"I am! I'm really excited to write about all the sports." I take a sip of the best coffee I've ever had. "Oh my God, this is amazing."

"I added a splash of brown sugar at the end. It brings a nice little kick."

It's heavenly. Seriously, I'm going to be here as much as I can. "This is absolutely my favorite coffee place I've ever been. I'm definitely going to put this in the article."

Her eyes brighten and she perks up. "Really?"

"Absolutely. Sports and coffee sound like a great mix."

"Well, you're welcome to spend as much time here as you want. I'm sure you're going to enjoy writing about his Ultimate Frisbee league."

She has got to be kidding. "Ultimate *what*?"

Hazel giggles. "Yeah, it's as stupid as it sounds, but they're very competitive. It gets pretty crazy around their tournaments."

"Wait," I say, putting my hand up. "You mean Lachlan West is playing on an Ultimate *Frisbee* team? The Heisman Trophy–winning ball-throwing guy?"

"Same one."

I let out a huff. "Oh. Wow. I didn't even know that was a thing. Who else is on this team?"

"It's mostly a college league, but they allow Lachlan's team in since he's really good at sports. He recruited a few other guys to play. Killian is a millionaire who owns a dating app company, Miles is the third guy, and he's a high school principal, and the last is Everett, who is the town veterinarian—and my best friend. All three of them were draft bound too. It's kinda crazy that they now do *this* for fun, but they love it."

If I didn't have bad luck, I wouldn't have any.

How in the ever-loving hell am I going to make this sound even remotely exciting? Ultimate Frisbee.

"Well," I say with a laugh, and doubt starts to creep in. "Okay then. I guess I have a lot to learn."

This is . . . terrible. I'm never going to be able to make this sound cool or interesting. It's a bunch of old guys who play against college kids.

I'm doomed.

My big break just became a sinking ship of misery.

"You're totally rethinking making the story about the fire, aren't you?" Hazel asks and then leans back.

"Kind of," I admit, my voice going higher at the end. "They want to know where he is now, so I guess this is just what it is. I'll find a way to make it sound more . . . stimulating."

"Then I wish you luck, and you're welcome to my writer's nook anytime."

"Thank you, I'll be back for more of this." I lift the cup.

I pay and then head out to start my investigation to learn more about this league and figure out how to get Lachlan to agree to this story, if there even is one.

———

"This is a disaster!" I tell Caroline on the phone. "An Ultimate Frisbee league?"

She laughs once. "I mean, too bad it wasn't old-man baseball. You could at least work with that."

I did a quick Google search on this league, and it's worse than

I thought. After I decided there was no way I could make a story out of that, I looked at the guys in the league. Now, there might be something, but still, it's going to be a damn stretch.

I groan and bang my hand on the steering wheel. "Seriously! Baseball, football, hockey, even that other game you made me sit through would be better."

"Tennis?" she asks as though I'm an idiot.

"Yes. Tennis. That was horrible, but at least it was a real sport. Ugh! I'm screwed!"

"You're not screwed. You just need to find an angle that makes it sound a little less ridiculous."

Like that's going to happen. "Where exactly is the less part? So far I have four guys who were literally draft bound or drafted into their prospective hobbies."

"Sports," Caroline corrects.

"Sports, whatever, and instead of going to the big leagues."

"Professional teams," she cuts in again.

"Right. Those. They're here playing Frisbee. Did you even know that was a thing?"

Caroline snorts. "Nope. So what are you going to do?"

I stare out the windshield, hoping for the answer to magically appear, but it doesn't. "I guess I have to call Mr. Krispen and tell him this is a nonstory. That Lachlan is just a former trophy winner who saved a kid and lives in a small town. There's nothing exciting here."

I hear something slam loudly, causing me to jump. "You will not do that, damn it."

"I won't?"

"No! You are Ainsley freaking MacKinley! You are going to write this article and you are going to make it your bitch."

I sit back, pursing my lips. "I am?"

Caroline's voice is firm. "You damn sure will. Are you one of the top reporters to ever come out of NYU?"

"Maybe. I don't know that I would say the top, but I think I was good."

She huffs. "You're killing me here. You know that?"

I'm totally bringing down her rather rousing speech and pep talk. I just don't know how I'm going to do this. It feels like everything is going wrong.

"I'm sorry."

Caroline's friendship doesn't waver, though. "Listen, all stories are hard. No matter what you're writing about. Do you think if this was about that senator that it would've been any easier?"

I think about that for a second and release a long breath. "Well, no."

"Exactly. So again, what are you going to do?"

That fire in my belly reignites, and I feel my confidence rising like the sun. I can do this. She's right. I don't give up. I'm the daughter of a freaking admiral. I'm totally going to write this article.

"I'm going to slay!" I say, letting myself feed into my inner power. "I'm going to give the best stupid sports story about a bunch of old guys, and it's going to sweep the nation."

"That's it."

"I'm going to give the people what they didn't even know they wanted."

"Damn right you are," Caroline echoes. "And what are you going to tell them?"

"I have no idea."

We both laugh and then she sighs. "You'll figure it out, Ainsley. You're truly gifted at writing, and you just need to dig in and get to work."

Which is exactly what I plan to do. "I can't wait for the world to realize what Ultimate Frisbee can do for them."

"Me either."

Now I just need to figure out how to do that.

━━━━━━

I've decided that the less time I have to spend in Ember Falls the better. So the direct and in-your-face route is my best chance at getting Lachlan to tell me all the things about how he went from being the number-one draft pick to playing in this league of unextraordinary men.

So glad he got a full ride to school, which I did not.

No, I have a mountain of debt to pay from what the military didn't cover.

"Can I help you, miss?" a very attractive Black man asks as he approaches.

"Hi, are you a fireman here?"

He nods. "I am. My name is Davidson."

I smile broadly. "Nice to meet you, Davidson. I was really hoping you could help me. I'm looking for the chief. He came by my place this morning and asked some questions that I didn't know the answer to."

He scratches his throat. "Lachlan West?"

"Yes, he said he needed to check if something was up to code in the cabin I'm staying in?"

"Oh! You're staying at the shit shack?"

The shit shack? Well, the nickname is pretty accurate. "If you're talking about the lodge that was advertised, but in fact is nothing like that, then yes."

His eyes widen and then he blinks, washing away the horror. "Right. Sorry. Did you want to come into the firehouse? He's most likely in his office."

"Is there any way you could ask him to come out here? I just ... I really want the chance of fewer people hearing."

Davidson gives me a wide grin. "No problem. I didn't catch your name."

"Painsley."

"Painsley. With a *P*?"

"Yes."

Poor Davidson, entering into a feud that he doesn't even know about.

"All right, *Painsley*, I'll ... let him know you're here."

"Thank you."

He heads in and I lean against his pickup, waiting for the

sexiest heroic fireman of the year to grace me with his presence.

It's really hard, because I never felt this way about Lachlan when we were kids. He was my friend, or, at least, friend by proxy. There were a lot of times when Caspian would be mean to me, tell me to do something stupid, that I would've absolutely gotten hurt doing, and Lachlan would come to my rescue.

He was my protective friend I couldn't wait to see.

Until my heart decided it loved him.

Traitorous organ that resides in my chest. Always trying to ruin things for me, I swear. The boy I knew was gone, and there was just a man I thought was so damn perfect. Even though he was four years older and never gave an inkling he was interested in me, I just wanted him.

The door opens, and all six foot three inches of him strides out like a fucking movie scene. His dark-brown hair is pushed back, brown eyes focused on me as he comes toward me, and then he flashes his stupid grin and I'm back to being that dumb girl again.

Ugh.

Focus, Ainsley.

"You told him your name was Painsley?"

"Well, you seemed to enjoy reminding me of it. I wasn't sure if you'd know who I was otherwise."

He chuckles. "He came into my office, slightly afraid, and said there was a girl named Painsley, with a *P*, here to see me. That she was incredibly beautiful, and I should prepare for that, but clearly be wary with a name that literally has pain in it."

"Aww, he thinks I'm beautiful?"

He huffs. "Of course you fixate on that."

"Yes, the horror that a girl wants to hear she's pretty. Whatever was I thinking latching onto a compliment?" I huff with a grin. "Did you explain who I was and why you call me that?"

Lachlan shrugs. "You'll never know."

"Yes, I'm sure Davidson will hold that secret close to his chest."

He shakes his head and leans against his truck. "What can I do for you, Berry?"

Ugh. The other nickname. "Why can you not just call me by my first name? I'm Ainsley. Not Painsley. Not Berry. Ains-ley. It's not that hard."

"I apologize. You're all grown up and I shouldn't tease you. Now what can I do for you, *Ainsley*?"

And here I thought I was going to have to work hard for this opening. "First, I brought you something." I grab the coffee that I had Hazel make and hand it to him. "Here, this is a peace offering."

Lachlan raises one brow. "Peace offering?"

"Yes, you know, a . . . I'm sorry for the fact that I showed up here, wouldn't let you in the shack thing, and that I haven't spoken to you in the last few years." *Because we're secretly in love with the other but can't admit it—or at least I am.* "So let's be friends and go back to the way it was."

"We've always been friends, Ainsley."

I ignore that because for the last four years we have definitely not been friends. And I've felt that void in my soul.

"Okay. Call it what you want, I just wanted to be *nice*."

He lifts the cup. "Thank you."

"You're welcome. Also, I might have spit in it."

"I expect nothing less." He laughs as he puts the cup on the hood. "Why else are you here?"

Ahh, Lachlan, always thinking there's an underlying reason someone does something nice. In this case he's kind of right, but still. "I'd like to come by and see Rose, if that's okay? It's been years, but hopefully she's at least heard my name from Caspian and . . . well, I just want to see her."

My brother is her godfather, and even though he lives four hours away in Nashville, he comes up at least once a month to spend time with them. I can at least hope he's talked about me.

"Of course you can, and yes, she knows who you are. I've shown her photos and talked about an annoying girl I know who used to torture me."

Well, that was unexpected, and then I actually let what he said sink in. "Torture you?"

He laughs once. "Did you think we liked you following us around and then tattling?"

I cross my arms over my chest. "I didn't tattle."

"Right. You just what? Informed the Admiral about what we were doing?"

"I like to think of it as a form of journalism." It wasn't like I enjoyed telling on them. My dad was just very firm that if you see someone doing something wrong, and you say nothing, you're equally guilty.

I couldn't help it that my brother and Lachlan seemed to be on the committee to commit crimes. The two of them were the reason they called us military brats.

They were brats.

I was an angel. Still am too.

Those two couldn't walk down the street without causing a damn problem. I felt it was my responsibility, as the youngest and more responsible of the trio, to ensure that I was not guilty by association.

Lachlan snorts. "Please, you loved it when our punishment was having to do whatever you wanted if Caspian and I wanted to hang out."

"This is true."

That was my favorite part. Our dads were diabolical. They didn't believe in corporal punishment or anything that required them to suffer. The idea of grounding them and forcing them to be inside and complaining was absolutely not their idea of a good time.

Therefore, they were forced to do whatever I wanted.

Which meant they had to play horrible games, where Lachlan was my husband and Caspian was our son. They had to play house and board games where it was required I win. They hated it, and for me, it was wonderful.

Lachlan pushes off the truck and takes a sip of his coffee, working to hide the grin behind the rim. "Oh, that's good. I'm wagering you met Hazel and found the coffee shop?"

"I did." I smile. "She's amazing and that store is . . ."

"Perfect for you."

"I'm going to take that as a compliment."

Lachlan nods once. "As you should."

I've always loved books. They're magical and amazing. No matter what I read, even books that aren't necessarily my genre of choice, books have some part of the author's soul in there. You just have to find it.

When I write an article, there's something about putting my own words into a story. There's an angle or a way that I work at picking the perfect descriptors to show what I'm trying to say. It's why some of my articles take me weeks to perfect.

And I don't even like what I'm working on most of the time, but it's my name under that title, and I'll never take that for granted.

Which is why I need Lachlan to be pliable and open to me writing this piece.

"Since you are in a giving mood, how about dinner one night this week?"

"Dinner?" he asks with a bit of hesitancy.

"Yeah, just . . . whatever night you're free. It's been forever, I don't know anyone in town, and I'll be here for at least two weeks. Monday? Wednesday? Thursday?" I ask, hoping he'll give away what day his practice or a game might be.

"I'm sure we can find a day."

"Are you free any of those?"

His eyes narrow. "I've known you pretty much our whole lives, you forget. I'm well aware of your attempts to get information."

I huff and lean against his truck. "I don't need to attempt a damn thing. I can get information a hundred different ways."

"I have no doubt you've honed your snooping skills."

Please, I've perfected them. He just throws me off balance a little, which is why I seem to be not as great at this moment.

"I'm going to pretend you mean that to be a compliment."

"Pretend away."

"So, dinner?" I bring the convo back around to what I want anyway.

Lachlan drains the coffee and smirks. "I'll let you know about that. In the meantime, you can come by tomorrow if you want to see Rose, maybe around four? Do you still have the same number?"

"Yup."

"Okay, I'll text you my address."

"Sounds great."

He grins. "It's eating you up, this trying to be subtle and not outright asking me whatever scheme you have cooking, isn't it?"

Maybe, but I'll never admit it. I give him a one-shoulder shrug and grab the coffee cup from him. "I'll see you tomorrow around four, and we can talk about the article."

Then I get in my car and leave him standing there, reveling in the victory that he's stunned this time.

five
Lachlan

"So who exactly is this girl?" Everett asks as he flicks the Frisbee to Killian.

"She's Caspian's little sister."

"You said she's writing an article on you?"

"Yup. Well, she wants to. I don't want any part of it."

"Maybe she'll write about us." Everett is trying to grow his business and would probably love the press.

"Trust me, you don't want to have her around."

"Well, if she met Hazel already, I'm sure her opinion of me is skewed. I need to do what I can to salvage that."

"Why does she hate you so much?" I ask.

They've been best friends since the fourth grade, but their friendship has shifted the last few months.

He shrugs. "Not a clue. This is why I prefer to work with animals. They're less ridiculous."

"Yeah, or you're a dumbass."

He laughs and then jumps to make a catch. "Keep it lower, Killian!" he yells and then turns to me. "Or that. It's you I'm worried about, though. You seem to want to avoid her. Why is that?"

After Ainsley left, I went to get another cup of coffee and talk with Hazel, see what information she would offer up. I played along where I could, and Hazel talked about how much she liked Ainsley and couldn't wait to see how the article shaped up.

Little does she know there won't be an article.

"Because I know her. There's an angle here, and I think we need to keep her away from the story as much as we can."

As soon as the words are out of my mouth, Everett laughs and then straightens up, his eyes shifting over to the side of the field.

"I'm going to say there's a fat chance of that."

Without having to look, I already know why he's saying that. She's here.

Sure enough, I turn, and there stands Ainsley with Davidson, who is going to find himself unemployed.

Ainsley waves and I sigh, waving back. "I should've known better."

Everett laughs. "So I take it *that's* your best friend's sister?"

"Yup."

"Dude, from a mile away I can tell she's fucking hot. I mean, I don't know how the hell you aren't—"

The look on my face says it all. I swear, if he finishes his sentence, my friend here won't have teeth left.

He raises both hands in the air. "Easy, brother. We all know I have no desire to date anyone."

"Doesn't matter. Don't fucking think it."

"I see. It's unrequited then?" he asks.

"It's not anything."

He chuckles. "Whatever you need to tell yourself, Lach."

I'm done with this conversation. I head across the field to where Davidson is standing with Ainsley. "Chief, Ainsley came to meet you for your dinner tonight, but she was confused where to meet. I brought her so she didn't get lost."

I force a smile and look to her. "Dinner tonight?"

She blinks a few times and clasps her hands in front of her. "Oh no, was it not today?"

This woman. "Nope. Definitely not."

Her jaw drops a little and she lets out a long sigh. "Oh, I

must've mixed the dates up. I'm so sorry, Lach. I just . . . you know, I swear you said to meet tonight. When you weren't at the firehouse, I thought maybe you wanted me to meet you somewhere else. Thank you so much, Danny. You're so nice and I'll be sure to bring Pricilla the steak sauce once I get it from New York."

"Not a problem, Ainsley." His eyes meet mine and he grins. "I better get back to work. Have a good practice, Chief."

"Thanks."

As soon as he's gone, Ainsley crosses her arms over her chest, and the grin on her lips makes me want to find ways to wipe it off —very creative ways.

"Pretty proud of yourself?" I ask.

"Why? I already knew that your practice was tonight, which is why I asked the questions."

Ainsley has always been a step ahead of everyone. She's brilliant, which is why when she talked about wanting to do journalism, it made perfect sense. She loves a story or a puzzle. The act of dismantling it and putting it back together was like a drug for her. Just like it was for me to watch her do it.

"So you found out about the league, happy now?"

She shrugs. "Maybe."

If I know her at all, she's practically doing a jig in her head. The best way to deflate her is to take the joy of the challenge away, which means it's my best scenario anyway. Ainsley is going to get the article, one way or another. The faster I get it over with, the sooner she'll leave Ember Falls, allowing me to go back to a world where I don't think about her.

The last few years, as hard as it's been, it's been worlds easier than seeing her. To try to forget the way she felt against my chest as she held me, offering me comfort when I sure as fuck didn't deserve it.

Ainsley has been that girl. The one that I knew would destroy my entire life and I wouldn't even care.

However, she has to tackle the world, and I would never fit into her idea of what life would be like. It's better for everyone involved if we never even enter a scenario where we could be together.

It means I need her to go, and I need her to go quickly.

I extend my hand. "Come on, you're relentless and I might as well get this over with."

"Where are we going?"

"To meet the guys."

Her hand fits like a glove in mine, but I focus on leading her across the field so she can get the distance we both need.

"Lachlan, who is this beautiful girl?" Everett asks, already knowing the answer to that one.

"Well, since you already know considering I was talking to you when she showed up, this is Ainsley MacKinley. She's a reporter, and everything we say is probably on the record."

She flashes them the most innocent smile. "It's not, but it's probably best to tell me when you don't want me to be in journalist mode." Ainsley shakes his hand. "I'm actually here to write about Lachlan and his life here in Ember Falls since his Heisman Trophy win. A sort of 'Where do athletes go once they've walked away from the sport they loved?'"

"All four of us have similar stories."

"You do?" she asks, glancing at me with a smile.

Great. Now she's going to rope them into this too.

"Yeah, Killian, Miles, and I were all draft prospects," Everett explains.

"This *is* a happy coincidence. I would love to interview you guys too. It would help with not only Lachlan's side, but a fresh perspective as well."

He looks to me and then back at her. "I see. I'd be happy to talk to you about my story."

"I look forward to it."

Everett calls Killian and Miles over. They all say hello, and Ainsley introduces herself. She immediately tells them her goal, and they agree.

Seems I'm the only one who is reluctant.

"Is this practice or warm up for a game?" she asks.

"Practice. We have a game in two weeks. You should come!" Everett says with a shit-eating grin.

"I'd love to." Her beautiful brown eyes find mine. "If that's okay with you?"

"Of course it is."

"Great. I'll let you all get back to your practice. I'm just going to watch and take some notes," she explains.

"I'll walk you over."

Her brows knit. "Because crossing the field is dangerous?"

"With Killian throwing, yes," I joke, but also it's not really a joke.

She waves and the guys do the same before I place my hand on her lower back and lead her away. When we're out of earshot, she clears her throat. "Do you have a reason why you don't want me to write this about you?"

I glance down at her. "Other than the fact that it's stupid, no?"

"Not because of . . . Rose's mother?"

I shake my head. "Claire and I are fine. She signed over her rights to Rose years ago, and there have been no issues."

Rose's mother and I were a drunken mistake that led to the best gift I've ever gotten—my daughter. Claire never wanted kids. She's a dancer and tours all over the world.

However, about six months after Rose was born, she started to question whether that was the right decision, and I'd prepared myself for a custody battle that never came. Claire got a gig with one of the top singers in the world, and we haven't heard from her since.

"Even though her tour is done now?"

"How do you know that?"

Ainsley's eyes widen for a second. "I may or may not keep tabs on her."

"Why?"

"I don't know, I just do."

We reach the side of the field and I sigh. "You don't have to do that."

She shrugs. "Maybe not, but I was there when you thought you were going to lose her."

It was right after my mother's diagnosis of cancer. Those were some incredibly dark times in my life.

"Thankfully, that didn't happen."

"No, it didn't." Ainsley lets out a long breath. "I would walk away from this story if it was that. I could make something up if it meant protecting Rose. You, well, you deserve a little pain and suffering."

We both chuckle at that last one. So Ainsley.

Even though I've hurt her, even though I took advantage of her when I was drunk, she always has my back. It's why I can never be with her.

"I know you would. Now I need to get back out there and make sure we impress you."

She bursts out laughing. "Yes, impress away while playing Frisbee. I can't wait to be dazzled."

And I can't wait for the day when she doesn't dazzle me.

———

"You're making me look like a fucking moron," I say, trying to catch my breath.

I've had four passes overthrown thanks to Killian and his horrific aim. "I'm trying. I told you to be the thrower this round," says Killian.

"It's because he was a quarterback. Lachlan has the arm strength you don't," Everett ribs him.

"Yeah, and you're any better?" Miles asks, already knowing that Everett is just as damn bad.

"Seriously, you three need to step it up. For all I know she has fucking cameras recording this. We look like a bunch of old guys trying to be cool."

Everett raises his hand as though we're in school. "Isn't that sort of what we're doing?"

I huff and drop my head. This game isn't complicated, but

we're making it look that way. Usually we are better than this. So far we've managed to be out of breath, we've been unable to catch, and we haven't scored once.

The four of us stand in the huddle, still struggling to breathe. "All right," I say when sucking in air doesn't burn. "We have one more play to practice. If we can get it right, maybe we can save some of our dignity."

"Considering we have none left, it'll be a nice try," Miles says.

"No matter what, for the rest of the week, we're doing cardio. Let's run the vert. We'll stack and then I'll pass it to Killian. We're the two who need the most redemption."

Everyone agrees and we line up. I run up and grab the disc. They start to run, only, once again, we don't actually look like the group I know we are. Instead, Miles trips and takes Everett out with him. I flick the disc to Killian, but the wind takes it, causing it to go way over his head, and we end up looking like idiots *again*.

The four of us stand on the field for a second, and then Miles bursts out laughing and falls back to the ground.

The other two also laugh, but mostly at him.

"So much for dignity," I say more to myself than anything.

Killian shakes his head and walks over to grab his bag, and the rest of us follow. We say our goodbyes and they head off while I make my way over to Ainsley.

"That was interesting," she says as I approach.

"It's not normally that bad."

"I wouldn't know, but I'm glad you said so, because I was worried. This is supposed to be an article about elite athletes, and you all looked like the backup to the JV team."

She's not wrong.

"We wanted to set the bar low."

"Good call," Ainsley says with a smile. "I'm glad I got to see this. I need to go back to my luxurious accommodations. I'll stop by tomorrow to see Rose and your place." She starts to walk away, and my chest tightens at the idea of her leaving.

"Ainsley, you shouldn't stay in that shack."

She stops and looks at me from over her shoulder. "Where would you recommend I stay then?"

"I don't know, but that place isn't safe."

Ainsley smiles softly. "I'm a big girl, Lach. I can take care of myself."

Yeah, but wouldn't it be nice if someone else took care of her for once. Someone like me.

six

Ainsley

My phone rings and I moan as I reach for it.

"Hello?" I ask groggily and half-asleep.

"Good morning, sunshine." My brother's annoying voice echoes through the phone.

"What time is it?"

"It's four a.m., time for you to get your little writer brain up and going."

I groan. "I hate you."

Normally I would just hang up on him, but Caspian, no doubt, knows I'm here and will keep calling back or send Lachlan here, because he'll make up some bullshit reason that I need help. My brother is fantastic like that.

I roll over, not too far or I'll fall off the tiny bed—again—and push myself up to a sitting position. "What do you want, Caspian?"

"For starters, I'd like to know what the hell you're doing in Ember Falls."

I sigh and lean against the cabin wall. "I'm working, which I'm sure you know."

"I do, but . . ."

"But what?"

My brother huffs. "Why?"

"Because it's my job. Why do you go into work every day? Because they pay you. Same rules apply with my job."

I know I'm a little testy, but, seriously, it's way too early for this.

"So you and Lachlan are talking again?"

I let that sink in a little, because in all these years, Caspian hasn't talked about it with me. He asked once what the deal was, but then dropped it. I have no idea whether he talks to Lachlan about it, but I had zero desire to bring it up to my brother.

In fact, I still don't want to talk about it with him.

Lachlan is his best friend. The only person that always had his back when we were kids. Being a military brat isn't easy. I had friends, and then they left. It was the way it was, but Lachlan never left. From the day he moved next door until the day our dads retired, they were together.

"Yes, we're talking. I plan to go over later to see Rose and do some of my interview."

"Good. She's gotten so big. I'm planning to come up in the next few weeks. Do you think you'll still be in town?"

I look around at this nasty cabin and shudder. "I sure as hell hope not."

"Where the fuck are you staying, anyway?"

"Oh, it's a cabin that is available for rent," I say nonchalantly, because if my brother knew what this place looked like, he'd be in the car on his way.

I don't need that. I need my story.

"Lachlan didn't seem too excited by it. I've been in town and there's really nowhere to stay."

"I'm fine, *Cas*."

"Okay, *Ains*," he relents. "How's Dad?"

I shift a little and pull my sweater around me. "He's . . . the Admiral. Still messing with the boat, pretending Mom is coming back to him, and letting me know all the things I do wrong in life."

"Better you than me."

I roll my eyes. "Yes, so much better. You should go see him instead of coming here," I suggest.

Caspian and our dad do not mix well. They're so much of the same person that when they're together, it's like someone spilled gas and we're waiting for a spark. Lord knows I'll be the collateral damage if I'm around.

Dad is tough. He believes that we're all soft nowadays, and if we just put our heads down and worked harder, life would be better. In some scenarios, he's probably right, but not in everything. However, according to my father, he's never wrong.

Ever.

He spent the last fifteen years of his naval career commanding a fleet of ships, and if you ask him, he was the best there ever was.

My brother, on the other hand, was destined to follow in his footsteps, at least according to Dad.

Caspian lets out a low laugh. "Has he stopped talking about what a fuckup I am and that I'm wasting my life trying to make it in Nashville?"

"Nope."

"Then I'll visit Ember Falls."

I figured as much. "If it makes you feel better, he thinks I'm a loser too."

My brother huffs. "I feel mildly better."

"I figured. It helps me to know that as much of a loser as he thinks I am, you've got the top spot."

"Fuck off."

I grin. "I love you too, Cas."

"Yeah, yeah. Well, happy writing."

"Happy being Dad's least favorite," I say with a smile he can't see. "It's really hard wearing this crown, if you could do something to ease my burden."

He snorts. "I'm perfectly fine being in last place in this race."

"Fine," I huff. "I'll continue to be his favorite."

Caspian laughs. "And I'm Mom's favorite."

I wish that was a lie, but it's true. "Lucky me."

"I think it's me who's lucky here. Now don't annoy Lachlan too much. He's my favorite out of you two."

"Har har, you're so funny."

Sad part is that I'm not even sure he's joking.

"Bye, Ainsley."

"Goodbye, my annoying brother. I love you."

"Love you too."

We hang up, and as much as I'd love to go back to bed, I need to send some emails and get my notes in order on how I'd like to approach the story. That means I need to get up and head to Prose & Perk.

First, to try to shower in this . . . mess of a cabin. Mr. Brickman told me that the water can be hot, but mostly it's just cold, and if I turn the generator on ten minutes before, I probably won't hate my life.

Yeah, that ship has sailed.

I pull my sweater tighter, pull my boots on, and head to the back. I'm supposed to press something, turn a lever, and then try to start it up.

I follow the steps as I remember them, but nothing happens. So I do it again, and this time the motor makes a sound as though it wants to start.

That's promising.

After the fourth time, it fully kicks up, and in the absolute silence of the woods, it sounds like it's waking the bears that should be asleep.

Back inside I go before I'm eaten.

I do my best to wait the ten minutes, but I'm really in need of coffee. I take what is probably the coldest and shortest shower of my life, convincing myself that cold water is good for my skin and hair—then I'm out.

I check my phone, and I have three calls from the office and an email, but my service sucks balls out here, so I can't open it. Therefore, I get dressed and head into the bathroom area to blow dry my hair.

When I push the button on my dryer, nothing happens.

I try again, and now the lights in the cabin go out.

"Great!" I yell and groan.

Back out to the generator I go.

Once again I have to basically say a prayer to get it to start. It does on the third try, and I go back in.

This time, with my wet hair, I wait the full ten minutes and then chance fate. I close one eye, waiting, but all the lights are still on, and everything seems fine.

Until it's not.

Suddenly sparks start shooting out of the outlets. The lights go out and there is a popping noise and smoke.

"Shit!" I scream, dropping the blow dryer.

I will not die in a shitty cabin in the middle of the woods.

I rush out of the room, grabbing some of my stuff and shoving it in my suitcase. I get through the front door, hair half-dried, in leggings, a bra, and flip-flops. I throw my small bag in my car, and then I see more smoke.

My hands are shaking as I dial 9-1-1.

The operator comes through the line. "Nine-one-one, what's your emergency?"

"Hi, I'm at 8223 Tiger Lane, in an off-the-grid cabin. Umm, I think it's on fire. I don't know."

"Are you in a safe location?"

I nod, but she can't see me.

"Ma'am?"

"Yes, I'm outside."

"Okay. I've dispatched the fire department. Can you describe what happened?"

I go through the generator experience with the dispatcher, telling her about my attempt to blow dry my hair before the popping and smoke experience.

"Is there still smoke coming out of the window?" she asks.

"Yes. No. Maybe. I don't know." My teeth are chattering as my adrenaline is starting to decrease.

"All right. Just please don't approach it. They should be there soon."

I have zero intentions of going back inside, and I stay on the line until I hear sirens. "They're coming."

"Good. Would you like me to stay on until they're fully on scene?"

"No, I'm okay. Thank you."

"Not a problem."

We hang up, and as the sirens become louder, I see a puff of smoke flying closer. At the speed it's approaching, they must be going incredibly fast on the dirt road.

Instead of a fire truck, it looks like a pickup truck breaking through the trees.

Sure enough, it is, and on the front it says CHIEF.

This is going to go over well.

Lachlan is out of the vehicle and running toward me. "Are you okay?"

"I'm fine, it's just some smoke. Maybe a fire, I don't know."

He grips both my shoulders and then pulls me to his chest. "But you're okay?"

"Yes, Lach, I'm totally okay."

His arms drop, and it looks like he takes a breath for the first time and then looks at the cabin. "Stay here."

Before I can say I had zero intentions of going anywhere, he's heading into the possible burning building, and every muscle of mine locks up.

No. He can't go in. There's a possible fire. While I know this is his job and he's a fireman, it doesn't do anything to quell my nerves. He doesn't even have all his gear on. He's in freaking basketball shorts and a T-shirt.

I start to go after him, but then he's coming out, his arm over his face, and then he goes around to the back. The generator noise stops, and he makes his way to me.

"There's no fire, but the electrical isn't meant for this. I'm going to kill Brickman. He never should've let you stay here. I never should've either." He heads back to his truck, clearly pissed off from the way he stomps, and grabs his radio. "I'm on scene. Fire isn't active. It's still smoking but doesn't require the tanker."

"Understood, we're five minutes out. Do we need medical on scene?"

Lachlan looks at me. "Yes."

"I don't need medical," I protest, but the way his jaw tightens and eyes narrow causes me to stop speaking. He looks murderous or terrified, maybe even both.

After a second of our standoff, he sighs. "Please, just get checked out. If the EMTs say you're fine, then you don't have to go to the hospital."

The defiant little girl in me wants to tell him exactly what he can do with his edict, but I decide against it. I'm pretty sure he was in bed and literally flew here. "Where is Rose?" I ask, hoping maybe her name will bring him back down.

"With the sitter. She watches her when we have a call I need to respond to."

"You didn't have to come for this. I'm completely fine."

He runs his fingers through his hair. "I'm not going to even dignify that with a response." He starts to pace and then turns to me. "Of course I had to respond to this, Ainsley! Did you really think I wouldn't? Don't even answer that. I'm sure you doubted I would, which I deserve, but fucking hell, of course I came for you." He keeps going in circles, having a one-way conversation. "Like I wouldn't come to make sure you weren't hurt. I'd have run through the burning house to get to you."

That's kind of nice. "I didn't say you wouldn't have."

"Damn right you didn't. Because I would."

"You'd do that for anyone," I remind him. "Since it's your job."

His brown eyes find mine, and they could probably set the woods on fire with the storm raging behind them. "Yes, but . . . it's not the same."

No, I would assume it wouldn't be. If it were him, I would go insane until I knew he was okay.

I take two steps closer. "Thankfully, none of that had to happen."

The sirens are in the background again, and this bubble will burst soon. He moves to me, lifting his hand to barely graze my cheek. God, he's touching me.

He's touching me and it's like lava being sent to every part of my body, warming me even in the cool morning air.

"Don't ever scare me like this again."

I fight back a smile. "You were scared?"

His eyelids lower, preventing me from reading any emotions. "You have no idea the level of terror I experienced when I heard it was the cabin."

My hand presses against his chest, feeling the heat of him and wishing that this was a million other scenarios and we didn't have a fire truck approaching. Although, the last time we had a similar moment, where we were close and emotional, it ended in disaster. So maybe it's not a bad thing this will end.

"I can imagine it was an inkling of what I felt when I saw you run in."

His thumb brushes my cheek, and then he steps back, putting distance between us as the fire truck enters the clearing.

seven
Lachlan

"You're going to the hospital."

Ainsley attempts to cross her arms over her chest, and it's funny to see her try, since she has on my fire coat to cover the fact she was in her fucking bra.

She started shivering uncontrollably and I bundled her up and put her in the back of my truck.

"No, I'm not."

"Yes, you are. You have possible smoke inhalation."

"That is *not* what they said!" she argues. "They said I might have inhaled a little smoke."

I raise one brow. "Isn't that the same thing?"

She groans. "I swear to God, you're maddening. When I told them that you went in there, they said you might have done the same. So are you going to the hospital?" Ainsley turns, smacking me in the face with her ponytail. "Of course you're not, because you're hardheaded."

Boy, that's hilarious coming from her.

I spit out some of the hair on my lips.

"No, I'm not going to the hospital," I inform her.

"Then neither am I. What I am going to do is find somewhere to stay while I work on my story. If you'll excuse me."

She shrugs out of my coat, but I throw it back around her shoulders. "Put a damn shirt on."

My guys do not need to see her like this. They're already falling over themselves to be near her.

"The rest of my clothes are in the cabin."

"Wear the jacket, Ainsley."

She glares at me, but pulls it taut.

There was no real damage to the cabin, just some smoke, and we've deemed it unsafe for occupancy, which means Ainsley will not be spending another night in this shithole. Not that the motel in the area is an option, either, which means she's going to stay with me and Rose.

Not an ideal situation when you're trying to pretend you're not in love with someone.

I'll deal with it for the short time she's here if it means she's safe and not dealing with generators and God only knows what else.

"I don't know when you became so damn bossy." Her head whips around and I avoid getting hit with her ponytail. Triumph. Only then she turns again and I get whipped in the face. "What does it matter to you anyway?"

"For one it's chilly. And the second thing is you're barely wearing anything." She pulls the jacket around her and flips her hair, giving me another slap in the face. "I'm going to cut your hair off if you keep doing that."

Her glare would melt a lesser man. Thankfully I'm not intimidated. "Try it and I'll cut something off you." Her eyes move to my groin, letting me know exactly what she'd like to remove from me. "I need to get my things and regroup."

"You're not going in there."

"Why?"

I don't have an answer to that other than I'm pissed off at her. "Because it's unsafe."

"Umm, I heard your men say it was perfectly safe. So which is it? Are they incompetent, or are you?"

"Are you trying to piss me off?"

She doesn't reply. She just heads into the cabin, and I follow like a stupid puppy dog. When she gets to the door, she stops, and I almost plow into her. She whips her head around, and I duck, avoiding her damn hair.

She sighs. "I'm not trying to do that. I'm just trying to get a grip because today was a little freaking traumatizing, you know? Like, I have to be here, and I don't know where to go now."

I open my mouth to tell her how there is no story here and she should head back to New York, but instead I say something else. "You'll stay at my house."

Her lips part, and she blinks a few times. "I'm not staying with you."

"Well, you're not staying here or at the motel in town. Do you have another option?"

"No, but . . . Lachlan, we haven't even spoken for the last four years. Rose doesn't know me, and it's just a bad idea."

I don't disagree with her, but there aren't any other options I can live with. As for Rose, she knows all about Uncle Caspian's sister. She's seen photos from when we were little, and he tells her all about the things I did to torment her when she was young.

She'll be more than ecstatic to have a girl in the house.

Plus, Rose is a great buffer and cockblock, if it comes to needing that.

"It'll be fine. Rose will love having you around, and I swear to God, if you fight me on this, I'll call your father and tell him you almost died in a house fire."

Ainsley gasps. "You wouldn't."

"I dare you to try me."

I have zero issues calling the Admiral, and she knows it. I'd much rather call her father and deal with his anger than have to call him if something actually happened to her.

"You are *so* going to regret this, Lachlan West."

I already do. Just not for the reasons she thinks. I step closer. "You can follow me over, and we'll talk about the rules when we get there."

Ainsley tosses my coat at me and saunters off in her bra and leggings in the cold morning air.

Rule number one—she has to be dressed from head to toe at all times.

———

We each pull up to my house, and for the first time I feel self-conscious. My home isn't a shithole, but it's not anything to write home about either. It's a three-bedroom modest farmhouse painted a terrible green with white shutters. I have more projects than time and more issues than money to fix them. However, it's a roof over our heads, and in this town, material things aren't what matter.

"This is your home?" Ainsley asks after we both exit our vehicles.

"It is."

She turns to me with a warm smile. "It's beautiful. It looks so cozy, and I imagine Rose running around the yard. We would've loved this space as kids."

Her voice is wistful, and there's not a hint of disapproval. I feel myself start to relax a little. "She loves it, that's for sure."

"Is that a rope swing?"

I nod. "I put it in last year."

"All you need is a pond."

"I have one and something better."

Her eyes widen. "You do not."

"I do."

"Where?"

"I'll show you another day. Providing you don't try to burn my house down."

She scoffs. "I didn't try to burn that disgusting cabin down. Hopefully you have power that's not run off a generator."

I tamp down my growing anger as I think about her out in that fucking cabin. "I have all the modern amenities. Plus, we have an activities coordinator in the form of a six-year-old."

"Oh, fancy."

I sigh. "Come on, let's go inside so you can meet her and she can inform you of the daily schedule."

We walk in and the neighbor is in the living room with Rose.

"Daddy!" She jumps up, like she always does when I come home after a fire call.

However, she stops dead in her tracks when she sees Ainsley behind me.

"Rose, this is Uncle Caspian's sister, Ainsley. She's going to stay with us for a bit because she tried to burn her house down."

Her eyes widen and she looks to Ainsley. "You did?"

Ainsley huffs and slaps my chest. "I didn't. It just started because I was trying to blow dry my hair." She squats in front of Rose. "It's so nice to meet you again. I knew you when you were a baby. It's been a long time since I've seen you."

Rose grins. "Daddy says I'm a menace."

She purses her lips. "Truth be told, he was the worst menace when he was a kid."

My daughter's hazel eyes stare at me. "You were?"

"Only with annoying little girls like Ainsley."

Ainsley shakes her head. "Don't let him fool you, Rose. He was always in trouble."

"All the time?"

"All the time," Ainsley echoes in agreement.

The sitter, Delaney, stands, grabs her bag, and walks over. "I'll need a note for school."

She is a sophomore in high school, and while I think her attitude could use an adjustment, Rose loves her. No matter what Delaney tells her, she does it. Her father took off a few years ago, and babysitting Rose has kept her out of a lot of trouble. The two of them are more friends than anything.

"Not a problem. I'll email Miles now."

She extends her hand. "That'll be twenty bucks for today too."

I hand her a twenty, and she stuffs it in her pocket. Her dour attitude shifts when she turns to Rose. "I'll see you Monday, okay, kid?"

Rose nods. "Monday. Don't get in trouble, Delaney!"

"Fine, just because you asked."

Rose is her mother's bargaining chip. If she skips school or does anything stupid, she's not allowed to babysit. Instead, Rose has to go to Mrs. Kimball, who watches her after school when I'm on shift.

Delaney heads out, and I shoot an email over to Miles, letting him know Delaney was babysitting for a town fire emergency.

I clap my hands. "Who wants breakfast?"

Rose jumps up. "I do, I do! Can I have pancakes, Daddy?"

"We don't have time. I need to get you fed and on the bus."

She groans and looks to Ainsley. "I hate school."

"You do?"

"There's a mean boy, and yesterday I got in trouble because I told him I was going to punch him in the eye if he kept taking my crayons."

Ainsley looks to me, clearly assuming that advice came from me. Which it did.

"I merely gave the girl some life skills," I say, not feeling the slightest bit bad about this.

She sighs heavily and turns to Rose. "I'm sorry a boy is being mean to you, but school was my favorite place in the world. You get to read, and learn, and make friends. Don't ever let anyone take that fun away. He'll stop, I promise."

Rose nods once. "I like my teacher."

"That's great! Do you like anything else?" Ainsley asks.

"Food. You need breakfast, and the bus will be here in fifteen minutes," I remind Rose.

Rose takes her hand and pulls Ainsley into the kitchen, chattering on about all the things she loves about school, her friends, and anything else she can come up with, because Ainsley is instantly lovable.

I put the bowl of cereal in front of her, which doesn't even get me an acknowledgment, and head back into my room to change. This day has absolutely not gone as planned. I was awoken to the tones, which usually aren't anything serious, but as soon as I heard "possible house fire" and Ainsley's location, I almost fucking lost it.

My neighbor came running over when I called. From the panic in my voice, it must've been clear that I wasn't dicking around, and then I was out the door.

I flew faster than I've ever driven to get to her. The entire time my mind played the worst scenarios I could come up with. When I arrived, the relief of seeing her standing there was so intense I wanted to fall to my knees.

Her being here, though, brings a whole new set of challenges.

Once I'm changed, I head back into the kitchen, where the girls are still sitting at the table. "All right, Rose, it's time."

She gives me a pouty look. "Do I have to, Daddy?"

"Yup. You do."

Rose huffs but gets off her chair, bringing the empty cereal bowl to the sink. "Will you be here when I get home?" she asks Ainsley.

"I think so."

"She will. She's going to stay here until she's done with her work." Which I'm praying is going to go fast. Our game is in two weeks, so at least that long.

Rose's smile grows. "Yay!"

Ainsley laughs. "Have the best day and I'll see you later."

I reach out and take Rose's hand, and we walk out to the bus stop. "Daddy, I like Ainsley."

"You like everyone."

She scrunches her nose. "Not Briggs."

"I stand corrected," I say with a laugh.

"She is pretty," Rose notes.

"She is."

"And smart."

I nod. "That too."

"You should marry her."

I choke and stop walking. "What? Where did that come from?"

Rose shrugs. "She's pretty and smart, Daddy. You should marry her."

"That's not happening," I tell her, hoping to squash this thought immediately. "You just met her. You have no idea how annoying she can be too."

My daughter doesn't look the least bit concerned. "I like her."

"Then enjoy the time you'll have with her when she visits."

Marry her. Seriously, where the hell did that come from? A few months ago, I kind of sort of was dating this girl from a few towns over. Rose met her when we were in a store and immediately disliked her. I don't know why. Valorie was perfectly nice, a little shallow, but not in a mean way. However, Rose told me when we got in my truck that she didn't want to be her friend. I didn't understand it but figured it was jealousy and she didn't want to share her dad.

Apparently I was wrong on that motive.

She has no problem with that regarding Ainsley. Of all fucking people.

"I still think you should marry her," Rose says as we come to the stop sign.

"I think that's not going to happen."

"Why not?"

I do not know what has gotten into my daughter, but I'm not having this conversation with her. "Because I said so."

Rose kicks a rock. "I want a mom. All the other kids have one. Well, not Gigi, but her dad has a new girlfriend already. My dad doesn't have *any* girlfriends."

I let out a slow breath and squat down. "Rose, you've never mentioned any of this."

"I know."

Here I thought she didn't care or want me to date. "Are you sad you don't have a mom in your life?"

She shrugs, but there's a layer of sadness in her eyes. "Sometimes."

My fucking heart shatters in my chest. "I'm sorry you're sad. You know I love you more than anything in the world, right?"

Rose nods. "I love you too, Daddy."

The bus comes, and I'm equally happy and worried with this conversation ending where it does. The driver stops and opens the door. I force a smile and kiss the top of her head. "We'll do something fun when you get home today."

"Can we get ice cream too?"

I laugh. "Sure. We'll get ice cream."

Hell, I'd buy all the ice cream in the world if it meant she wouldn't be sad. Rose turns, heads up the steps to the bus, and turns again and waves, like we do every day. Then the door closes, and I stand here feeling a myriad of emotions.

As I walk back to my house, I do my best not to let the events of the day already feel crushing. It's not even nine in the morning, so God only knows what else is going to happen. When I walk in, Ainsley is sitting on the couch with her glasses perched on her perfect little nose and face buried in her laptop.

God, she's so fucking cute. Why couldn't she be an ogre or something? Instead, she has to be the most beautiful woman I've ever seen.

She's always been, though. Her dark coffee-colored eyes, long brown hair, and light olive skin have always appealed to me, even when I did everything I could to convince myself it didn't.

Ainsley is so much more than just gorgeous, though. She's smart, funny, and has a huge heart that is impossible to resist.

God knows I've been trying for years to do exactly that.

She looks up and smiles. "Everything okay?"

"Yup," I lie.

"Good. Listen, I know this situation isn't ideal, but I was thinking, if we can get the interview done quickly, I can spend more of the time with the other guys."

I don't want her spending any time with the other guys. I also don't want her to write this stupid story. "There's no story here."

Ainsley pulls her glasses off. "I disagree."

"I'm sure you do, but what the hell is the point? I graduated from college. I won the Heisman. I didn't get drafted. So what?"

"That's what I'm trying to find out," she says and then leans back. "I think there's a story here, Lach. You were supposed to be playing pro ball right now. You were destined for the pro-thingy, I mean league, it was all anyone could talk about."

I huff and pinch my temples. "I'm aware."

My entire life, it was all anyone fucking talked about. I was good, I get that. I went on to play in a national championship. Sure, we lost, but I played my heart out. I was ready for the future with the NFL, but then . . . . I had Rose.

She became my world. I was not going to give her a life even remotely close to what I had.

And I saw it.

Right there.

A mother who wasn't there. A father who traveled for work and was never around. A kid desperate for a different life.

I would never do that to Rose.

"So don't you think people want to know why? Especially now that people know you're amazing?"

I let out a long sigh, smile, and shake my head. "Nope, I was amazing then, too, and it got me nowhere. Third door on the right is the guest room. You can stay there. I have to go to work now."

"Lachlan!" Ainsley is on her feet, following me into the kitchen. "I need this story."

"So get the story without me."

She groans. "You are the story!"

I'm not. No one really gives a shit about a washed-up college football player. "Sorry I can't help you."

"You are so maddening! You're not leaving without telling me why."

I grab my keys and start to move to the right, but she blocks me.

"Move," I say, leaving no room for argument.

But this is Ainsley, and she isn't the slightest bit scared of me. "Not until you tell me why you're being such an ass about this."

"No."

"Yes!"

The tension in my jaw is so tight I could shatter my teeth. "Move, Ainsley."

She shifts to the left when I do. "Just let me interview you."

"If you don't move, I'm going to pick you up and move you myself," I warn.

Ainsley crosses her arms over her chest. "I'm not moving."

"Suit yourself." I take the two steps to her and lift her, but when I grab her, she wraps her arms and legs around me, plastering herself to me.

I try to adjust, but instead I now have her pinned against the wall. Her scent is everywhere, that jasmine and vanilla that she's worn forever. Her brown eyes are locked on mine, and there's a hitch in her breathing.

My hand is under her ass, holding her body to mine, and suddenly the antagonism between us is lost, and in its place is desire.

So much fucking desire.

The events of the morning, the fear, the need to save her, have morphed into this—a want that is bone deep.

I start to release her, but she grips me tighter.

"Don't," I say to both her and myself.

We stare into each other's eyes, and I see the same emotions mirrored in hers. For years I've thought about that night, when I was drunk and alone in that garden. When she was against me, just like this, kissing me.

Then pushing her against that stone wall, driving into her mouth, taking everything that she offered and drowning in her, until I realized what I was doing and had to stop it, forcing her to leave me, but I didn't know she'd never come back.

She leans her forehead to mine and loosens her grip. The loss of her body around mine causes an ache in my chest that makes me want to scream out.

"One day we're going to have to figure this out and stop dancing around what we feel," she says as she lifts her head from mine. "Just not today, it seems."

I take a step back and shake my head. "No, because our dance ended before it began."

With that, I throw the door open and head to my truck, where I can berate myself on the way to work.

eight
Ainsley

T*ap, tap, tap.*
 I bounce the pencil against the table over and over.
Tap, tap, tap.
Come on, ideas. I need you. Come to me.
Tap, tap, tap.
I stare at the screen, willing the words to magically appear, but they don't. How the hell am I going to write a story about Lachlan and where he is now when he won't let me interview him? I could write about what I do know, leaving out any freaking commentary from him. Which will be a boring and absolutely basic story. I could always make it more about the Ultimate Frisbee players who once were deemed the top athletes of their time. That way it could kind of be a much broader article, even though that's totally not what my boss sent me here for.

Ugh.

I'm so going to fail.

My email pings, and I've never been happier to stop staring at a blank screen. Only when I see it's from my boss, I no longer feel relief, because today I need to send him my top six angles.

I don't even have one, so this is going to be a shit show.

Ainsley,

I will be traveling this week and I need your storyline proposals by four.

The clock says it's two, so . . . I'm screwed.

"More coffee?" Hazel asks, coming around the partition.

"Sure. Maybe coffee will perk my brain up," I say, holding out my cup.

She gives me a refill and then puts the pot on the counter. "Everything okay?"

"I just have two hours before I need to submit something that sounds Pulitzer winning about heroic former athletes or Frisbee."

She lets out a soft laugh. "That doesn't seem all that difficult."

I drop my head on the table. "It's impossible."

"It can't be that bad!" Hazel says with some gusto. "Come on, tell me what you have so far."

I lift my head just enough to see her face. "I have nothing."

"Oh."

"Yeah."

Hazel pulls the seat out across from me. "Okay, this isn't the end of the world. You have two hours. I've seen writers pull things out of their ass in minutes. What usually gets your brain working?"

"Talking it out," I admit. I'm so much better when I can think aloud, which is why I love writing in my office. Caroline is an amazing sounding board and always helps me work through the wormholes in my brain.

"Then let's hear it." Hazel lifts both hands.

It's great that she wants to help, but I don't even have a jump-off point. "I can't give you anything because I have nothing."

Nothing except replaying that moment when he held me against the wall. When I was an idiot and thought that maybe he was feeling the same thing I was. Once again, I'm a freaking dumbass.

"Okay, so what's rattling around in your head? Is it the fire at the cabin that has you messed up?"

"I wish," I confess under my breath.

Hazel's eyes widen. "Something else?"

"Someone else, more like."

While I don't know Hazel, I like her a lot. She's incredibly sweet, and I hope that at the end of this, we can remain friends.

"I thought that might be the case," she says with a smile as she leans back. "Lachlan is a great guy."

"He's also my brother's best friend and has always seen me as a little twerp who he had to be nice to."

She shifts forward. "But that's not the case, is it?"

I shrug. "I don't know."

"Do you like him?"

What a loaded question. "I've always loved him. Not in the way that I feel now, but Lachlan will never see me that way. He's basically told me so in a hundred different ways."

Like how he never should've kissed me. How he was sorry.

God, that was the worst.

To be told they were sorry they kissed you.

I wasn't sorry. I was . . . shattered.

"Can you use that to write about?"

"Use what?"

"Your feelings. Look, I think the best stories come from what we know, right? You don't know sports, but you know Lachlan. You know what that time in his life was like, and you can understand what it must've been to see his football career go up in smoke. It's clear you care about him."

"I do, but I don't think he wants me to talk about that. He refuses to even discuss it. However, the other guys seem all for it."

Hazel purses her lips. "Could you have the guys focus on what they miss?"

I think about that for a second and write it down. "I could try to have them talk about the brotherhood they experienced, teamwork, and how it shaped them into who they are now."

She nods. "Yes, I mean, that has definitely guided them into their daily lives, right?"

"With Lachlan being a fireman—definitely. Killian is a business owner, so surely he has experience with building a team. Miles has to rally an entire faculty and he served in the military, which I know a lot about. The only one I don't know about is Everett."

Hazel immediately stiffens. "He's an idiot. Just leave him in that box."

I smile. "I think they're all idiots."

"I would agree. Especially if Lachlan fails to see how amazing you are."

If only it were that simple. "Lachlan has his reasons."

"Do you know what they are?" Hazel asks.

"Nope." Although I'm assuming something with the loss of his mother.

"Then we'll put him in the idiot box too."

I lift my coffee cup and cheers to that. "To the idiots who drive us bonkers."

Hazel grabs the coffeepot and lifts it in solidarity. "And to the women who are slowly learning their lesson."

"*Slowly* is definitely the word of the day there."

We spend the next hour drinking coffee, and she lets me bounce my ideas around, interjecting when she sees a flaw or another angle to consider.

I fire off my email just in time to Mr. Krispen, and then I head off for another thrilling Ultimate Frisbee practice.

I have the green light on three of the six. Whichever of those feels the best, Mr. Krispen wants me to run with it.

He's hoping that the article will be more personal interest than sport, but he wants a really good stronghold on sports in general.

Which, you know, is so not my thing.

His parting line in the email still has me rattled.

Ainsley,

All of these are good, but these three are the best options from

*what I can see. The story will be more full circle if we can focus on
how they started playing sports and ended the same way. So I want
sports involved in this no matter what. You know the stakes, if you
nail this assignment, we'll be able to open new doors for you. I like
that you're turning this into a bigger story than just one guy.*

Good luck and I have faith in you.

Mr. K

I read it again, waiting for the words to scramble themselves to
say: *You're a dumbass. Good luck with the sportsball.*

But they don't.

I glance back up at the field, seeing the guys coming off
laughing and pushing each other around.

Practice was exactly like the last, a bunch of older men trying
to throw a Frisbee, missing a lot, and then blaming the other.
However, I really wouldn't even know if they were missing or if
that's supposed to be what happened.

There's no clear offense or defense. It's just one . . . fense.

They run back and forth, and sometimes they're flicking?
Throwing? Airing it out? Then suddenly they're batting it to the
ground and whooping.

I watched about twenty videos online to see if I could figure
out the sport, but . . . these guys don't seem to be following those
rules.

"Did you enjoy practice?" Everett asks as they're grabbing
water and toweling their faces.

"I did. It was . . . thrilling."

He snorts a laugh. "Embarrassing is the word we all used."

"Hey!" Miles jumps in. "I had that rather spectacular catch."

I grin. "I did notice that."

"Do you have questions about the sport?" Miles asks.

"Is it a sport?" I figure we might as well start with the one
most people will ask.

Killian tries to hide his smile. "It's something."

I turn to him. He's the oldest of the bunch and has a dusting
of silver mixing with his dark-brown hair at the temples. When I
did my research on him, he was destined for great things in foot-

ball. They said he had one of the best hands the sport had ever seen. He could catch a ball no matter where it was placed on the field and was drafted, but then never played and left after one season.

"Why do you play, Killian? I know you're a successful businessman and you don't live in Ember Falls full-time, but you never miss practice or a game."

Killian pulls his duffel bag onto his shoulder. "For fun. For friendship, and because there's nothing I love more than kicking a bunch of college kids' asses who roll onto the field thinking we're an easy win."

"You guys have won?" I ask with obvious surprise. Not that I know much about this sport, but it doesn't seem to me that they're any good.

Miles laughs and clasps Killian's shoulder. "We're undefeated."

Well, this just keeps getting worse. "There are teams worse than this?"

Oh, Lord. I'm never going to be able to sell this story as a legitimate sport angle if this is the best the league has.

It's fine. It's fine. I'll just stage photos if I have to.

"Believe it or not, yes," Killian confirms.

"Awesome, I can't wait to see it all come together in a game because . . . you know, this must just be different."

I'm hoping this isn't it and they're saving it all for the big game. Otherwise, this story is dead in the water, and I need to scrap the sport angle completely. Which is the one that Mr. Krispen underlined and bolded.

Even when I explained the sport was Ultimate Frisbee.

So I need to play up how great they still are, even though they're all in their thirties.

I turn to Lachlan. "Do you guys play often?"

"Yes."

"Okay, how often?"

"Biweekly."

Doesn't give me a ton of time to write about the games. My

story is due by the end of the month, which gives me three and a half weeks, and I really need it to run in the next issue.

"That's good, and you practice twice a week?" I ask.

"Yes."

His one-word answers are grating on my nerves. However, I just brighten my smile more because, while he might be a grumpy bear, I do not have to be.

"I see. Can you tell me what drew you to the sport of Ultimate Frisbee?" I ask, knowing a one-word answer is not going to suffice here and maybe I can get *something*.

"No."

I huff. "Really?"

"Really."

The urge to stomp my foot on his grows, but I tamp it down and turn to Everett. "What about you?"

Everett launches into a story about how after he graduated from college and entered the draft, he realized it wasn't what he wanted to do anymore. He played through broken bones, concussions, and a never-ending stream of pain. "I just knew that I wanted more than a career cut short from an injury."

"So you turned to healing animals," I say with a smile.

"I did, and Ember Falls is where I spent a lot of time growing up, so I came back and met this fool at a town meeting." He grips Lachlan's shoulder. "Instant best friends."

"Oh? I can imagine you were drawn to his sunny personality."

Lachlan rolls his eyes. "I'm pleasant to *most* people."

I scoff. "Lachlan West, I've known you since you were eleven, and I've never heard a single person describe you that way."

His eyes narrow and he leans in. "Maybe it's only the people you talk to."

"Yes, maybe it's that," I concede with sarcasm dripping on every word. I give my attention back to Everett. "How did the Frisbee thing come to fruition?"

"Well, there weren't enough of us for a baseball team. Then we thought about flag football, and then we heard about a couple of colleges in Virginia that were starting a Frisbee league, and we thought it would be fun."

I nod, writing all this down. "Was it more of a joke then?"

"No. Considering our injury lists, we figured it was no contact and should be easy, especially since there weren't going to be a ton of teams."

"I see," I say, taking notes. "Sounds like it would be difficult to get a spot since you're not an actual college."

"Difficult, not so much, but we had to do certain things to get into the league."

Now my interest is piqued. "Oh, like what?"

Lachlan steps in. "All right, Lois Lane, let's go. We have to get Rose before her babysitter files a missing person report."

I roll my eyes. "Yes, I'm sure your practice has never gone over five minutes."

He grabs his bag. "See you guys later."

"Bye, Lach! Don't forget to stretch or you might not be able to walk tomorrow," Everett taunts as he's heading to the truck. Then he leans into me. "He went pretty balls to the wall. I'm going to suspect it was to impress someone."

I laugh softly. "Lachlan never works to impress me. If anything, he tries to pretend I don't exist."

My eyes move to where he's going, hating that it's always been that way. We dance like this, where there are some days that I swear he wants me, that he sees me, but then he shoves me away so hard, locking every door I could ever think to open. For four years he went on with living his life, trying to reach out only once in the beginning.

I know it was me who ran away, but I . . . I don't know. I was young, stupid, horrified, and then I was too embarrassed to go to him. A part of me wanted him to chase me.

Which is even stupider. But it hurt so much more than I think I ever allowed myself to admit.

To love someone who doesn't even acknowledge your existence is devastating, but I learned to just live in the pain. To remember that Lachlan never wanted me. That it was a mistake and the best way to not make them is to learn from them.

Everett waits until I turn back to him. "Well, it's a good thing he became a fireman, because his acting skills suck. The man clearly has feelings for you."

I smile and shake my head. "No, he doesn't."

He laughs softly. "Sure he doesn't."

He may want me, but he doesn't love me the way I love him.

nine
Lachlan

"Daddy, we're going to be late!" Rose yells as she's standing at the front door on this fine Saturday.

Today is her first official cheer competition, and she is very excited about it. She was brought up to a higher-skilled team, which doesn't happen normally. Apparently she has natural athletic ability, which doesn't surprise me.

I was pretty good at football, and her biological mother is a dancer. Both of us were at the top of our sport.

"You're not going to be late." I tap her head as I walk past her.

"Dad! My hair!"

"Rose! It's on your head," I toss back, feeling a little too close to my father in that moment.

"Daddy, please, we can't be late. I still have to find Emma's mom so she can do my makeup and put the glitter in my hair."

She has over two hours before we have to be there, and it's a thirty-minute drive. We're fine. Also, I need more coffee.

Glitter. Makeup. Red lipstick. I can't handle this. She's six, for fuck's sake, but I was told that competition cheer is a sport and these are the rules.

"We won't be late."

She doesn't look all that confident in my promise. The guest bedroom door opens, and Ainsley comes out wearing shorts and a tank top.

Thank God I don't have coffee in my hand, because I would've dropped it. She yawns, lifting her arms up, and I want to fucking pour the hot liquid from the pot into my eyes, because that is a sight I will never get out of my head. Maybe I can burn it out.

Rose calls her name and rushes to her. "Do you want to come to my competition today?"

Please. God no.

"Wow! Look at you in your outfit. I'd love to come watch a West play a real sport," Ainsley says with a grin as she looks at me.

"Great." I turn to pour the coffee in my cup and down it.

Big mistake.

Holy fuck.

It's scalding.

I do everything not to cough or show any discomfort because I will not look like more of a moron in front of this girl.

I just barely have it under control when I feel a hand on my shoulder. "Oh, coffee." The gasp that comes out is loud, and Ainsley turns to me. "Oh my God, are you okay?"

I nod, tears stinging my eyes from holding my breath, and I cough. "Yup. Fine. Great."

She stares at me, concern in those doe eyes, and then smiles. "Coffee is hot. Do we need to put a warning label on your cup?"

"No."

It's her who should come with a warning label.

Ainsley laughs softly and turns to Rose. "What time is the competition?"

Rose nearly bounces. "Two hours, but we have to drive there, and I need to warm up, and I need one of the moms to do my makeup, because Daddy can't."

"Okay, let me go change. I want to make sure I look presentable."

I clear my throat, which is still burning. "You look good in anything you wear."

"Aww, is that a compliment?"

"It could be."

"Could be? Then I really have to find something to wow you."

I chuckle. "Ainsley, you've been doing that your whole life."

She smiles and blinks a few times. "Thank you . . ."

Rose huffs. "We're never going to make it on time!"

"Never fear, I hate being late," Ainsley tells her. "I'll change and we can head out. Do you mind if we do one thing on the way?" she asks Rose.

"What?"

"Can we maybe stop for coffee?"

Rose seems to ponder that. "If you promise we won't be late."

Ainsley lifts her hand. "I swear." She taps Rose's nose and heads back into her room to change.

I stare at the door, doing my best not to imagine her pulling her shirt off while she was definitely not wearing a bra. Then removing those shorts. I wonder what kind of underwear she has on, or does she not wear that either? Is she completely naked? If there was a fire and I went in there, would I get to see everything I've dreamed of, only just barely gotten to touch?

"Uhh, Daddy?"

I blink and move away from that line of thinking and see my daughter with her hand on her hip. "What?"

"I asked if you packed me a snack?"

Right. A snack. "I did."

"A good one?"

"I packed the one you're going to eat," I say with a shit-eating grin. Rose opens her bag and sighs in relief when she sees the bag of Cool Ranch Doritos, her favorite. She launches herself at me, wrapping her arms around my middle. "Oof, what is this for?"

"Being the best dad in the world."

"The world? All for a bag of chips?"

Rose looks up at me and nods. "My favorite chips."

"Even if you worry that you're going to be late?"

She nods. "I love you."

"I love you more."

A second later, Ainsley opens the door. "Was that fast enough?"

"Yes!" Rose releases me and runs to her. "Can we go now? Please!"

I release a sigh. "Fine, let's get Ainsley her coffee, and then we can get you to your competition."

We head to Prose & Perk, where she comes out with coffee for the both of us. "Thank you."

Ainsley smiles and I feel it in my chest. "Of course. Now, I warn you, this coffee is hot too. So, you know, don't try to do it as a shot." She tucks her hair behind her ear and turns to Rose, ignoring my glare of annoyance. "Tell me all about this competition."

Rose launches into the details and explains the costumes and how she's the youngest on the team. Seeing her this excited makes all the craziness worth it. Rose has always been an easy child. She was a great baby, never had tantrums, and when we moved to Ember Falls after my mother died, we were all each other had.

Which further solidified why my choice to walk away from a career that would've had me gone all the time was worth it.

"I love my team and the friends I have," she says with joy in every word.

Ainsley smiles. "That's the best. I can't wait to watch you!"

We pull up to the large building, which is where the competition is being held, and find her coaches.

"Why don't you double-check your bag so we can go?" I suggest.

Rose lifts her bag. "It's good."

"You have your makeup, extra hair ties, uniform, warm-ups, and anything else I forgot to mention?"

Rose nods. "Yes. Bye, Dad."

"Bye, Rosebud, break a leg."

She wraps her arms around my neck and then hugs Ainsley.

"Good luck, sweetheart."

"Thanks!" Rose says before she runs off.

I stand here next to Ainsley as I watch my daughter give hugs to all the other girls. When I turn, I see Ainsley staring at me with a strange look on her face.

"What?"

"You're a great dad, you know that?"

I don't think of it like that. "I want her to be happy. If it means carting her to cheer competitions or if she wanted a pony, I'll do what I can for her."

"Keep saying things like that and all the women will be falling all over you."

"I don't care about other women." I say the words and wonder whether she hears the double meaning. I don't care about them because I care about you.

"Who do you care about, other than Rose?"

"You."

She gasps slightly and leans back. Her lips are parted, and she stares at me with curious eyes. "You do?"

"You know I do."

Before we can get any further into this conversation we probably shouldn't be having anyway, Rose's team's name is announced over the loudspeaker, stating they should head to the ready room.

"Lachlan . . ."

"Come on, we need to find our seat. Rose will be competing soon."

I place my hand on the small of her back and lead her to the stands, kicking myself once again for letting my feelings show.

———

"Hey, Lachlan!" one of the moms—I think her name is Debbie—says with a wave of her fingers.

"Subtle," Ainsley says with a laugh.

"What?"

She raises her brows. "Don't even tell me you don't know when a woman is hitting on you."

I glance over at Debbie, who is sitting with four other moms. "She's being polite."

"I bet she is."

"Jealous?"

"Yes, I'm brimming with it."

Oh, how I missed her sarcasm on a daily basis.

We find a seat up at the top of the stadium and Ainsley grabs the blanket, draping it over her legs. "What else do you have in that bag?" I ask.

"I have some snacks, wipes, another blanket, because I never know when I might get cold, my phone, a portable charger, and my book."

"When the hell did you have time to pack all of that?"

Ainsley shifts. "I prepare. You know this. I changed quickly and then laid out all of my possible needs before deciding which would be the right things."

Caspian used to joke that if Ainsley didn't go to college or the military, she'd be a great doomsday prepper. We would ride bikes, then randomly have the idea to head down to the beach, but if Ainsley was with us, it required a detour. She'd have to go home, change, and pack a new bag that had all kinds of crap she never needed.

It wasn't until I played sports that I ever appreciated it. She'd always come with a bag, and it usually contained whatever we needed.

"I see you've perfected it—time-wise," I clarify.

"I'd like to think so."

"What book are you reading?" I ask.

She leans back, adjusting her blanket. "I just finished one last night. I've decided to start a new one later, but I'm not sure what my mood is."

"A bad one," I say under my breath.

Ainsley slaps my chest. "Ass."

"I've been called worse. So what are the choices?"

She pulls out her reading device and opens it up. "First, I felt like maybe I needed some historical romance—that's usually my jam. Then I thought some alien romance might be what I'm feeling, but then it recommended *this* book."

I take the device and eye her suspiciously. "A book about a girl loving her brother's best friend."

"Well, if you read the synopsis . . . clearly, he's in love with her and she's totally not."

I'm reading something clearly and it's not the story. "I see, well, good luck to her."

"Or to him," she adds on. "Most of the time it's the guy who is the idiot."

"Yes, women are always the sane ones."

"I would agree to that."

"I was being sarcastic," I inform her. "You, especially, are not of sound mind."

"You think about me a lot, huh?"

I laugh. "No."

I think about her all the damn time.

She stuffs the e-reader back in her bag. "Like I said, not sure what I'm in the mood for. I might go for the aliens. Maybe they have higher cognitive functions than the men on this planet."

Pretty sure that's a jab at me, but I let it go. "Happy reading."

"What about you?"

"What about me?"

Ainsley shifts to face me a little more. "Please, you have always been a reader too, Lach. What's on your TBR?"

Sometimes I forget just how much she and I shared over the years, the friendship that we formed on our own. Times when the forced trio became just her and I. We talked about things I never imagined I would with her.

Ainsley became my friend as well. I've missed her.

I've hated that I've missed her.

"I'm reading another thriller."

"Anything good?"

I shrug. "They're all starting to feel the same."

"Maybe it's time for a genre switch," she suggests. "You know

Hazel has a ton of options at her store. I bet there's something there you could try."

I give her a mischievous smile. "I could read one of your books."

"You should. It's like a how-to guide on women. More men would probably be much happier if they read romance. Lord knows you've had a pretty shitty go at it. Can't make it any worse."

I laugh once. "You think they'll fix me?"

Ainsley shakes her head. "I don't think there are enough romance novels in the world to fix you."

"You have no idea what I'm like anymore," I remind her. "Four years can change a man. Make him see the error of his ways and give in to love."

Her brown eyes widen a smidge. "You? Give in to love. Oh, please tell me about the woman in your life who has guided you toward this newfound place of awakening. Is she young? Older? Maybe she's a firefighter? Teacher? Or . . . maybe she's fictional."

She damn well knows there's no one else. Caspian would've told her, or any member of this town would've when she rolled in.

"I didn't say I had someone, just that I'm not the same guy you knew back then."

I learned how to shut down, how to turn off my desires, how to forget that the only woman I want isn't meant for me—until Ainsley walked back into my life.

"Then I stand corrected. Tell me about you." She leans in, all her attention focused on me.

I narrow my eyes because I don't think this is Ainsley wanting to know all about the last four years. I'm pretty sure this is Ainsley wanting information regarding her freaking story.

However, I'll play along.

"Let's see, I'm a Virgo who loves adventure and thrills, but also enjoys a night in where we watch a movie and I can feel all the butterflies when the guy gets the girl."

She rolls her eyes. "First of all, you're not a Virgo. You're a Libra. Secondly, shut up."

I laugh. "You asked."

"About you, not some stupid bio that's fake. We have four years of gaps to fill in."

"Tell me about you first," I say, leaning back in my chair.

"What do you want to know?"

"Anything."

Everything.

Ainsley sighs. "Let's see, I graduated top of my class from NYU. I had these grand plans that I was going to get a job in New York, write stories that people would frame—people other than my father," she clarifies. "That was just a young girl's dreams, though. Instead of a paying job, I got an internship in Manhattan, but couldn't take it because . . . bills. The Admiral said my freeloading days were over and he wasn't going to pay for me to enjoy a stress-free life."

We both laugh at that. "He's so predictable."

"Right! I swear, if Caspian or I would've agreed to wear a uniform, it would make his life so damn easy. He'd know what to do with us if we were sailors. Anyway, no amount of begging or batting of my eyelashes was enough to let me stay in that job. I got a job in the city, which was . . . freaking amazing, or at least I thought it was. My boss is nice, but I keep having to write about fashion and trending hairstyles."

She makes a pinched face at that last part. "And that isn't what you want?"

She shakes her head. "I want to write about politics and foreign policy. I want to tell stories that matter and can change someone's mind because I was able to provide an alternate view or because the facts were laid out in a clear and concise way. Most of the time I read articles and have no clue what's real, because it's an opinion piece."

"So what's stopping you?" I ask.

"You have to be assigned those stories."

The defeat in her voice makes me want to let her boss know he's a fucking idiot. Doesn't he see how brilliant she is? Ainsley was meant to set the world on fire and create something beautiful from the ashes.

She's a force that can't be contained.

"Get the stories then."

"Yes, just like that," she says on a huff.

"I'm serious, Ainsley. You're not a sit-back-and-wait girl. You've always charged ahead and gotten what you wanted. It's one of the things that I love about you."

"Again with the profession of emotions. Who are you?"

"Wouldn't you like to know."

Ainsley leans in. "It's why I'm here. To uncover all your layers."

"There's not much you don't know. Besides, I don't have layers."

"I think you do. You're a great dad who loves his daughter with all he is. You're a fireman who is willing to put his life on the line for anyone in need. You're a former elite athlete who walked away from the sport and never looked back. Most importantly, you're the captain of a college Frisbee team. Very many layers there to take off."

"Are you propositioning me to get undressed? Because I'll take my shirt off right here." I stand and she grabs my arm, pulling me down.

"Lachlan!" Her cheeks turn bright red. "You know that's not what I was saying."

"Do I? I thought you wanted me."

"I do. I mean, I don't! Not like that. Oh my God. We were having a perfectly normal conversation, and then it went pear shaped."

I grin. "It's fun making you blush."

I'd like to see her blush in other ways. Not that there can ever be an us. She's in New York and I'm in Ember Falls. It would never work, and I'm not stupid enough to think there's a way around it.

I moved here to set down roots, which were something I never had. For the first eleven years of my life, I moved every three years.

I didn't know what a home felt like. My dad was climbing the ranks of the navy, which meant we were following along with him. It was hard. I never had a sense of home, not until we finally moved to Norfolk. Once Dad was there, we bought a house next door to the MacKinleys.

My life changed because Dad decided to end his career there. That meant I got to spend seven years in one place. I had friends, and a best friend I didn't have to say goodbye to.

All my life I watched people leave.

My father for deployments. My friends when they had to move. My mother when she chose to give up on life. Rose's mother when she walked out.

I will never do that to my daughter.

Ever.

She comes first. She's always my choice. I'll choose her because I know what it feels like to never be chosen.

I've provided that stability, and I'm not going to move to the city, and I will never ask Ainsley to give up her world for me.

It's just better this way.

Her brown eyes meet mine. "I'm glad one of us enjoys it, but seriously, I want to write better pieces, only the opportunity hasn't come to me yet. I'm hoping this article opens the door for me."

I inch closer, inhaling her perfume and fighting the desire that is a constant around her. "No one ever gets everything they want, but if it matters to you, if it's something worth fighting for, then put your gloves on and get in the ring."

"And if I get knocked out?"

"Then you get up again and punch back."

She gives me a sad smile. "One day I hope you're willing to take your own advice and fight for what you want."

"I have everything I'm allowed to have."

That causes her to shift in her seat and then look at the mat. "They're starting."

And just like that the conversation is over.

ten
Ainsley

I can't sleep.

I can't stop thinking about the things he said about the girl I am.

He's right. I never was a sit-back-and-wait girl. I was raised by a father who literally commanded a fleet and who demanded his kids be leaders.

I always tried to please the Admiral. I worked hard to get good grades and be the class president, editor of the school paper, and anything else. Accolades were what got my father's notice. My mom could not have cared less. She stayed with my dad until he retired, and then she was done trying to be the trophy wife he kept on a shelf.

Still, I've always done what I can to make my parents proud.

Other than pop out a few grandchildren for my mom.

I get out of bed, grab my laptop, and head into the kitchen. On nights like these, the only thing that will settle my brain is to write.

In order for me to write, I must have sustenance.

Thankfully, on the way home from the dance competition, we stopped to grab some groceries.

I quietly open the cabinets, trying to see where he stuffed my chocolaty goodies. As I open the cabinet where I think it was, a bag of chips falls out. I freeze, looking around to see if that woke anyone. Not that it was super loud, but in the dead of the night, everything sounds ten times worse.

Nothing stirs, and I let out a sigh of relief and continue my quest for the contraband. I finally find it in the fourth one, and as I go to reach for it, the kitchen lights flick on.

I gasp, covering my mouth so I don't scream.

"What are you doing?" Lachlan's deep voice fills the silence.

"Trying to *not* have a heart attack." My heart is thumping. Jesus, he scared the crap out of me.

"Why are you up?"

"I was getting a snack."

"At three in the morning?" he asks with apparent frustration.

"I didn't realize snacks were time specific."

He walks closer. "They are when you're being loud."

I crinkle my nose. "I wasn't being loud. I'm as quiet as a mouse."

Maybe a larger mouse, but still I wasn't banging things around.

"Your version of quiet and mine are clearly different."

"Or maybe you sleep incredibly light," I say, offering another option.

Lachlan sighs and walks into the kitchen, reaching for the cabinet right behind me. I try not to let my heart speed up just a little at his closeness, but I've learned I can't ever get a grip around him.

His bare chest brushes against mine, and I wish I had a freaking sweater or jacket on so my nips wouldn't be pointing straight. As soon as he leans back, I cross my arms over my chest to hide that little hint at what I'm feeling.

"Come on, let's go out back so you don't wake Rose while you eat," he suggests.

I stay here, not sure I really want to go anywhere other than in my bed, where I can contemplate my life choices.

He stands there, lifting the bag of chips, and pushes something behind his back. "I have snacks."

I purse my lips. "Do you have chocolate?"

Lachlan snickers. "Come and find out."

He totally does, and if he doesn't, I'll find a way to punish him. I follow him out back, and he heads to the left, where there's a large bed swing.

"Oh my God!" I say, moving quickly. "I love these!"

"So does Rose. It's our favorite place to hang out."

"For a good reason."

He flips a switch for the two heaters above the bed area. "Climb up."

I don't argue. My apartment is modern and great, but it's the uniqueness of my childhood home I miss. We didn't have fancy appliances or new flooring, but we had old charm. The Admiral installed a porch swing, pool, and basketball hoop so Caspian and I had things to do at the house. We loved all of it, but what we really loved were the nooks in our home.

There was a little door under the stairs that my parents let me turn into a hideaway. I had pillows, a light, and books piled in the corner. It was tiny, but it was my safe space. For hours I'd hide under there, getting lost in a make-believe world where I could pretend to save the innocent people from darkness.

I long for that little nook most days.

Or the garden next door. The one I would go to when I wanted to feel the sun and see the boy on the other side of the fence.

"You look like you're somewhere far away," Lachlan says, drawing me from the memories of home.

I smile and shrug. "More like the past."

"What about it?"

"I was thinking about how great this house is for Rose. How much, when we were kids, our homes were really special. I don't remember much about moving around from base to base, but Caspian said the one before it was terrible."

"I hated moving. I loved my house next to yours," he says, his voice wistful. "It was a home."

"You moved more than we did."

Caspian and Lachlan are four years older, so I got to enjoy the feeling of a home more than they did.

He lets out a long yawn. "Yeah, it was horrible."

"I'm not complaining, I'm just saying that what you're giving Rose is better than we had or . . . different at least."

"I'd agree with different. I want her to have roots. She's not worried about her friends leaving after she gets close with them, or about her leaving. We didn't get that."

"No, we didn't. I didn't worry about us moving, but I remember when some of our friends moved."

Lachlan nods. "It's why that life was never for me. I went from being the kid leaving to always having people around me go. Military life is odd."

The Admiral was already pretty set in Norfolk when I was a kid, and he could pick his duty stations much easier since he was the Admiral.

"It really is. Not something you can easily explain to people either."

"Nope. I'm just glad that Dad bought the house next to you guys. Our lives changed for the better."

I shift, tucking my legs under my butt. "Well, of course, you met me."

He snorts. "Yes, that was really when my life took a nosedive."

"You meant to say 'high point.'"

"Did I?"

I nod. "Yup. Glad I could correct the error of your ways."

"Yes, you're a saint that way."

"Glad you think so," I say with a grin.

Lachlan laughs under his breath. "It was a high point."

His confession stuns me. Lachlan has never been one to toss compliments out for no reason.

"So you're saying I'm a delight?" I ask, knowing I'll get a smart-ass comment back, because he's Lachlan.

"You're something."

I smile and lean in, brushing my shoulder against him. "I knew it. I'm the sunshine of your life."

"I'd say that title belongs to Rose."

"Fine. I'll accept losing it to her."

"You never had it to begin with," he says, nudging me.

I sit up, feeling rather affronted by that. "Then who did?"

"Caspian," he says deadpan.

I laugh because, of all the things my brother is, the sunshine of someone's life is definitely not it. He's more like the dark cloud that keeps dumping buckets of rain on your head and keeps moving where you go to ensure you look dumb.

"I can't wait to tell him you said that," I joke.

"Do it and you're dead."

I raise my hands. "I'll let you keep this secret."

Lachlan places the tray of cookies in front of us, and we both grab one. It's like being kids again, and I wish, so much, that I knew what to say. I want to tell him how much I've missed him. How I would go back in time and change everything if it meant I could have him and Rose back in my life.

Yet a part of me doesn't think I would actually do that. To take it all back would change the trajectory of my life, and we wouldn't be sitting here now.

"What's wrong?" he asks, causing me to jump a little.

"Nothing. I was just . . . drifting."

He grabs another cookie. "So why couldn't you sleep?"

That's a loaded question. "Just a lot on my mind. I need to write, and I've been struggling with the right angle for the story."

"Maybe you should write about something else then."

I laugh once. "You'd like that."

"I would."

I shift to face him, crossing my legs in front of me. "Why?"

"Why what?"

I swear he does this just to piss me off. "Why would you rather I not write about this?"

Lachlan pops another cookie in his mouth, and once he's

done chewing, which takes for-freaking-ever, he sighs heavily. "Because I don't want to think about the past anymore."

"It's not about the past."

"No? You aren't going to talk about all of our glory days? How we're just a bunch of stupid jocks who can't let go of the time when we were kings?"

"I mean, that might have been in there a little. But what's the big deal? You were those things. You were destined for a life that people dream of."

Lachlan huffs. "*This* is the life that people dream of, Ainsley. Where they have a little something that's theirs. Where they can raise a family, build a life. The legacy is in the little moments, not the big things."

I disagree. "Legacy is what we leave behind, Lach. It's not moments, it's everything we are. The life we had, the things we did, the people we touched. You don't get to define that. Your past is what made you the man you are today. The things you've learned, the way you chose to follow different paths, are all part of the greater story."

It's why I love writing about people instead of fashion accessories. There's a nuance about uncovering layers of a person's life. It's all part of the threads that weave a story. Without those differences and colors, you have a muted and boring article that leaves the reader unfulfilled.

I don't want that.

"Have you forgotten what that time was like for me?"

I try to remember back that far, but it's a blur. First of all, I was so damn in love with him that I probably couldn't see anything other than a heart each time I saw his face. Those rose-colored glasses were thick too.

"I guess I have," I confess.

"I hated everything. I was so fucking sure I was going to be drafted. It was all anyone could promise. The coaches, the scouts, my teammates, and then I found out that Claire was pregnant. I walked away. I just knew that my life couldn't be that. I saw what being away does to a kid."

"I'm sorry, Lach."

He shakes his head. "You know what I hated most?"

I stay silent because I'm pretty sure it's rhetorical.

"Having to see your face after I dropped out of the draft."

I rear back slightly at that. "Me?"

I don't even remember him telling me about it. Sure, I was sort of busy with college, but still, I don't know why I would've been a worry at all.

"You thought Caspian and I were fucking heroes, and here I was, letting you down."

Without thinking, I move toward him, resting my hand on his arm. "You didn't let me down by not going into pro sports. Let's be real. It's not like I'm a fan of any sport. I go to games with friends and I'm lost."

He chuckles. "I know."

"I'm just saying that I should've never been a worry."

"I think it was just the idea of you thinking I was a loser."

The way he says it makes my stomach clench. I need to bring this conversation back to the witty banter we're both known for. Otherwise I'm going to say something stupid like: *You could never be a loser, I love you. Marry me. Let's have babies.*

I shift back to my original position and grab a cookie from the tray. "Well, you are a loser, but not because of football. Just because . . . you are."

I pop the cookie into my mouth, and Lachlan lunges forward, catching me before I can jump off. He pulls on my hips, the two of us laughing, and pins me beneath him.

"Take it back," he teases.

I wiggle, but there's no moving. "Never."

"Berry, take it back. Say, 'You are not a loser, Lachlan, you are amazing.'"

I laugh at that one. "Do you know me at all?"

He moves and holds both of my wrists in one hand. His other moves to my side, and I know exactly what he's going to do.

"Don't!" I warn.

"Don't what?"

"Don't even think about tickling me. I will scream."

He grins, leaning down closer. "No one will hear you."

"Rose will," I remind him.

"She sleeps through anything."

Great. I try to pry my arms out of his hold, but all it does is press my boobs up against his chest.

The light, fun mood of this little moment shifts.

I do not think about the fact that I'm under him.

I do not focus on his weight above me.

I don't imagine how easy it would be for him to kiss me.

None of those things I allow my mind to work through. Instead, I try to calm my racing heart.

Lachlan stares down at me, his brown eyes full of passion and something else. Something I've seen before, memorized and felt—desire.

It's there, shimmering on the edges.

Kiss me. Kiss me. Please kiss me.

I beg it in my head, knowing it must be written all over my face.

The indecision wavers between us.

However, I will not do it this time. We're not drunk. We're not young. We both know what's happening, but it has to be him.

"Fuck it."

His lips crash down on mine, and I tear my arms out of his grasp, my fingers moving to the back of his head. The silky strands slide through my fingers exactly like I remember.

He moans against my mouth, hands gripping my sides, and I want him to bruise me, mark this moment in time, but he never would. I don't think it's possible for him to hurt me, unless it's pushing me away.

That thought has no space here, though.

I open my mouth and feel his tongue slide against mine.

God, it's even better than I remembered.

eleven
Lachlan

She feels like home.
I should stop.

I need to stop.

But, fuck, I can't.

She shifts her body, wrapping her leg around my hip, kissing me as much as I'm kissing her.

For years I've done my best not to remember how her body fit so perfectly with mine.

I pull her tighter, wanting to absorb her because for the first time in so long, I feel alive.

My lips leave hers and kiss down her neck, absorbing every sigh she lets out. Just one more second of this. Just one more and I'll stop.

The lie isn't even believable. Ainsley takes my face in her hands and pulls me back to her mouth. My hands roam over her perfect body, taking in each curve and dip. I kiss her deeper as my fingertips breach the hem of her shirt, wanting to take even more from her. She moves one hand to cover mine, pressing it upward. Just as I'm starting to move higher, I hear the sliding door open.

Like cold water over our heads, the moment freezes. We break apart immediately, and I roll her behind me, shifting to my side so Rose hopefully won't see her.

"Daddy?"

"Hi, baby, what's wrong?"

"I had a bad dream."

I'm having one right now. "Go back to bed and I'll come in."

She rubs her eyes with the back of her hands. "Okay. I was scared."

"I know, I'll be right there."

Rose goes back inside, and I breathe a sigh of relief, as does Ainsley.

Fuck. Ainsley. I was kissing her and . . . Jesus Christ. Did I learn nothing from the last time?

She shifts into the corner of the bed swing and wraps her arms around her legs. I turn to her to say something, anything, because I was so fucking out of line, but Ainsley speaks first.

"Go check on her. I'll clean this up."

"Ainsley . . ."

"Don't say a word, just go."

She seems upset, and once again I fucked up. I never should've kissed her. I've spent years perfecting my ability to resist her, but this . . . I couldn't do it.

I stand, feeling like the biggest piece of shit. "We're going to talk about this," I tell her. "Tomorrow, we're going to have a conversation."

Ainsley clears her throat. "Rose needs you more than we need to discuss any of this."

"Don't run away again."

I run my hands through my hair and head inside to hopefully do right by one of the women in my life.

———

"Daddy, where's Ainsley?" Rose asks.

"Probably sleeping. I don't know."

I've done my absolute best not to think about Ainsley since

last night. After I got Rose to sleep, I went out back to talk to her, but she was already gone. Instead of making another mistake by going into her room, I went to bed, ready to have it out today.

However, it's almost ten in the morning, and she still hasn't come out of her room.

Rose runs to the front of the house and yells back. "Her car is gone!"

I let out a long breath and look heavenward. She fucking left? Jesus. Again? Are we going to go back to another four years?

I walk over to her room, open the door, and breathe a sigh of relief. Her stuff is still here.

Hopefully that means she's returning and didn't just leave her stuff for me to mail back.

I turn to Rose. "I'm sure she went for coffee or something."

I grab my phone and text her.

> Hey, are you okay? You left and Rose is worried.

I am, too, but I leave that part off.

I wait for a reply, but she doesn't answer.

Great.

Just before I can start to really freak out, the front door opens. "Good morning!" Ainsley's voice is bright and animated. "I brought cake pops!"

"Cake pops!" Rose yells and rushes toward her. "I love cake pops."

"Because they're amazing," Ainsley agrees and brings the box to the table.

Her eyes meet mine, and I wait for her to glare or tell me I'm a fucking prick. Instead, she smiles. "I brought our morning person some coffee too. Maybe that'll make you nicer."

"I'm always nice."

Rose laughs. "You're always mean in the morning, Daddy."

"He really is," Ainsley agrees.

"I am not."

"You are," Rose tosses back.

I grunt.

The girls share a look, and I now understand why some animals eat their young.

"Enough talking about my mood, which is perfectly fine. I have to get ready to head to the field."

Rose groans. "Can I go to Becky's and play?"

She truly hates going to the field. "If her mom says it's okay."

Rose turns to Ainsley. "Do you want to come to Becky's too?"

Ainsley laughs softly. "Normally I would totally take you up on that, but I think I'm going with your dad today. I need to watch their practice."

"Why?" Rose asks with her nose scrunched.

"Well, if I need to write about their sport, then I have to observe."

Rose shrugs. "Daddy? Can I use the tablet to text Becky?"

"Yes."

She runs off, leaving me alone with Ainsley. The two of us don't say anything for a few seconds. Her eyes move to me, and then she looks away before letting out a sigh. "I think we should talk about last night."

"Okay. You're right."

Ainsley takes the seat across from me, her eyes full of worry. "I think we should get married."

I choke on my coffee. *"What?"*

"Married. We should get married. I mean, I'm ruined now. You owe me as a gentleman. I'm spoiled goods, and you have to marry me. We were caught, and my reputation is at stake."

My head is spinning, and I'm not even sure what conversation we're having. "Ainsley . . ."

"I'm serious, Lachlan. I'm a lady, and you totally took advantage of me. That comes with consequences. We'll marry quickly and it'll all be fine."

I stare at her, my jaw slack, and then I rub my temples. She's got to be joking.

She starts again. "I told the Admiral and Caspian this morning that I've been compromised and there's no other way to fix this other than marriage. They both agreed. Caspian will be here today to give his blessing, and the Admiral will be here tomorrow for the wedding."

"Tomorrow? What?" I stand, pushing the chair out behind me.

Ainsley places both hands on the table, entwining her fingers. "It's the only way. You kissed me. You almost touched a boob, that's . . . marriage, buddy."

I wait for the punch line, or maybe I'm just waiting for her brother to come punch me because . . .

A loud, long laugh falls from her lips. "You should see your face! Ha!"

I'm going to kill her. "What is wrong with you?"

"Me? You're the one who looks like you might pass out. Relax, Lachlan. I'm well aware that last night was something you regret, or whatever you've convinced yourself of. I'm completely fine. We're fine. You don't need to be worried that I have some grand ideas about what last night was. I'm not doodling your name in my notebook or hoping for anything. It was just a kiss."

"It was."

She nods. "Yes, and don't worry, my dad won't be coming. He has no idea how many boys I've kissed or hooked up with."

The idea of other men anywhere near her makes my jaw clench. "Right."

"I mean, we're not in the eighteen hundreds. It's fine."

"Sure."

It's completely not fine that other guys took advantage of her. None of that is fine. It's not fine that I did it, either, but at least I love her. I would fucking lay down my life for her, even if we can never be together.

Ainsley leans back in her seat. "Now, let's talk about practice today. Is it the last one before the big game?"

The fact that she just changed topics like that has my brain unable to keep up. However, this is Ainsley, and she's always been this way. Although it's probably a good thing we don't talk about other men kissing her, because my ego can't take it.

"Yes."

"Okay. I'll observe. I talked to Everett, and he said after practice we can grab coffee and talk, so I'll take my car."

The fuck she is going with Everett for coffee—alone. "I'll drive us both."

"Why?"

"It's better for the environment." I give the absolute worst excuse.

Ainsley's brows furrow. "Umm, I drive a hybrid and you're in a pickup. I'm pretty sure your car is the offender here."

"Doesn't matter. No need to double it."

I really should slam my head against the wall to hopefully knock some sense into it. Seriously, I look like a babbling idiot.

She opens her mouth to say something and then stops. "Okay then. Maybe while we're doing the interview, you can chime in with your one-word answers, and that'll really add to the conversation."

Instead of speaking, because I seem to be unable to say anything intelligent around her, I nod, get up, and head into my room, where at least I know she won't be.

twelve

Ainsley

After my freak-out this morning, which led me incredibly close to running away, changing my name, and never returning to my current life, I got a grip and came back—with cake pops.

I've spent most of the last four years trying to forget what kissing Lachlan West is like, and this time it was even better.

And worse.

Because now I have a new memory to rattle around in my stupid brain for years, hating that I'll never have more of it. I have a new taste and smell to obsess over. He's pretty much ruined mint and chocolate for me, thanks to the cookies we were eating.

Now every time I have freaking ice cream, I'm going to think of his lips.

He's ruining everything for me.

And I hate him for it.

We just dropped Rose off and I'm doing my absolute best to be normal.

Whatever that means.

"How long will your practice last?" I ask, breaking the awkward silence that has been building in the thirty seconds since she left.

"About an hour. What about your meeting with Everett?"

"My interview could be an hour or more. Depends on how forthcoming he is and what we discuss."

I'm hoping I can get a good backstory on each of the four guys. Then I can build off a similarity between them.

"You know this story of yours isn't going to work?"

I sigh. "That's what you keep saying. You also know I don't need you for this story, right? I can very easily call your dad and talk to him. He was a huge part of your college career."

Lachlan snorts. "Yeah, what he thought he could gain."

I hate that, even after these four years, Lachlan and his father still haven't found a way through their past issues. When his mother died, Lachlan blamed him. If his father had cared about her, been there for her, not let her basically fall apart when he left, then she'd be around.

"You should talk to him, Lachlan," I urge gently.

He turns his head to me. "No."

I wait a second, trying to think of the right things to say. Lachlan's father and mine are close friends. I've heard conversations that weren't mine to hear, but I know how much his father aches for her. How much he misses her and how much he blames himself without the addition of Lachlan's rage.

"I know you're angry and I get it, I really do, but I think he tried. I think he loved your mother and wanted her to get better, but . . ." I stop when I see the way he grips the wheel. I can't fix this. I shouldn't even try. "I'm sorry. I shouldn't have said anything."

His fingers loosen just a touch. "I was there, Ainsley. I lived in that house and saw how much he *tried*."

"You're right. My perspective is skewed."

He lets out a long breath. "You've always wanted to fix the world, but some things just can't be repaired. They're too broken, and that relationship was buried alongside her."

I reach out, resting my hand on his arm. "She loved you very much. I remember her telling me when she brought over my birthday cake each year."

Isabelle West thought her son hung the moon. That boy could do no wrong in her eyes, and I understood her, since it was the same in my book.

She was the kindest woman, but she struggled so much with depression, and when she found out she had cancer, she decided to give up. Ultimately, it was like when that choice was made, she was just done.

I was at the house with my family when Lachlan was told. I heard the screams and absolute agony as he raged about his father not doing enough. It broke every part of my heart, seeing him fall apart.

Lachlan takes my hand in his for a moment before releasing it. "She loved to bake for every kid in the neighborhood, but most especially you."

"She was so good at it, and I loved her."

His mother made the absolute best cakes. They were weird flavors, but so damn good. She made me a pistachio-and-chocolate cake every single year. It was my favorite, and even when she tried to teach my mom, it wasn't the same. After that, Mrs. West made everyone's cakes. Everything was from scratch, and she designed elaborate decorations representing the year.

"Other than when she put all those lips on yours," he reminds me.

My cheeks flame and I cover my face. "Ugh, I tried to forget that one!"

"You never should've let her know you kissed John."

"I didn't let her know! She caught me!"

Talk about mortifying.

Lachlan laughs softly. "She walked in on me once."

I gasp. "Like, doing it?"

He nods. "It was . . . a lecture I never wanted to repeat."

"Well, considering I had a two-hour lecture on what boys really want, I can imagine yours was even more in depth."

"It was, and then my father got home and I got round two, which was more about what I put my mother through."

I laugh, trying to imagine how that went over. "I remember

when Caspian went to prom and my mother and father sat him down for an hour to talk about condoms. I think he wanted to die."

His gaze turns to me. "I was there next to him!"

"Oh! That's right, I remember that. I'll never forget when my mom got a banana and talked about how I wasn't allowed to eat it because it was for Caspian to practice with." God, my parents were strange.

"I got the cucumber. English style," he adds on as though he's so proud. "She knew I needed the extra length."

"Oh, were they teaching to scale?"

He shrugs. "Not saying a word."

I laugh. "No, not a word. I'll find out the truth."

I grab my phone, and Lachlan keeps glancing at me and the road as I dial my brother. "Who are you calling?"

"Caspian."

"What up, buttercup?" my brother answers way too joyfully before Lachlan can grab the phone.

"Hey, did Mom teach you how to put on condoms based on size of vegetables? Lachlan says he was more English cucumber, and you needed the smaller fruit?"

"What the fuck?"

"I did not!"

They both yell at the same time.

"I'm asking because Lachlan was pretty proud of his cucumber."

"Why the fuck are you talking about the size of your dick with my sister?" Caspian asks, and I lean back with a grin.

Lachlan glares at me. "We weren't. Calm down, asshole. We were talking about embarrassing parent shit."

Caspian sighs. "Prom?"

"Yup."

Lachlan's eyes are full of warning. "Once again, Berry is causing issues."

Well now I really plan to. I hit the mute button without Lachlan knowing. "Cas, I just wanted you to know that last night, Lachlan pinned me down on the bed swing, made out with me, and dry humped me a little." Lachlan nearly runs off the side of the road as he grabs for my phone. "It is on mute!" I yell.

"Fuck! Are you trying to get me killed?"

I shake my head. "No, but you're trying to kill us both!"

"Hello? Lach? Ainsley?" my brother says.

I sigh heavily. "Sorry, I hit the mute button. Anyway, I just wanted to annoy you both. Love you."

"Love you, too, and please don't talk about your dick with Ainsley."

I roll my eyes. "Yes, because I know nothing about that. I guess we're back in the Victorian era? Should I marry Lachlan?" I grin, loving how this has come full circle.

"I swear, Ainsley, you get worse as you get older," Caspian complains.

"On that note, I'll talk to you later with Dad on three-way!" I hang up before he can complain, and I feel quite proud of myself.

Lachlan parks the truck and turns to me. "You're a troublemaker."

"I try."

"Try to *not* be one."

I shrug. "There's no fun in that."

"I'm going to need to start therapy after this."

"I have a few names," I offer helpfully.

Lachlan exits the truck, and I giggle before following him out. Today is sweltering hot. I don't know how anyone would willingly come play a sport in this heat, but the three other guys are standing outside their cars along with about ten new guys.

Okay . . . this is interesting.

"Ainsley, this is the rest of the team."

"Oh!" I say, walking to them. "Hi, I'm Ainsley MacKinley. I'm writing a story on the four elderly gentlemen on your team."

"Elderly," Lachlan scoffs.

Each introduce themselves and shake my hand. I ask how they all came to join the team. The one—I think his name is Tate—

looks to be maybe twenty-two, and he speaks first: "We all attend community college."

I wonder whether that's how they justify this as a college team.

Another one of the college kids nods. "Yeah, since all of these guys are enrolled in a class, it gives us the ability to play against other teams."

Well, well, I was right.

I turn to Lachlan, Everett, Killian, and Miles. "So you're all taking classes?"

"For professional development, yes," Miles answers. "My military time affords me the right to free college, so . . . I'm taking it."

"I see. We wouldn't want the government funds to go to waste."

Lachlan huffs. "Enough with the inquisition. We need to practice to be ready for next week."

They grab their bags and Frisbees and head off to the field. This time it actually looks like a team. They line up in different ways and start the game, tossing the Frisbee. Is it tossing? Chucking? Maybe it's something else. I make a note to ask them the correct terms.

After about thirty minutes, I think I might be roasting. I wore a bathing suit under my clothes because I knew it was going to be so freaking hot. It was like the heater got turned on and now I miss those cool mornings. I pull my tank top off and respray my sunscreen. There is literally nothing happening that I need to pay attention to, so I pop my earbuds in and take advantage of the sun.

Just as my favorite song about tortured poets hits the bridge, my sun is gone.

I open my eyes to see Lachlan standing over me.

"What are you doing?" I ask as I pull my earbuds out.

"I was going to ask you the same."

"Isn't it obvious? I'm tanning."

He sighs and wipes the sweat off his forehead. "Put clothes on. I really don't want to have to kill anyone today."

I smile and then hide it before he can get too mad. "Lach, it's freaking gross out. I'm enjoying the sun." I glance at the guys from around him, and no one is paying any attention to me. "From what I can see, you're the only one fazed by this."

"I'm not fazed. I'm irritated because instead of focusing on the game, they're all trying to get an eyeful."

"Maybe you all should learn to avoid distractions. Now please stop blocking my sun, since I have another hour of waiting for this to be over."

He shakes his head, probably realizing he's not going to get anywhere with me, and heads back onto the field.

I stand and spread the blanket out beside my chair and pull my shorts off, then lie on my stomach. There, that should be better.

With my eyes closed, I let the lyrics lull me into a state of nothingness. It was an exhausting night where I got no sleep and was hit with a lot of anxiety.

"Ainsley."

I hear Lachlan and feel additional heat on my shoulder. "Go away, sleeping."

"Come on, you need to get up. You got one hell of a sunburn."

"Sunscreen on," I mutter.

"Well, someone should tell your ass that, as it's rather red."

I go to roll to my side, but as soon as I do, I feel the burn. "Oh my God! I burnt my ass!"

I push up and turn my head to look. It's red. Like *red* red. This is going to be horrible.

"I have aloe at home," says Lachlan.

That's not going to help me now. "That's great, but I have a chapped ass. Literally!"

He tries not to laugh but fails. "Sorry, well, not really."

I give him a good glare. "This isn't funny. How the hell am I going to sit?"

This is going to be miserable. I carefully slide my shorts on and bite my lip when the material just barely grazes my skin.

Stupid me for not spraying the damn sunscreen on when I took my pants off. Ugh.

"Are you going to be all right?" Lachlan asks with way too much humor in those brown eyes.

"Don't even pretend you don't think this is funny."

He lifts both hands. "I never said anything of the sort."

Everett walks over with a huge smile. "Are you ready?"

Damn it, the interview. I need to do this, but . . . how am I supposed to sit? I look at Lachlan's grin and smile back at Everett. "I am. Can you drive? I don't have my car."

"Of course, consider it a date."

I glance back to Lachlan. "See you later."

And I walk away with so much pain on my chapped ass.

———

"Why are you standing?" Hazel asks as she hands me the coffee. "Does he smell?"

"Because my butt is burned." She blinks a few times and I sigh. "I laid out while they practiced, and I didn't sunscreen appropriately."

She snort-laughs and then tries to cover it with a cough. "Sorry, I'm not laughing."

"You totally are."

"All right, I am. I have burn cream upstairs. I'll go grab it."

"You are an angel," I say before drinking the coffee.

"It could happen to the best of us."

I laugh under my breath and then head over to where Everett is sitting. "Hey, thanks again for this."

"I'm happy to help, and it gives me the opportunity to try to force *someone* to talk to me."

I glance over to where Hazel disappeared, which is where he's also staring. "She said you guys were best friends?"

"We were—we are. I don't know what we are, but the woman is maddening and holds grudges like no one else in the world. Be careful if you get on her bad side."

I grin. "I'll keep that under advisement."

"I heard that!" Hazel yells from the back.

"It's not like you can punish me worse than you are!" Everett calls back to her.

"Challenge accepted."

I giggle. "Now you've done it. Never challenge a woman who is already pissed."

He sighs heavily. "One day I'll learn. Until then I have you here, and you happen to be interested in my life."

"That I am."

"Are you going to sit?"

I glance at the metal chair and internally groan, but I managed to handle the car, so I need to suck it up. I gingerly sit down and try to focus on the cooling effect of the metal, not the searing pain, and force a smile.

"Okay, let's talk about sportsball."

He raises one brow. "Sportsball?"

"Whatever one you played."

Everett chuckles. "I played baseball, but I threw out my shoulder three times during college."

"That must've been hard."

"It was, but the worst was the last time. I was a catcher, and if you can't throw, you can't do a lot of things."

I do my best to school my features, because what the hell does throwing have to do with being a catcher? The job description is right there—catch.

"It sounds like a career ender," I bluff, as though I have a clue about sports.

"It was and it wasn't. I think *I* was the reason it ended."

"Why is that?" I ask.

Everett leans back and sighs. "I was in love with the sport. It was my wife, mistress, and only love. I didn't care about anything else other than making it to the majors. Baseball is . . . it's hard to explain, but it can be the most amazing thing, and it can also destroy you. Most guys never see the MLB. They spend their best years fighting in the minors for a chance to be brought up. Sure, there are those stories we see, but it's not the norm. It was actually Hazel who helped. She sat me down after my last surgery and asked one question: Is this pain worth the possible price?"

"Good question."

He nods. "Right. Immediately I was like, of fucking course it is. No one could tell me that baseball wasn't worth every ache and pain I felt. Three days later, the doctor explained how I'd have loss of motion or strength for at least six months, and he didn't think playing ball was going to be possible for at least a year. I knew at that moment there was no amount of work that was going to put me back in the running for playing professionally. I had a year left of college, and my coach allowed me to stay on the roster, so I kept my full ride, and I applied for vet school."

His story is definitely not what I expected. "If someone had told me my junior year of college that my dream of being a journalist was no longer an option, I don't know that I would've had the foresight to change gears so quickly."

Hazel approaches with the bottle of aloe. "Don't let him fool you. He didn't handle it well. He went through a ridiculous party phase, drank himself to sleep for weeks."

"She was there," Everett adds on. "I wouldn't have survived if it weren't for Hazel."

I smile. It's so clear the two of them deeply care about each other. "Friendships often save us when we're at our lowest." I try so hard not to let my mind drift to Lachlan and how hard it was after our rift, and while I don't know Hazel or Everett well, I do know genuine kinship when I see it. "I don't know why you two are upset with each other, but as an outsider, I would beg you both to take a good hard look and ask yourselves, if something happened to the other tomorrow, would this reason seem silly or worth the strain?"

Hazel looks to him and he grins at her. "Come on, Hazel, forgive me."

She rolls her eyes and shakes her head. "You were forgiven weeks ago. I just like seeing you sweat it out."

He turns to me. "See what I deal with?"

"Yes, because you're a walk in the park?"

"I'm like sunshine and rainbows."

Hazel scoffs. "More like storm clouds and tornadoes."

"All right," I say, breaking it up before it becomes a hurricane. "I'm glad you're both talking. Is Hazel why you came back to town?"

Everett shifts, and I wonder whether I hit a sore spot. "Partially. I grew up here, and my family moved when I went to college. After I finished school and became a veterinarian, I planned to stay in Texas, but the town needed help, and Hazel convinced me to give it a few months, and it's been five years."

"Can I ask one more thing about baseball?"

"Yeah, sure."

"Why did you deserve a full ride to college, because you could play sports, over someone else who planned to be a vet all along?"

He clears his throat and takes a second. "I didn't. I just could play ball."

thirteen
Lachlan

Today is the day.

It's the day where I am going to annihilate these little college kids and show them that age is nothing but a number.

When I head out into the kitchen, Ainsley is sitting at the table with a cup of coffee and her nose deep in a book. So much that she doesn't even notice me.

She's so beautiful sitting in my kitchen. Her dark-brown hair is in a braid that doesn't really look like a braid, but works. Ainsley pulls her lower lip between her teeth as she turns the page, almost as though she's living it with the character.

I watch for a moment, wishing that circumstances were different and that this could be my life in some way, but it can't.

I learned a long time ago that we don't get what we want in life, and people may have good intentions, but their wants may not align and I've gotten hurt.

Pessimistic? Maybe, but it's honest.

Besides, I have a feeling it's going to be a good day and I'm not going down the shitty roads with my thoughts.

I clear my throat.

"Oh! Good morning, my little adorable Frisbee player."

My good mood disappears just like that.

"There's nothing little about me."

She rolls her eyes. "Such a man. So what's the plan?"

"The plan?"

"For today."

I shrug. "Not sure what part you're questioning. We get our team opponent in about five minutes. Then we head to the tournament grounds to prepare for the day."

"Oh, this is, like, an all-day thing?"

"Yes, it's the best out of three."

Her brows shoot up. "You all are going to do this multiple times?"

"Yes . . ."

"Is there medical on site? I mean, I'm not a doctor or anything, but you're all a little . . . you know, old."

I huff, but . . . yes, we already made sure. I'm not going to lie, I'm a little worried one of us might pass out trying to impress her.

Not a chance in hell I'm going to let her know that. "And you're a little annoying, but here we are."

"*Anyway*, is Rose at her friend's house for the day?"

"Yes, she hates coming to the games."

"Boy, I wonder why," Ainsley says with a grin.

I grab my massage gun, supplements, phone, and knee brace, further making me wonder whether I am going to need the medical tent.

My phone pings, and I groan when I see Everett's message in the group.

EVERETT

Schedule is out, we're playing the Swift-bees in round one.

MILES

I wonder if they're going to shake it off when we show them we're the masterminds.

I roll my eyes.

> **KILLIAN**
>
> I'm not even going to ask why you're talking in song titles.
>
> **MILES**
>
> Well, I'm a school principal, what the hell do you think I hear all day?
>
>> Yes, but you don't have to repeat it.
>
> **EVERETT**
>
> Is anyone else going to point out that Killian knew these were song titles?
>
>> I was leaving it to you.
>
> **KILLIAN**
>
> Dickheads. All of you.
>
>> You're just pissed we caught you.
>
> **MILES**
>
> I have the best idea! You guys are going to think I'm a fucking genius.

There's not a chance of that happening, since most of the time he's a dumbass.

> **EVERETT**
>
> Oh, this should be good.

Suddenly I feel warmth at my back and turn to see Ainsley peeking over my shoulder. "Excuse me?"

"Just keeping up on the gossip. A group chat about Frisbee—scintillating. Did you find out who you're playing?"

"Yes, nosy ass, we did."

She grins. "And?"

"The Swift-bees in the first round."

Ainsley's eyes go wide, and I really wish I didn't have to say that aloud.

"*Wait*. You have team names?"

I failed to mention that, and for this reason. Although, after today, there's no way we're going to be able to hide it from her. So I go with being proud. Sure, we're older. Sure, we have the most ridiculous name, but we didn't have the option to change it, because Hazel is who registered it for us.

"We do."

She silently laughs, covers her mouth, and then drops her hand. "I'm sorry, I'm sure you all have rather respectable names. Something like Ultimate Manchildren or Frisbros or Floppy Discs."

That second one would've been good. "No, it's much more dignified. We're the Disc Jocks."

Ainsley holds it together for about two seconds, which is more than I thought she would anyway, before bursting out laughing. "Oh my God! I'm starting to really be excited about this now. I mean, this article is going from a boring follow-up about a football god who walked away to a thought-provoking piece about why schools should give scholarships more on merit instead of sports."

"You do know that sports are what brings money into those colleges so they can give academic money out, right?" I ask.

She crosses her arms over her chest. "I'm well aware of that."

"And since you got that off the hard work that me and my other athlete friends provided, I'll happily accept an apology," I say with a brow raised.

There's about a snowball's chance in hell of getting that from her, but I wait.

And wait.

Ainsley snorts. "Dream on, buddy."

Figures as much. "Ungrateful to my contributions to your life, as always."

"Umm, I'm sorry, what the hell have you contributed ever?"

"I just told you. My physical prowess has allowed you to go to school at a reduced rate."

"You didn't even go to NYU!" she yells and throws her hands up. "We didn't even have a football team. Jesus."

I shrug. "Semantics."

"Okay, Mr. I-Am-So-Sports-I'm-in-Community-College-to-Still-Play, what exactly are the hopes of the Disc Jocks?"

"To win."

I mean, is there even any other option? I don't think so.

"I guess I'm trying to ask what exactly you all hope to gain out of this."

I narrow my eyes a little, wondering whether this is Ainsley, my longtime friend, or Ainsley, the reporter who is trying to get ahead in her career.

Either way, I'm the Lachlan I've always been and love nothing more than pissing her off.

"Fun."

And with that I grab my things and head into the living room.

In normal Ainsley fashion, she doesn't like not having the last word and grunts, storming in behind me.

"What was Miles's genius idea?" she asks.

Ugh, I forgot about that text thread. I open it up to several more messages, which means I missed any chance to veto this.

MILES

We all wear different Taylor Swift shirts. We can psych them out.

KILLIAN

I'm sorry, what?

MILES

You know, I love this idea. My sister is a huge fan and has shirts. I bet I could get some.

EVERETT

We can all be a different era.

KILLIAN

Again, what the hell are you talking about?

MILES

Listen, Grandpa, you just wear the shirt. Maybe you should be the first one since . . . you're the oldest.

KILLIAN

Fuck off. You're the worst on the team.

EVERETT

Ladies, focus. Okay, shirts. Let's make this happen. We can walk on with background music too.

MILES

Done. I'll bring the shirts, someone get a boombox.

EVERETT

Do they still make those?

MILES

I don't know, but if they do, I'm sure Killian has one.

KILLIAN

* middle finger emoji *

I swear they are trying to find new ways to torture me.

. . .

> Absolutely not happening. Do you all forget we have Ainsley writing about us? No way are we going to embarrass ourselves more.

EVERETT

> It was decided on. Sorry, bro, those are the rules.

What rules? He's out of his damn mind.

MILES

> Got the shirts!

Fucking hell. This day just can't get worse. I turn around, and Ainsley is leaning against the wall. Here goes the worst.

"His idea was Taylor Swift shirts."

She starts a smile, then pulls her lips tight. Then her hand covers her mouth as she almost doubles over. Her whole body is shaking, and then she looks up at me, letting her laugh fly.

Yeah, I would be doing the same.

"Please can I pick which one you'll wear?"

"No."

"Please? I promise it'll be a good one."

I roll my eyes. "You are out of your fucking mind if you think I'm going to let you pick my clothes out."

She grins, grabs her bag, and winks. "We'll see what the other guys think."

Then she walks out and toward the truck.

I stand here for a second, groan, and get ready to head to what is sure to be an absolute shit show.

fourteen
Ainsley

When we get to the field, groups of college teams are spread out all over with their little pop-up tents.

I follow Lachlan, taking photos as we go to help with remembering all of this, because it's a lot to take in.

Off to the left, Everett and Miles call us over.

"Hey there, Ainsley."

I smile at Everett. "Hello there, boys. Are you all ready for your big day?"

Miles nods. "We are in our winning era."

Lachlan sighs heavily. "I'm not wearing a shirt."

"I think he should be the *Lover* era. He's totally in his happy mood."

He side-eyes me. "Shut up."

"Make me."

"So many ways to make that happen," Lachlan says with a laugh.

I know which way I'd like to choose, but that's neither here nor there. I turn to Miles. "I hear that you're responsible for this brilliant plan to psych out the other team?"

"Is it psychological warfare, or did I just want a way to embarrass Lachlan?"

"Either one, I'm on board," I tell him. "Do you have a shirt for me?"

"Of course. Take your pick."

I look through the pile and opt for *Reputation* because . . . I love me some angry girl power music.

Just then Killian comes over with a bunch of the other guys who are attending community college to play in this league.

"Well, well, if it isn't the old-man team." A young kid comes up behind us, crossing his arms and fighting a grin.

Oh, this is so going to be fun to watch. Immediately the four men in question posture a little. Lachlan's chest puffs out, and Killian seems to grow taller.

"Come to see who is going to defeat you, Grant?" Miles asks.

"Defeat us? Please. We're going to wipe the floors with you."

"Sure, kid."

"Whatever, pops. You're so old you won't even be able to see the disc."

Oh, for shit talk, this is sad.

I turn my head to see what the guys are going to come back with. I really hope it's better than his volley at them.

Lachlan faces Everett. "Didn't he say that last month? I swear he did. He came over here, talking shit, and then we annihilated them. Do you remember that? I know I'm old, so maybe my memory is off."

Everett purses his lips and pinches his chin. "No, I'm pretty sure you're right. Miles, do you remember it?"

"You know, we beat so many people, I can't remember if Total Discbags was below us, but . . ."

Killian jumps in. "Wait, wait, wait, they had to be because we won! That's right. Grant, were you there?"

Grant seems to fume a little, and I almost feel bad for the kids since . . . you know, these are grown men and all. "Not this time."

My face falls, and I almost want to hug him because he really needs to work on his game if he's going to come over here. "Grant, is it?" I ask. "Honey, these guys have decades on you in the shit-talking game. Next time talk about the fact that one has a knee brace or threaten to kick him."

"Ainsley," Lachlan says with a warning in his tone.

I ignore that because . . . what's he going to do? Pin me down and kiss me? I'm all for that. I keep talking to Grant. "Maybe watch some videos for tips or something. Better yet, leave it on the pitch and just kick their ass that way."

Grant looks slightly offended, but I'm just trying to help him out. He leaves without another word, and I hope he takes my advice. Sparring with these guys is a sport in itself.

"It's a field not a pitch. We're not playing soccer," Lachlan says after a minute.

"Is there a difference?"

He rolls his eyes. "I'm really confused why you were chosen for a sports piece."

"Well, my decrepit friend, I'm not writing about sports. It's more like sports with a twist of human interest and a splash of money for colleges."

"Money for colleges? I thought we already talked about why athletes get scholarships."

"You can't tell me there's not some backdoor dealings with this stuff. Everett and I talked at length about his offers. I think there's a story there," I tell him. "I'll learn more after my meeting with the others."

Since he's no help.

Lachlan pinches the bridge of his nose. "Some days, I wonder about you."

"What I'm hearing is that you think about me often."

"I don't."

I shrug. "That's what you just said."

"I said I wonder about you, meaning I wonder how you get through life without walking into walls."

"Easy, I just keep my eyes open," I explain.

He sighs. "Let's get set up."

When he said "set up," I really thought it would be like the others. A tent, a blanket, maybe a chair or two, but oh, no. It's nothing like that.

These are grown men who know how to do a tournament setup.

There are four tents tied together, each having a quadrant where there are specific uses—one with chairs and a table, one where the food will be handled, one for stretching and an array of things I have no idea about, and another for overflow.

The food side is especially amazing, with a grill, chips, soda, waters, and all kinds of fruits and veggies.

"Are we tailgating?" I ask.

Miles laughs. "That's after. The beer has to stay in the truck since this is a college event."

"Yes, and you're all such doe-eyed college kids."

He opens his eyes wide. "Aren't we?"

Fools. They all are, but I really like these guys and see why they all get along so well.

"All right, explain how today works. Let's say you beat the Swift-bees, then what?"

"It's pretty easy. We play them, win, and go on. We have three games total, and if you lose two games, you're out completely. We've never experienced that, so . . ."

"I forgot, you guys are, like, a *huge* deal in the Frisbee world."

Miles grins. "We sure are, sweetheart."

I laugh and shake my head. "You're trouble."

"You have no idea."

Lachlan comes beside me. "Don't you need to warm up?"

Miles salutes his friend. "Sure thing, coach."

He heads over to the stretching section, and they all start to warm up.

"Shouldn't you be joining your team?" I ask.

Lachlan clears his throat. "Someone has to make sure you're not accosted."

"By the feral Frisbee players?"

"The ones on my team, apparently."

"What does it matter to you?"

He jerks his head. "What does that mean?"

Exactly what I said. Why is he worried about anyone talking to me? He and I aren't together—we've never been. I'm at worst his best friend's sister—at best, his friend. Neither of those titles gives him the rights to anything. Still, I'm pretty sure I know why, and while I'd love to push him and force him to say he wants me, I know Lachlan.

He won't.

His deep issues regarding people choosing to leave him will never go away, and I'm not meant to stay.

"It means it really isn't your business if someone does flirt with me. You had your chance to marry me after you kissed me, and you passed on it."

"It's a wonder why."

"See! Even you get it. I'm happy to call the Admiral and let him know your hands touched my person."

He rolls his eyes. "Heaven help me."

"Yo, Lach! Let's go. It's time to show these Swift-bees it's about to be a cruel summer."

"That was just bad, Miles!" I call back.

"Really? I've been working on it for our trash-talking during the game. I thought it was a good one."

I giggle. "Maybe start with asking if they're ready for it!"

"Oh! Good one." He puffs out his chest, showing off his black shirt with a snake on it.

Miles runs off and Lachlan lets out a deep sigh. "I regret this more than ever."

"Is it because now there are witnesses?"

"Yes."

I bump his shoulder. "Don't worry, no one really reads my articles anyway. Let's just hope it doesn't go viral."

"Knowing my luck—it will."

Knowing my luck—it won't.

"Well, either way, you better get out there and show those little girls what you're made of, big guy."

Lachlan grunts and then rushes onto the field, and I grab my chair to watch the shit show.

The thing is, it's not a shit show. It could be, but I'm not watching the game. I'm watching him. About ten minutes into the game, he ripped his shirt off, tossing it at me as he ran past. Now he's shirtless, and every glorious muscle is on display. His arms are huge, and he moves with such grace it's making me hotter than I'd care to admit.

After about an hour of them running back and forth, yelling at each other, and yelling when they get a point—*Touchdown? What the hell do they call it? I really need to learn these freaking terms before the article*—they form a huddle.

His back is to me, that perfect ass pushed out, and I want to bite it.

Where the hell did that come from?

I shake that thought away and have to get control when he comes to the sideline.

"Hey, I need my shirt back."

The one I'm clutching to my chest like a two-year-old with her blanket. Yeah, that shirt.

"Oh, here." I hand it over and he winks at me.

I melt. Because I'm a dork.

Or because it's a thousand degrees out, but I'm pretty sure it's the dork part of me.

"If we score in the next five minutes, it's over. It'll be a mercy rule," Lachlan explains, but I'm too busy staring at his chest before he covers it with the shirt again.

"Cool," I manage to get out.

Cool? Seriously? I have no game at all. Not that I think I need game, because since our kiss nothing has happened.

He winks. "Don't blink or you'll miss the good stuff."

"So you've been holding back?"

"Just watch."

Sure enough, about two minutes later, they come running off with huge smiles. The sad part is that I did, in fact, miss the scoring.

"That was great. You guys did amazing," I say, hoping it sounds sincere, because honestly, I wouldn't have known who won if it weren't for their singing "We Are the Champions" at the end.

None of them look like they're about to keel over, so that's promising. When they get close, Lachlan pulls me in for a hug, plastering me to his nasty, sweaty chest as he walks.

"Lach! Eww! You're so gross!"

They all laugh, and he keeps walking, forcing me to go backward as I try to pry myself out of his grasp. "Hey now, if you're going to be a part of the team, you need to suffer too."

After another second of struggling, he releases me, and I glare at him. "Ick. I need a shower now."

"Me too."

Maybe we can take one together . . .

No, no, we are not thinking these things. But . . . you know, I am.

I clear my throat. "Well, now what?"

"Now we wait. We have an hour to eat, hang out, and rest before the next game."

"And just how bad did you beat those girls?"

He grins. "We destroyed them."

"Feel good about that, huh?" I ask, crossing my arms over my chest.

Not that my competitive edge doesn't love a good spanking, but still. They're a bunch of middle-aged guys beating up on college girls. I'm not sure this is where I'd want that part of my personality to shine through.

"You know, in fact, I do. You make me out to be this ancient old dude, and look at what we did."

I nod slowly. I can see his point. "Fair enough. You guys were really good—I think. It was much better than the practices."

"We did that for your benefit," he lies.

I know he's lying because Everett told me how bad that was, and they were really pissed that they couldn't get it together.

"Oh." I say the word as a sigh as I place my hand over my

head. "Thank God you did. I was really worried for today, but . . . due to your absolute suckage the other days, I'm just . . . impressed."

He wraps his arm around my shoulder, pulling me back against his sweaty side. "Good. I'm rather impressive."

"Sure, we'll go with that."

We make it to the tent. Everyone is sitting, eating, and talking about the game. I grab a plate, loading up with veggies, dip, and some chips. Because I eat like a twelve-year-old. The area is packed and there's nowhere to sit, so I stand over to the side.

"Here," Lachlan says, getting to his feet. "Sit here."

"No, I didn't play. You need to sit."

"Or just let her sit on your lap," Killian suggests.

"Right, let her just sit with you," Miles piles on.

Not wanting to let on that this is even a little uncomfortable, I say, "I'll just stand. It's fine."

Lachlan shakes his head. "Stop, come sit. It's not a big deal."

Yeah. No. Not a big deal at all. In fact, it's such a small deal, it's not even a deal. Nothing to see. Nothing to think about.

I walk over, because if I do protest, they'll all think it matters. So I smile and sigh as I sit on his leg.

His very strong leg.

I turn to look at him with a stern face. "I swear, if you do anything stupid like bounce your knee and make me drop food, I'll cut your balls off in your sleep."

The guys burst out laughing, and then the conversation turns to the game. We sit here, and they explain more of the rules. Really, the rules are crazy. The disc must always be moving forward. They can't pass it backward, and the referee on the field is really just for show, because they call the penalties. The other team can argue it or accept it, and most times they just accept, unless it's blatant they're trying to screw each other.

The referee is there to sort of mediate, I guess. Regardless, dude is getting an awesome cardio workout.

As we sit here, the awkward feeling of being on his knee stops being awkward. I move so that I can see the guys better, which means my legs are draped over the side of the chair and I'm leaning into the crook of his arm.

Lachlan moves a little, and his hand rests on the top of my thigh.

I do my best to not think about it until it moves just a little higher.

My eyes find his for a heartbeat, and there are a million questions there. I pull my lower lip between my teeth, and he moves his hand higher again.

Without a word, I ask him what he's doing. Not that he can read my mind, but he smirks a little after I say it in my head.

It's like he's daring me to tell him to stop.

Lachlan West knows there is not a dare in the world I'll ever back down from.

I nod my head a little, telling him to go ahead.

His thumb brushes the sensitive skin there, stroking ever so slightly.

My breathing gets just a little shallower, and then Lachlan juts his chin toward the guys. "Are you going to answer him?"

Answer who?

People are here?

Shit. Yeah, they're all getting up, cleaning their mess, and starting to get ready for the next game.

I turn to face Miles, praying to God it was his voice I heard. "Sorry, I missed what you said."

His brows furrow and Everett laughs. "I asked if you needed me to throw away your plate, but I see your mind is elsewhere."

I force a smile and push off his lap. He grunts when I push off, and he grabs my hips, pulling me back down, and that is when I feel his erection.

"I'll throw her stuff out. I need to talk to her."

Everett laughs. "I bet you need to do something to her."

"Fuck off."

"Well, that first word was what I was going to tell you . . ."

"Go." Lachlan's voice is low and commanding.

I really hate that it turns me on.

They all file out of the tent area, and I sit here, waiting until the last person leaves. "We have to talk?"

Lachlan brushes something off my lips. "Yeah, after the game, we're going to come up with a way to deal with this."

"We are?"

"Yes."

"Lachlan, let's go!" Killian yells, and Lachlan pushes me so that I stand.

I face him and stare up into his brown eyes. "And how exactly do we deal with it?"

He adjusts himself. "I'm not sure, but I'll let you know when I figure it out."

Well, now I'm excited to hear this, because I know what I'd like.

fifteen
Lachlan

"You guys were truly amazing!" Ainsley says as she runs over to us. "I actually could follow that last match."

"Amazing might be a stretch, but we definitely were better than usual," Everett says as we reach her.

"Well, I was impressed. I think I understand a little more about the game too."

"You do?" I ask.

She nods. "Yes, you guys run a lot, chucking the Frisbee and yelling at each other."

"You've got the basics," I reply with a chuckle.

"Hey, your phone rang a few times."

Ainsley hands me the phone.

It's Becky's mom. I dial her back, and she answers on the second ring.

"Hey, Lachlan, sorry to bother you."

"Is everything okay with Rose?"

"Yes, she's great. I wanted to see if it was okay with you if she stays with me for the night. I need to go help my mom on the farm, and I'll probably be there late. It would be a huge help if Becky had Rose so she wasn't driving me up the wall."

I glance over at Ainsley, who is laughing with the guys. All night alone in the house. No distractions. No one to walk in and stop us.

I should do the smart thing and tell her I need Rose home to keep me from being an idiot. Although it's a little late for that.

I clear my throat. "Yeah, that's fine. Let me know when to come pick her up tomorrow."

"Thank you. I appreciate this so much."

"Of course, I'm sure Rose will love it. She adores your mom's farm."

She loves animals, and getting to spend the night with Becky will be an added bonus.

"Hope the tournament went well. Do you want me to grab Rose so you can talk to her?"

"No, it's okay. I'm sure she's playing with Becky. Tell her I love her and she can call me later if she wants."

"Will do."

"Thanks, Mary. Talk to you tomorrow."

I hang up and walk over to where the guys are talking to Ainsley, and she's got the biggest smile on her face. She looks so happy and free, so fucking beautiful it makes my chest ache.

Tonight, we're going to figure this out.

Tonight, before I do something really fucking stupid.

She looks over to me. Her eyes are soft, and she gives me a sweet smile. Yeah, tonight I'm absolutely going to do something stupid.

───────

"And when is the next tournament?" Ainsley asks as we are about fifteen minutes from the house.

"In two weeks."

Since we got in the car, she's been nonstop talking. I swear she's going to lose her voice at this rate. She's asked every question about the rules, why we kept dropping passes, and what the point of the referee is.

I've been able to supply her with at least a few two and three-word answers instead of my normal one-word ones.

"Oh! Good! By then I should have a ton of information on the four of you, so the last tournament will be a good ending part to the piece that I can add during edits."

"You mean three."

She huffs. "Yes, I forgot. You're a pain in the ass and won't comply."

"Comply with what?"

"Helping me. You know how much this all means to me, Lach. I've wanted this since I was a kid."

"To write about the sportsball, as you call it?"

She wants more than this. She's better than this too. She is meant to take the world by storm, to win prizes, to show people just how damn smart she is. I've read and saved every article that she's ever written, and even when talking about hats, she makes the words come alive and jump off the page. Ainsley MacKinley is one of the most talented writers I've ever read.

"You know I want more than that."

"And yet you're writing about Frisbee."

"The world doesn't work like that. We have to prove ourselves, and that's what I'm doing. *Without* the help of someone I know."

"As you just said, you have to work. What makes you think every person you want to interview or expose is going to be helpful? Consider this training."

Ainsley snorts. "Do you remember who my father is? I've been training for this my whole life. The Admiral is the most evasive human ever known. He never answers a question without making you think you asked something else."

That's accurate. He's also not a man you want to piss off. Ainsley, though, was able to say anything and never get in trouble for it. She somehow cracked the code to be able to always be on his good side.

"He also always indulged you."

"I can be persuasive when I need to be. Most people have a weakness. You just have to find it."

I smirk. "And what's mine?"

She shakes her head and looks out the window. "I don't know."

I laugh at that. "You do. Go on, tell me."

"You don't have one."

She's lying. I know because that's her weakness. She sucks at it. Her pure heart doesn't allow for the deceit easily.

"Ainsley," I say her name carefully. "Don't lie to me, please."

The long sigh that falls from her lips is filled with frustration. "You're not going to like it."

"To be fair, I don't know that anyone likes their weaknesses."

"True, but one of your many weaknesses is that you don't think you have any."

I huff. "I know I have them."

"Name one."

You.

You are my biggest weakness, and it's why I tried so hard to shut you out of my fucking world.

"I'm stubborn," I say instead of that thought.

"That's an understatement."

"I'm always right."

Her eyes narrow. "That's not a weakness, that's bullshit."

I laugh. "Fine. I don't trust easily."

Years and years of people proving that they aren't trustworthy have made that my reality. I've tried to see past the broken promises, but after a while, you can't. People show you who they are—I just choose to believe them instead of deluding myself they'll change.

My mother suffered with depression throughout her life. She fought as hard as she could, until she decided she didn't want to anymore. No matter how many times she promised me she'd try again, she would go back. I didn't have friends, other than Caspian and Ainsley, who came to the house growing up, mostly because I never knew if she would be dressed, awake, or functioning.

"No, you don't, but you have your reasons."

Ainsley and Caspian know. They were there, and it wasn't always bad. She had good times. Where she baked cakes and threw elaborate garden parties. Those were the times I had my mom, the woman who loved me and did anything to make me smile.

I'd miss her when she'd fall into the abyss.

"It's not that I don't want to," I tell her.

"Lachlan, I'm not saying it's a bad thing. I know why you don't trust people. Your whole life has been a series of letdowns. I get it. Your mom, Rose's mother, your college girlfriend who tried to take money from you . . . I was there. I know all about it. However, you trust some people."

"Your brother, that's about it." She flinches a little. "And you, you know that."

"Do I? I'm not trying to make myself a martyr here, but I'm not sure you do. Four years ago you didn't trust me. You pushed away and told me I was a mistake."

I put the truck in park in the driveway and turn to face her. "I didn't trust myself."

"Why?"

"It never should've happened that night."

It never should've happened, period.

She turns, pulling her leg up onto the seat. "It happened again, though."

"Yes."

"And today, you . . . we . . . if we weren't in front of your team, I think it would've happened then."

I nod slowly. "Yes."

"So you said we were going to find a way to deal with it?"

I inch closer. "We need to establish some kind of . . ."

"An agreement."

"Rules."

"Boundaries," Ainsley says as she moves closer. "So no one gets hurt."

"You're going to leave here," I remind her.

"And you're going to stay."

Her brown eyes are trained on mine, the tiny flecks of yellow almost glowing. "Yes."

"What's your plan?" she asks softly.

"I have several of them." One is that I strip her down and kiss every inch of this woman until she begs me to stop. I'm going to bring her so much pleasure that she'll never want another man to even look at her. I plan to take her over and over again, fuck her out of my brain because she's embedded herself there.

I plan to do a lot to her, but that's not the plan I think she's asking for.

"You matter to me, Ainsley. You aren't just some hookup that I'll never see again. You're my best friend's sister and you matter, understand?" I need that to be fully transparent. "If any of this idea doesn't sit right, we figure something else out."

Like I bribe Hazel to let her live there, because we can't keep doing this dance. One way or another, I'm going to end this madness.

"And the same for you."

I almost laugh, but I hold it in. "I want you. I have for a long time, but because you're who you are, I've done my best to stay away."

"I'm pretty sure you know where I stand."

Again she moves an inch closer. Any more of this and she's going to be plastered against me.

Which wouldn't be unwelcome.

I need her to say the words, to tell me exactly what she wants. "I don't know anything that goes on in your head, Ainsley, but here's what I want . . . you. I want you while you're here. After you leave, we go our separate ways and remain friends."

"So it's just for while I'm here?" She licks her lips and I feel my cock harden.

"That's it."

"And after we pretend it didn't happen?"

I'm pretty sure she's going to fuck my entire world up when she goes, but that's not her problem.

"We will always be in each other's lives, and I don't want to complicate that."

She laughs softly, her lips a breath away from mine. "I'm pretty sure we're about to complicate everything."

"Are you okay with that?"

"Sex? With you? Until I leave . . . yeah, I'm okay with it."

"Good."

And then I lean the rest of the way in and kiss her.

sixteen
Ainsley

The calluses on his thumb brush my cheek, and I am so lost I don't even remember we're outside his house, in the truck, until he pulls back. "We need to get inside."

I look around. "Right."

I'm out of the truck before he has time to change his mind, and as I'm starting toward the house, he lifts me up, tosses me over his shoulder, and takes the stairs two at a time.

"I guess the fireman carry really does come in handy."

He chuckles and then we're in the house, alone, after just making an agreement I am pretty sure I'm going to fail at.

After these few weeks, there's no way I'm going to be the same.

Lachlan destroyed me for any man four years ago, and since then I've lived in that memory.

Having him fully—yeah, goodbye life as we know it.

I'll take every ounce of pain if it means I get to have him, even if only for a while.

Those memories will carry me when I'm old and alone with fifteen cats. I'll look back and be like: *Remember that time you got your brains fucked out by Lachlan West? Good times.*

And I have zero doubts that it will be Very. Good. Times.

I stand against the wall. Lachlan's chest heaves, and I would give everything I am to know what's in his mind.

Is he going to pull away? Is he going to gain control of whatever is driving him to this and tell me it was a mistake again?

"Lachlan?" I breathe his name, begging with every part of me for him to not push me away.

He shakes his head, and my stomach falls to the floor. I knew it. I was prepared and still it hurts so much. "I don't deserve to take this from you, but I'm not strong enough to turn away."

Relief washes over me, allowing me to breathe and also know what has to happen. I'm going to need to push, and he's going to have to allow it.

I stay here, knowing if I go too fast, he'll spook. "Why do you put me on some pedestal?"

"I don't."

"No? Then why would you say that?"

"Because, Ainsley, you're better than a few weeks and a hug."

I smile softly. "Then how about a kiss instead?"

"You know that's not what I mean." Lachlan takes a step toward me.

Good, this is progress.

"I'm not asking for anything more than we agreed on. Now, you have two choices," I say, pushing off the wall and taking three strides toward him.

"Oh?"

"You can follow me to your bedroom, strip me down, and make good on every fantasy I've had." I have to keep myself in check when I see his eyes flare with desire. "Or you can use that fireman carry you're so good at and take me to my room, and I'll invent some new fantasies."

He grins. "Either way, this is happening."

"Either way."

"Well, then." He takes that final step and once again throws me over his shoulder. "I'm going with the last option. You're going to my bed, and we're going to invent all kinds of fantasies together."

Being the smart girl I am, I don't say a word as he carries me through the kitchen and into the back area, where his room is.

When he opens the door, I don't have any time to really take in my surroundings because he tosses me on the bed and then grabs my ankles, pulling me to the edge.

"I've dreamed of you in here."

I've dreamed of him as mine.

"And what was I doing in here?" I ask, lifting my shirt off and tossing it on the floor.

"What weren't you doing?"

"I wouldn't know. It's your dream."

He takes his shirt off, giving me the most amazing view. His body is fucking perfect. I'm a girl who has a thing for big arms, and Lachlan delivers. His chest is broad, and his stomach is rock solid. If this is a dream, I'm perfectly fine never waking up.

"First, you were naked."

"That can be arranged."

He shakes his head. "Not yet. I want to take everything off you myself, like unwrapping a present."

I lean back on the bed, my arms behind me, holding my weight up. "Okay, then tell me more about this dream."

"Once you were naked, I spent a lot of time exploring you, licking you, tasting you, and the sounds you made, sweetheart, when I sucked you . . . I'm looking forward to seeing if I was remotely correct."

I let out a soft moan at his words. "Was there a lot of talking in this dream?"

"Not on your side."

"Why not?"

"Well." He steps to me, hand moving to brush my hair back. "For one thing, you had my cock in your mouth, so it's pretty hard to talk then. Secondly, you were screaming more than talking."

"I like that," I say with a grin.

"Lastly, when you're panting, it's hard to speak."

I lean forward. "Right now, all I'm hearing is a lot of talking."

"Then I should start getting to the doing."

I'm totally on board with that. Lachlan doesn't waste time, his hands roaming up my body until he reaches the straps of my bra. Slowly, he pulls them down, and our gazes connect. This is really happening, and my heart is pounding.

The cool air hits my chest and he looks down. "You're fucking perfect."

"I'm not."

My boobs are way too small. I'm like the president of the Itty Bitty Titty Committee, but the way his eyes are drinking me in, I don't feel anything but beautiful.

He lifts my head a bit to meet his gaze. "You're perfect, Ainsley. You always have been."

There's a tightness in my chest that grows, spreading out like vines wrapping around my heart and squeezing.

Why does he do this? Why does he affect me so much? Why have I believed that I loved him with all my heart when that was a lie?

I've loved him with more than that.

Knowing that I will probably start crying, which will lead to clothes going on and me being packed up and sent to my room, I speak before that can happen. "Lachlan, your present is waiting to be opened."

His smirk is full of mischief, and I see the boy I've known my whole life. "Lie back, sweetheart, I'm going to unwrap every layer of you."

I do as I'm told, mostly so I can get out of my head, and he pulls my shorts off, leaving me naked.

"Commando?"

Now it's my turn to feel smug. "I never wear underwear."

"Noted. Don't start now. I'd like easy access to fuck you anytime the opportunity arises."

Yeah, these next few weeks are going to be amazing.

Before I can say anything more, his lips are on my calf, slowly moving up as he spreads my legs apart.

I try to keep still, but I start to tremble in anticipation. His tongue makes circles going up my thigh. Without preamble he's lightly flicking my clit. I let out a soft moan, and my whole body is tight as a bow as he delves between my legs.

Lachlan doesn't do anything in his life without a full commitment, and dear God, I didn't know how much I've been missing out. He licks, sucks, and circles my clit, drawing pleasure from me I didn't know was possible.

My fingers move to his hair, sliding my nails against his scalp. This seems to excite him, because the softness I had before is gone, and now he's a man on a mission. He sucks harder, and then I feel his finger enter me.

"Oh God!" I arch my back and contract around him.

He does it again, pushing even deeper.

"Lach!" I call out, knowing I'm going to fall apart.

I'm not going to hold out much longer. I try because, God, it feels so good. Everything is perfect. He's perfect. I never want this to end, but my body is on that precipice, and it's going over the edge without any ability to stop it.

My fingers grip the sheets, tightening as every muscle clenches. The delicious pain is a prelude to the pleasure that I know is coming.

Lachlan's teeth just barely pinch my clit, and I detonate.

Warmth flows through my veins, searing me with an unimaginable euphoria far beyond what I've done for myself—and worlds beyond what the one guy I was with did for me.

I lie here, panting, struggling to get my mind to work, and he kisses his way up my body.

"Part one of the fantasy done," he says against my ear.

"I like this fantasy," I manage to say between breaths.

"Me too."

I roll onto my side, pressing my hand to his chest. "I have dreams too—about you."

My dreams aren't just of a sexual nature, but I lock those deep in the vault. No way am I going to spill my stupid ideas of marriage, of us raising Rose, and of us living in marital bliss.

Lachlan doesn't think there's such a thing, and I really don't want to screw up tonight.

The tip of his finger slides up my arm, over my shoulders, and then back down. "I'm really hoping they're dirty."

"Oh, they are. Very dirty."

He grins. "Who would've imagined that under your poised exterior lies a very dirty girl."

"What is it they say? It's always the quiet ones."

Lachlan lets out a laugh and then rolls me so I'm on top of him. I lean up, straddling him, hating the damn fabric between us.

"This is one of my dreams. You under me while I ride you," I confess.

"Mine too."

"Seems your imagination has been very busy."

Lachlan palms my breast. "You don't even know the half of it. Take my pants off, Ainsley."

I shift so that I can do as he asks, kissing my way down his perfect body as I do. I don't actually need to get off the bed, but I do, pulling his pants with me.

His cock springs free, and those dreams I had . . . yeah, didn't do it justice.

I've been with only one man. It was my junior year of college, and I was starting to panic that I was still a virgin, so I dated one of the frat guys.

Big—or I should say *little*—mistake.

It was terrible.

Absolutely awful.

We didn't have any chemistry. It was literally just to get it over with, and while he tried—he failed.

Thankfully I knew what an orgasm felt like beforehand so I could fake it after twenty minutes of him attempting to get me off.

I did not have to fake a single thing this time.

I move my hand up his leg and wrap it around his dick, pumping. He makes a hissing noise and pulls me back up toward him.

Our lips meet again, and I kiss him deeply as I continue to stroke him. He breaks away, groaning as he does. "You feel so good."

"I want to make you feel good."

"You are, sweetheart. So much."

He kisses me, breaking off any chance of a retort. Then he flips our positions and he's on top of me. He reaches over and grabs a condom out of the drawer, then slips it on. I lie still, not letting my mind start to wander.

However, I'm freaking out a little.

Lachlan stares down at me. "Ainsley . . . are you sure?"

"I am."

"It just feels like . . . it'll change everything."

It will. I'll never be the same, but that's okay.

There will be two halves of me. The before Lachlan made love to me and the after. This girl, in this moment, doesn't actually know what it'll be like. I can live in a pretend world where I can lie to myself about what he'll feel like inside me.

After, I won't. I'll know what his weight feels like, how he will make me feel whole, full, and his.

I bring my hand to his cheek and smile. "Change is good."

"I don't want to stop now."

That's a damn good thing. I sigh, wanting to lighten the mood so he doesn't stop. "Really?"

"I want you too much. God, I want you so fucking much, Ainsley."

"Good, because I want you to be my first," I joke.

His eyes widen and he pushes up farther. "What?"

Okay, maybe this was a bad joke. "I'm kidding! Relax."

He laughs once, dropping his head to my shoulder. "Fucking hell. You literally are going to be the death of me."

"I don't know whether to laugh or be offended."

Lachlan lifts his head. "You swear you're joking?"

"I swear." I don't tell him it's only been once. I'm pretty sure that will equally horrify him. "But I wasn't lying when I said I wanted it to be you."

"I would've hated myself if I took that from you, not when I can't give you everything."

Meaning his heart.

I push that aside, brushing my thumb against his cheek. "This is enough."

The lie slips from my lips far too easily.

It will never be enough, but it'll be enough as far as he knows.

I'll find a way to endure a life without the only man I've ever loved.

God, I sound like a country song.

Lachlan shifts and I feel him start to push inside. My heart is pounding, and I close my eyes, trying to focus on anything other than what's happening. Lachlan moves his hips, sliding deeper. I suck in a breath, and he pauses.

It feels like the first time. He's so big, and I may have joked before about the whole virgin thing, but right now it sort of feels like it.

"Ainsley?" His voice is strained.

I look up at him. "It's been a long time for me and . . . you're much bigger than my last."

He grins. "Touch yourself."

"What?"

"Touch yourself, sweetheart. I'll go slow." I move my hand between us, rubbing my clit slowly. "That's it. Feel how good it is? Relax and let me in." The sound of his voice is almost as arousing as what I'm doing. "I'm going to slide deeper and deeper, and you're going to open and let me." I whimper as the pleasure starts to build. "Good girl, you're so tight it's like heaven."

"Lachlan," I breathe his name.

"Just a little more. Keep rubbing your clit. Remember when my tongue was there, licking you until you screamed?"

I moan. "Yes."

"Yes, that's it," he croons and then thrusts his hips forward, stopping when he's fully seated. I gasp, gripping his biceps as I try to acclimate to the feeling of him inside me. "Tell me when I can move."

I clench around him and he groans. "Move."

He sets a pace, slow at first, probably making sure I can handle him. While the beginning wasn't great, once he was in, the pain was gone. Now all I feel is . . . Lachlan.

Our eyes connect and my emotions bounce around like a Ping-Pong ball. I'm happy, worried, hopeful, aware this won't last, and my emotions swirl with each thrust. It's as though I'm a snow globe that can't settle after being shaken up.

"Stay with me, Ainsley," he says, brushing his nose against mine. "Don't go inside your head."

I hate that he knows me. "Make it stop," I challenge.

He moves his hand between us, pressing against my clit. Yeah, that'll do it.

Lachlan increases the pace, and I feel a second climax lingering. "I feel you tightening around my cock. Let go, let it all go."

I shut my mind off, allowing the sensations to take over. "I'm close."

"I feel it. Your cunt is so hot. So fucking tight."

I hold on to him because I need something to tether me. It builds faster than the last and maybe it's everything. The way he's inside me, the heat of his body, the smell of his cologne mixed with sex in the air. Everything is more intense.

Lachlan leans down, kissing my neck before he moves to my ear. "I want to hear you, Ainsley. I want you to scream and clench around me. I want your moans to echo in the room as I fuck you into another orgasm."

The low growl of his voice sends me over and I scream out as my orgasm takes me under, drowning me into the oblivion that is Lachlan West.

And I really don't care if I ever come up for air.

seventeen
Lachlan

We just finished showering and having sex again thanks to Ainsley very seductively washing herself.

I couldn't resist the temptation.

She grabs one of my T-shirts for her sleepwear and I'm in boxer briefs.

There's really no reason to get dressed fully because I'm pretty sure I'm going to wake her up with my head between her legs in an hour or two.

We climb into my bed, and I pull her to my chest. I'm not sure what to say, so I opt for nothing.

This has been the most incredible sex I've ever had.

She lets out a long sigh, running her finger in a circle along my chest. I take her hand in mine, and she lifts her head. "Hi."

I grin. "Hi."

"We had sex—twice."

"We sure did."

Ainsley bites her lower lip. "Did you . . . enjoy it?"

Is she unglued? "Do you think I didn't?"

"I don't know. It seemed like you did."

"I enjoyed every damn second—twice."

She smiles at that. "I did too. I didn't know it could be so . . . intense."

The way she says it makes me wonder something about her joke before.

"Just how many times have you had sex before this?"

Ainsley clears her throat and looks away. "Once."

So she wasn't a virgin, but she sure as hell isn't exactly experienced. How every man in the world isn't banging down her door to have a chance to even know her is beyond me. She's the whole package, and while I thought that prior to having sex with her, now there's one more reason to hate that we can never be together —she's amazing in bed.

That said, I'm not sure how I feel about the fact that I'm only her second time.

"How?" I ask her, keeping my voice careful.

She rolls over, staring up at the ceiling. "First, I wasn't stupid enough to sleep with anyone in high school. The Admiral would've killed them, and I would've been locked in a nunnery or something. When I got to college, I kind of felt like I'd held out, and I wasn't in a rush to sleep with any of those guys. Sophomore year went without dating. You know me"—she rolls over to face me, head propped up on her hand—"I'm nerdy. I like books and asking a million questions to get to the heart of an issue. I was the sorority girl who never really drank or went to bars. I was happy watching a movie on a Friday night with popcorn and skin-care masks."

"So that means you didn't date anyone?"

"Pretty much. It wasn't until my junior year that I started getting concerned there was something wrong with me. I mean, I'd never had a boyfriend. My friends were on rotations and sleeping with random guys at the bar. I wanted to just get it over with. So I met a guy, we had sex, and I decided the only thing wrong with me was wanting to sleep with someone just to do it."

"There was nothing wrong with you," I reassure her.

Something flashes in her eyes, but she covers it quickly.

"That's not exactly true. I have a lot wrong with me, but it wasn't that I was a virgin in college."

I cup her face. "You can count this as your first time if you want."

She smiles brightly. "So I can tell the Admiral I was a virgin until you?"

I laugh and shake my head. "You really should never mention this to anyone, you know that, right?"

"So you don't want me to call Caspian and tell him about the intense sexfest we shared?"

Sometimes I can't tell if she's actually serious. She and Caspian are those siblings that actually would tell each other about this kind of thing. At least, he'd tell her. From the sounds of it, Ainsley didn't have much to spill to him.

"I'd rather we keep this between us. That is, if you want to have another night like this."

She taps her finger against her chin. "Let me sleep on it."

I grab her, rolling her to be on top of me. "You can sleep on me."

"You're like a rock."

"Something is definitely hardening," I tease.

"Already?" Her eyes widen.

"I'm finding it harder to stay unaroused lately."

"Oh, I bet it's because of me."

I grin. "I would say you're correct."

"Has it always been this way?" Her voice is tentative.

"Since you were about eighteen, yes."

"So, wow, before your mom died?"

I brush her hair back, tucking it behind her ear. "I'm not sure how much to tell her. "That's why I was so angry with you. You. Ainsley MacKinley. My friend, my best friend's sister, was not supposed to be the girl I was lusting after. Then I got drunk, thinking I could numb the pain of my mother and the feelings I had for you. It was supposed to help."

"But I came out there."

"You came out there, smelling like jasmine and vanilla with the purest of intentions."

She lets out a loud laugh at that. "Umm, I wouldn't exactly say that. Not that I thought you were going to maul me against the stone wall, but my intentions around you haven't ever been pure and innocent."

"And all this time you've been mentally undressing me?"

"And you haven't been doing the same?"

I grin. "I never said I wasn't."

Ainsley leans in and kisses me. "Now we have a few weeks to actually undress each other."

My hand moves up to grip her ass, sliding her closer. "We sure do."

Just as things are starting to move in the right direction, the fire tones ring out through the radio, and I groan, breaking away from her delicious mouth.

Ainsley rolls off to her side of the bed—great, I'm already thinking of it as her side—and I sit up, waiting to hear the announcement.

"Station 13, Battalion Chief 2, Truck 689, report of a building fire at 188 Main Street. EMS en route."

I'm pulling my shorts on before it can start the repeat message for those who missed it the first time. "I have to go," I tell Ainsley.

She sits up, pulling the blanket with her. "Of course, Main Street . . . is that Hazel?"

"No, but it's close. Stay here. I'll be back as soon as I can."

Ainsley nods. "Be careful, Lach."

I wink as I grab my radio. "Always." I get halfway out the door and turn back, walking to the bed. She blinks a few times as I lean down. "Don't leave the bed. I want you here when I get back." I kiss her and then head out.

———

"Good job, everyone," I say as we're standing outside the fire truck. When we got here the fire was already out thanks to the overhead sprinklers. What sucks about those is that they cause more water damage than anything. The only way to shut the water off is if we do it.

"Thankfully it ended up being nothing," Davidson says, cracking his neck. "Just sucks they'll need to replace the whole first floor."

"Still, the sprinklers did exactly what they were supposed to."

Lopez nods slowly. "It would've been bad if not. The owner said it went up fast, and he didn't have time to think."

"Yeah, it was a grease fire and he put water on it," Davidson says with a huff. "We do training on this with all the restaurants here to avoid this."

I place my hand on his shoulder. "We do, but we're trained to stay calm in crisis. Not everyone else can take that second to pause prior."

"Hey, boys," Hazel calls, coming out with a tray in her hand.

"Hazel, my favorite woman!" Lopez says when she gets close.

She smiles. "You say that to every woman who has coffee, Edgar. I know you say the same to Margaret from the diner too."

He clutches his chest. "You're my favorite—always."

"Yeah, yeah." Hazel extends the tray. "Here you go. Coffee for everyone."

We all take a cup, thanking her as we do. Her coffee is hands down the best I've ever had. "I'm assuming we woke you up?"

"Well, being that Main Street is pretty small, yes. But I heard the smoke alarms as well. It ended up being nothing?"

"I wouldn't say that. The restaurant sustained damage, but nothing that can't be fixed."

She nods. "Well, that's good. I'm sure the community will help. We always do. You guys be good. I'm sure I'll see some of you in a few hours."

Hazel heads back to her house, and it's already ten. We need to get off the street to let people get back to bed.

"All right, guys, let's get back to the station so you can write your reports." And I need to return to where a very gorgeous woman is waiting for me.

"Sure thing, Chief."

I get in my truck and see I have a text from Ainsley and two missed calls from Caspian. He's usually just getting to work around this time and doesn't often call.

Normally I would call him back, but now . . . I'm not sure what the fuck to say to him. It's not that I think I did anything wrong, but still—she's his sister.

It's not like I haven't spent years coming up with every possible way I'd handle this, but now that it's in my face, it feels different.

Now it's reality.

I check the text first.

AINSLEY

Call me before you come home.

As I'm staring at the phone, getting ready to call her, it rings, but it's Caspian.

Shit. I'm just going to be normal, because it seems he's not going to stop calling, so I might as well get this out of the way.

"Hey, Cas."

"Hey, dickhead. You know, I had to tell you something," he says, his words slurring at the end.

Great, he's drunk.

"Did you?"

"Yeah, but I think you're sleeping."

I've never been happier that he's totally shitfaced and I don't actually have to have this conversation about Ainsley.

"I could be sleeping right now," I say, fucking with him.

"Shit. Sorry, bro," he whispers. "I won't wake you up."

I laugh once. "Listen, you should go to bed. You sound pretty fucked up."

"I am." I'm not sure whether he's agreeing that he's in bed or fucked up or both. "The Admiral came for an inspection."

I blink. "What?"

"Yup. He came here, with his endless supply of disapproval."

No wonder he's drunk. Caspian is the son that the Admiral tried to break. My dad, for all his endless faults, didn't try to make me into someone I wasn't. He let me play sports and be a kid. Caspian didn't have the same freedoms. I think a lot of it came to optics and goals that his father had.

"You're not a kid, Cas. You're a grown-ass man who doesn't ask your father for a fucking dime. Don't let anything he says change the way you're living."

"I'm not. I just had a few shots when he left and then some beers. Then I told him the truth about Ainsley. So he's going to fix her next. He'll tell her *all* the things she does wrong."

Fuck. I have a feeling I know what he's implying. "What do you mean he's going to fix her?"

"I tried to call you, but you are sleeping. But I might have slipped that Ainsley was staying with you, and he was not happy."

I pull down my driveway and see a white Mercedes with the plates RADM and . . . there goes my night.

eighteen
Ainsley

"Daddy, hi!" I say as I open the door, completely out of breath from running around to not look like I was waiting naked in Lachlan's bed.

"Hello, Ainsley Christine," he says, disapproval ringing in every syllable.

It's amazing how easily he can make me feel like I'm six and in need of a lecture.

"What are you doing here?" I ask, wishing to God I put on more than just a pair of shorts after Caspian called literally one minute ago. I didn't have enough time for much else, and I'm still wearing Lachlan's T-shirt.

This is so bad.

So. Bad.

"I could ask you the same," the Admiral says as he takes in my attire.

"Well, I'm here because I'm working on an article. I told you that."

"Yes, but you failed to mention you were staying in the house with Lachlan."

I sigh, feeling like screaming and also still battling the desire to please him. "I didn't know I had to mention it. He's Lachlan."

"Yes, and you're my daughter. You didn't mention it because you didn't want me to know. You said you were staying in a log cabin."

"That was the original plan, and I did stay in one, but there was an issue, I needed to leave, and Lachlan told me I could stay here. I figured you'd be happy since I'm not alone in the woods."

He crosses his arms over his chest. "I'd prefer that to you staying in a house with a man."

I shake my head. "Daddy, I'm staying with Lachlan and Rose. He's not just a random guy. Not to mention, how many nights did he stay at the house when we were growing up? I've slept in the same house with him a hundred times, and it's been fine." And we just had dirty, sweaty sex in that back bedroom, but . . . you know, I'm not mentioning *that* to him.

"Why didn't you just tell me?"

Oh, I don't know, because you're an overprotective lunatic.

I sigh and take a seat on the couch. "Because I really didn't think it was a big deal. You and I haven't really spoken since I told you that I was coming here for work."

We don't talk about anything by choice. I love my daddy. I really do, even though he's very difficult to love.

"You don't tell me anything, Ainsley. You or your brother."

I want to ask him why he thinks that is or why he feels that it's his business, but my father doesn't believe in faults. Asking him to even consider that he has any is not in his range of possibilities.

Still, he demands honesty. It's what I constantly combat in this relationship. Telling him the truth and how I feel or lying to soothe his fragile ego.

"We don't tell you things because you're often disappointed in us. You drove at ten o'clock at night to come here to what? Scold me?"

He straightens his back. "I came to make sure my only daughter was okay."

"Daddy, be honest for a second. Do you think Lachlan would ever hurt me?"

"Of course not."

I raise one brow. "Well, then why did you really come here?"

"I . . . I don't know."

The way his shoulders drop makes me sort of feel bad for him. "For twenty-six years you took care of countless men and women. Your whole life was about making sure people were safe and came home to their families. I can't imagine it's easy to let that go."

I can truly empathize with him. He always believed he'd done the right thing, the noble thing. He thought if he worked hard, gave us a life that he could be proud of, that when he retired, it would all pay off.

Instead, we were grown up, my brother can't stand him, and my mother left.

"No, it's not." He looks around. "Where is Lachlan?"

"He had a fire call. Rose is staying with her friend tonight."

He nods slowly, and then his blue eyes meet mine. "All I've ever wanted was for you to be honest with me."

"And also for us to do what you want."

The Admiral chuckles but at least looks chagrined. "That too."

"Well, that's not going to happen all the time," I say with a soft smile.

Sometimes I get to see the soft, insecure man that's under all that gruffness.

His sigh is heavy, as though he's letting out a lifetime of worries.

Just then the door opens and Lachlan enters. However, he doesn't exactly look surprised at seeing my father's car. I'm really hoping my brother gave him the same heads-up. He nods once, staring at my father. "Admiral."

"Lachlan," Dad says and walks over to take his hand. "Everything okay with the fire?"

"Yes, sir. Thankfully the sprinkler system did its job, so we didn't have a real tragedy."

I mouth to him: "Sorry!"

He gives me a wink and then looks back at my dad. "Is everything all right here? I didn't know you were coming by."

My dad shakes his head. "Surprise inspection to check in on Ainsley."

Always the Admiral.

God only knows what my stupid, drunk brother said to make him drive here. I tried to get the whole story, but he just kept telling me that he was going to date a bartender so he had beer all the time.

Which then morphed into some other ridiculous statement.

Lachlan clears his throat. "As you can see, I've managed to make sure she hasn't done anything too stupid."

I roll my eyes. "Yes, because I'm just the most irresponsible out of the group of kids."

You know, if I could go back, I wouldn't have warned Lachlan and would have made him think we really were going to be forced to marry. That would've been funny.

Instead, I'm the one caught in this strange joke.

My dad shakes his head again. "I know the truth, princess."

I grin. "Yes, Caspian and Lachlan are always at fault."

"Well, since I know you're okay, I should head home."

Lachlan speaks first. "It's late. If you want, you can stay."

My father lifts both hands. "Absolutely not. Thank you, though. I need to get home tonight. Ainsley, the Strawberry Festival is next weekend. I assume you'll be there?"

I nod enthusiastically. "Of course. I'll be there, like every year."

Dad straightens slightly. "Maybe you can see if your mother will come this year?"

Oh, Daddy. His regrets aren't long. They really are just singular—my mother. He loved her the only way he knew how, and she was just so tired of being an afterthought.

"I don't think she will, Dad." My voice cracks just saying it.

"Okay. Maybe you can come stay at the house and help me with a few things?"

The defeat in his voice breaks my heart a little.

"No problem."

He turns to Lachlan. "Take care of my girl."

Lachlan dips his head. "Of course, Admiral."

I wrap my arms around my dad. "I'll see you next weekend. I'll beg Lachlan and Rose to come too."

He smiles. "I'd love to see her. Your dad would too, son."

Oh, Jesus. There goes that idea.

My dad leaves, and after his taillights are no longer visible, I let out a long sigh. "Well, that was unexpected."

Lachlan's heat presses against my back, and I lean against him. His arms come around the front of me, and I tilt my head up to look at him. "It doesn't matter that I'm thirty, own my home, have a good job, and am raising my kid without help, your father fucking terrifies me."

I smile. "Imagine how it would've been if he came here a few hours earlier."

"I'd rather not."

I spin around, my hands resting on his chest. "I can give you something else to think about."

"What's that?"

"While you were gone, I was lying in that bed, completely naked, thinking about all the things I wanted to do while we had the house to ourselves."

Lachlan smirks, his hand pressing against my lower back. "Knowing your very active imagination, I'm going to assume you had some good ideas."

"Oh, I definitely think so." My fingertips gently scrape the exposed skin by his collar. "I wonder, though . . . which one you would've liked the most."

"Why don't you give me my options," he suggests.

"Hmm." I gaze up into his brown eyes. "We could go back to the bedroom, and I could show you."

"Or I could strip you down right here and see if I can guess them."

Not a bad idea. I lift up on my toes. "We have a limited amount of time. How about we do both?"

"Be prepared to be naked a lot."

I grin and press my lips to his and then step back. I strip right in front of him before he chases me into the kitchen, where we make very good use of the table, which definitely was my idea.

———

I'm so exhausted, but I'm sitting in Prose & Perk with unlimited refills and a very rough first draft.

Last night, Lachlan and I stayed up almost all night, just touching, laughing, and talking about random things and memories that have long been forgotten. We slept for a few hours before he had to leave to get Rose, and I informed him I wanted to come write.

I need to submit a draft to Mr. Krispen this week, and now that I have a game under my belt, I can at least write about that.

However, the focus of the story isn't really about Frisbee, more about how young athletes who go on to play in college have skills that academic students alone don't usually hone. I'm learning so much about the sports world and the different kinds of coaches. Each of the guys feel very different about their experiences which is giving me a very rich story that shows how strong and resilient they are.

I'm lost in my laptop, letting the words come, not caring about sentence structure, just needing my thoughts on paper, when I hear someone clear their throat.

I look up and see Killian there. "Hey, Ainsley."

"Hi, Killian! It's good to see you."

He smiles warmly. "Do you mind if I sit?"

I nod quickly. "Of course not. Please do."

"I know we were going to meet tomorrow, but I need to head up to our headquarters and didn't want to stand you up," he explains.

"Oh, no problem. Do you have a few minutes now?"

I really hope so because I need all the parallels I can get.

"Sure."

"Great." I grab my notebook, where I have my interviews with Miles and Everett, and glance through the questions again. "I asked the other guys the same things, but I think your situation is a little unique. You were actually drafted, correct?"

"I was. I was drafted third round into the NFL and played one season."

Incredible. "But you consider yourself not to have played since college?"

"When I say I played one season, I mean that I was on the roster. I never stepped foot on the field during that season. I trained, got my ass kicked quite a bit, and hated every fucking minute of it."

"Wow." I'm honestly shocked how many of them disliked the sport once they got to this point. "Why did you hate it?"

He rubs his chin before wrapping his hand around his coffee cup. "Have you ever idolized something or someone?"

Yeah, his friend.

I nod. "I think we all have."

"That was all I did throughout college. I went to classes, got my degree in accounting, and was really apathetic to it all. I only cared about football. Truly cared. I was that guy up at four in the morning, first in the gym and last out. Being a tight end meant I needed to be able to catch, block, run routes, be a sort of jack-of-all-trades. I was good or at least good enough to be drafted, but once I actually got there, it was like the fairy tale ended. I didn't want to spend sixteen hours a day focusing only on football. I didn't want the stress of being afraid during training camp I'd get cut. It's like living on adrenaline and stress, all day, every day."

I jot down notes and then glance up at him. "There were no good parts?"

"The good part was college for me. I loved my coaches, teammates, and that feeling of accomplishment. That was all gone once I was drafted."

"Any idea why?"

Killian smiles and shrugs. "I think, for me, there was this drive to achieve more than anything. Which may seem stupid since once I got to a professional team, you'd think I'd want to prove myself there, but I just didn't. I was watching these guys talk about their pay, injuries, failed marriages, kids who they never see. I have a grown adult son who I never see, and I think a lot of that was because of football. His mother became pregnant in high school, but moved without telling me about him. When I found out, it was right after the draft and I knew there was never going to be a relationship between him and me if I was always gone. What the hell was the point in that? About six months into it, my college roommate called me because he'd created this app and needed someone with a head for numbers to step in. It was the first time I felt excited about anything and it gave me a chance to know my son."

"So you decided to leave football?" I ask.

"I think football left me."

I lean back, trying to gather my thoughts. Nothing about these guys is what I assumed. I knew they were all successful in their current lives, but in my head they were "washed up" athletes who couldn't hack it. So far, all of them have left by choice.

Each for different reasons.

"Do you think you'd feel the same way if the choice wasn't yours?"

Killian stays quiet for a moment. "You know, I never thought about that. If I would be okay with this life if I hadn't been drafted. Knowing Lachlan, Miles, and Everett, I want to say I would. I probably wouldn't have taken it well in the beginning, but there's a part of us that are poets."

"Poets?" I can't keep the surprise out of my voice.

"Not the literal kind, but athletes are all about fate, destiny, answered prayers. We live in the abstract and can convince ourselves of just about anything, regardless of the outcome. We are masters at convincing ourselves that words in the right order can make or break a play or a game."

My smile is wide and only grows when he dips his head a little. "Superstitions and prayers are a huge part of sports."

"I wore only one brand of briefs when we were winning. As soon as those were cursed, I would find another. My coach wouldn't wear gold-toed socks, and if we were caught wearing them, we had to do one hundred jumping jacks to get the bad luck out of it."

I snort at that. "I remember Lachlan always ate a bag of Cool Ranch Doritos an hour before gametime. Once, someone took his Doritos, and I thought he was going to kill. I had to literally run to the gas station to get more."

That was the day he kissed me on the cheek, and I thought I was going to expire on the spot. Little did I know that we'd do a lot more—and hopefully will again tonight.

nineteen
Lachlan

"Hey, Chief," Davidson says as he enters my office.

"Hey, what's up?"

"You have a visitor."

That can only be one person. I'm smiling before I can even stop myself. Sure enough, Ainsley enters, carrying a bag. "Thanks, Davidson."

He closes the door, and Ainsley places the bag on my desk. "Hello, Chief West."

"Ms. MacKinley," I say with a grin. "To what do I owe this honor?"

"I could say so many things, but I'm here for several reasons."

"And they are?"

She sits in the seat and inhales deeply before blowing that breath out. "I need your help, Lach."

Those four words tear at my heart. "With what?"

"I have a rough draft of the article, but it's not good. I know good and I know bad, and this is just . . . not good."

"I see."

"So I need your help. I want this to be something more than just a 'where are you now.' I want to talk about sports overall, the things it does for kids and adults. To do that, though, I need you."

I hate that I struggle with this. Talking and thinking about the past causes me stress that I've worked hard to avoid. It's not that I regret any of it. I just don't want to go back and remember the way it felt at that time, but then I look at Ainsley, and there's no way I can deny her.

I will hurt myself a million times before I sit back and let her suffer.

So I'll help her. I'll give her the interview and make her happy. I'll do whatever she needs because I want to be the man who makes her happy.

"Then you have me."

Her eyes widen. "I do?"

"Yes, I'll do the interview."

She jumps up, rushing to me, and throws herself in my lap. Her lips find mine, and I sort of hate myself for not agreeing to this sooner if this was going to be the reaction. She pulls away much too quickly for my liking. "You mean it?"

"I mean it." She squeezes my cheeks and then kisses me again, not a long, sexy kiss that I really want, but more of a long lip-slap kiss, and then she pushes herself off my lap. "Do you do that with all the people you interview?"

She giggles and goes back to her seat. "Since you're my first assignment, I wouldn't know."

"What's in the bag?"

She shifts in her seat a little. "I wasn't sure you would say yes, so I came prepared with a bribe."

"A bribe?"

"Listen, you haven't been all that cooperative so far. I needed backup."

I go to grab the bag, but she snatches it quickly. "No, sir. You don't need the bribe now."

"I'm not sure what's in there, but if it's food, I definitely need it."

She lets out a long sigh. "It is food, but I think it's better if I use it as leverage in case you become difficult."

"Me? Difficult? I'm a hero who saves children and puppies, remember?" I tease.

"Oh, now there are puppies?"

I shrug. "Rolls off the tongue easily."

She bursts out laughing. "Who are you? You're never in this good of a mood."

"I'm always in a good mood."

When I'm not pining after her. When she shows up here and kisses me. When I'm just near her, suddenly it's like the sun peeking over the horizon.

Ainsley chases away that dark cloud that's hung over my head for years.

"That is a lie, but I'll allow it."

"Thank you."

Her eyes are bright with happiness, and I feel like a damn king, knowing I put it there. "All right, we should get down to it."

"We're doing this now?" I ask.

"Are you busy?"

I look at the stacks of paper on my desk and then back to her. I'm swimming in a never-ending sea of bureaucracy. My chief retired a year ago, and since then we haven't had anyone permanent in this spot. The two other captains and I rotated, but no one ever handled anything fully before we had to pass it to the next guy.

Which means everything slipped through the cracks. Since I was appointed chief after that stupid fire, I've been doing nothing but cleaning up messes and finding new ones.

However, the way Ainsley is staring at me with pleading eyes, I know I'll let it all build up to make her happy.

"You know, I was just thinking that it's nice outside today and I should take a break," I say as I get to my feet.

"You were?"

"Let's go get lunch."

She grabs the bag. "I have one better for you. Is there a park or somewhere close?"

"No park, but I have a good friend who owes me a favor."

Her brows lift. "Oh?"

I grab my phone and send a text to the group chat.

> Killian, are you cool with me having a meeting at your ranch? I'd like to take the horses out for a ride.

KILLIAN

Meeting with who?

EVERETT

And since when do you have meetings in barns? That's usually my gig.

> t's for an interview. I'd like to take Ainsley to see the horses and take her for a trail ride.

EVERETT:

Now it makes sense.

MILES

He needs a barn to show her the hayloft. You know what they do up there . . .

EVERETT

Nothing says love like hay in the ass.

> There's something wrong with you.

KILLIAN

We knew this. You're welcome to ride any of the horses. I'm back in Boston for the week, but I'll have the trainers saddle up two if that works.

> Thanks, Killian, that's perfect. At least someone in this chat is helpful.

EVERETT

I'm helpful. Listen, once you get her in the "saddle," you want her to ride the . . . horse . . . in an up and down motion.

You like to play with the horses a lot, huh?

MILES

Fighting words there. So, you and Ainsley?

We're doing an interview. That's it.

EVERETT

Miles, is that what the kids are calling it these days? Hey, baby, come meet me for an interview at the barn, I'll show you my stallion.

KILLIAN

Ainsley is great, don't fuck it up.

Thanks for the unsolicited advice.

EVERETT

It is you. The chances he's going to fuck it up are pretty high.

MILES

This is true. You are a pretty big idiot.

I huff and put the phone away. "Okay, let's go."

"I take it the Frisbee team is involved in this?"

"Not even a little. Other than we're going to Killian's ranch."

"There's a park there?"

I grin. "Come on, I'll show you."

After we arrive, we go through the huge gates, and her eyes are like saucers. "This isn't a ranch. This is like a compound for the rich."

I snort a laugh. "You don't even know the half of it."

"Why did you bring me here?"

"Just let me surprise you for once."

She sighs but doesn't press me for more. I take her hand, pulling her back to the barn. The trainer exits. "Hey, Lachlan."

"Good afternoon, Pete. This is Ainsley."

They shake hands. "It's nice to meet you. Do you work here?"

He nods. "I'm the head trainer for Mr. Thorn."

"Killian runs this ranch and boards his racehorses here," I explain.

She looks to Pete. "You do? Wow. I love horses. I had one until I was in high school, but . . . that was a long time ago."

Until Peaches had to be sold because Ainsley was getting ready for college. The way she cried when the Admiral told her it was time to let her go. I remember the tears, the way she curled up in my mother's garden and sobbed. Mom wouldn't let me go out there, saying that sometimes girls need a real good cry and we needed to give her space to grieve.

I'd like to take that pain away, because as far as I know, she hasn't ridden since.

"Pete, could you show us to the horses you saddled?"

Ainsley's head whips to me. "What?"

I step closer, a smile on my face. "We're going to ride."

"But . . . you hate horses."

"You love them."

"I repeat, you hate horses."

"I don't hate them. I've learned how to ride since living here."

"I . . . didn't know that. Wow. Lach, we don't have to do this. I know you . . ."

"I know that I want to take you riding. I know that you loved your horse when we were kids. That every Sunday you woke before the sun came up, dressed in your fancy riding gear. Mom used to say she thought you slept in it." I chuckle.

"Well, she wasn't wrong. I did sleep in it. When I was really young, I even slept with the helmet. I didn't want to forget anything." She steps closer, taking my hands in hers. "You remember that?"

I nod. "There are a few regrets I have in this world, Ainsley, and one is the day you had to let go of Peaches, that I didn't come out to the garden."

"You heard me?"

"Yes, and my mother told me to let you cry it out." I shake my head. "I never should've let you cry alone. You wouldn't have done that to me."

She looks off to the side. "I would've soaked your shirt with the amount of tears I cried that day."

"I wouldn't have cared."

Ainsley leans up on her toes, pressing her lips to mine. "Thank you."

"Don't thank me yet," I joke. "For all I know, Killian put us on two crazy horses."

She giggles. "I'll protect you."

I kiss her again, tugging her against my chest. She pulls away, resting her hand over my beating heart. "You stole my line."

She shrugs and then walks toward the barn, turning before she enters. "You stole my heart, so it's only fair."

No, she stole mine, and we're going to have two hearts broken when this ends.

———

"That was the best ride ever. It's been so long and . . . it was just like riding a bike."

I'm glad one of us is happy, because it sure as hell isn't me. I may have learned how to ride in the last few years, but that wasn't what I did.

She's a goddamn maniac on a horse. She was going full speed and not having a care in the world.

It's going to take me weeks to recover from this.

"It was something."

She laughs. "You didn't feel free? Like there was nothing that could touch you as we raced through the fields?"

"I felt like if we hit the ground, the only thing that was going to touch us was God."

"For someone who literally walks into burning buildings for a living, you're a chicken."

"Completely different."

Which to some might sound ridiculous, but it's true. That's

my job. I am trained to go into that building and do what I can to save lives and property. This was for fun and was terrifying.

We walk the horses back to Pete, who informs Ainsley she's welcome anytime to ride.

"Thank you for this, Lach. I didn't realize how much I missed riding until I got on the horse. It was like a part of me returning."

I throw my arm over her shoulder, tugging her to my side and kissing her temple. "I'm glad it made you happy."

"It did. However . . . I'm the one who planned to bribe you. How did I end up coming out on this side of the deal?"

"I'll think of inventive ways to let you pay me back."

She grins. "I bet you will."

"You owe me nothing, sweetheart. This was because I wanted to see you smile."

It's what I always want. When Ainsley smiles, all the bad in the world disappears, leaving nothing but beauty and joy. She's everything to me, and while we are in this arrangement, I want her happy.

"Well, I smiled a lot."

"Good."

"So where are you taking me now?"

"I'll show you." We walk down to Killian's dock. He has incredible views from here, and you can almost hear the falls. It's a great spot for fishing and hopefully a serene place to talk about some of my past.

"Wow, his views are spectacular," Ainsley notes.

I try to look at it from her view—the river that runs from the mountains through the town, the way the mountain peaks look as though they can pierce the clouds, and the sun behind acting as a beacon on all the beauty of this area.

But then I look at her.

I no longer see any of it, just Ainsley.

"Yeah, the views are spectacular."

She glances back at me, her lips tipping up as though she knows I'm not talking about the landscape. "Did you want to see what I brought for you?"

That's right, she has a small paper bag in that gargantuan purse of hers. We head over to the large Adirondack chairs, where we can look out at the river. She's digging in her bag, and I lean back, hands laced behind my head.

"Since it was supposed to be a bribe, I'm hoping it's good."

Ainsley wiggles her brows. "Oh, it is."

"I'm hoping it's lingerie."

"Uhh, no. Sorry to disappoint."

"I'll survive. You do go commando, and knowing you're walking around with nothing under those leggings is good enough for me."

"Glad to be of service."

I jerk my head to the bag. "What's in there then?"

She grins. "Something you love."

"I love a lot of things, but most don't fit in bags."

"This does."

"Okay, let me have it."

"Close your eyes and put out your hands." I do as she says, waiting for this gift I love, and it feels like a plastic container. "Okay, open them."

When I do it's a slice of cake, but not just any cake. It's strawberry shortcake. The kind like my mother made for me every year. While the other kids wanted her strange blends, I just wanted this.

"I haven't had this since she died," I admit.

"I drove an hour and a half to find the bakery that Hazel said makes the absolute best pie. I called there first, and they said they didn't have any of that this week, but I explained what I needed it for, and she specially made you a cake. The rest is at home."

I glance up, my chest feeling as though someone is squeezing it, and I can't breathe. "Ainsley, this is . . ."

"Sometimes the past belongs behind us, and other times we need to visit because there's a part of us that isn't healed yet. While it's not your birthday, and it's not your mother's baking, it's a piece of our life that we can still enjoy. I know this article feels like we're going back, and all those things are going to be opened again, but, Lachlan, you should know I would never do anything to hurt you."

I lean forward, taking her hand in mine, and kiss her softly. "I'd break myself open for you. You've always been my weakness."

"Let me be your strength."

I kiss her again. "What do you want to know? I'm an open book."

And then we have the longest interview of my life.

"Can Ainsley do it?"

"Do what?" I ask.

"Can she read me the story tonight?"

I glance over at Ainsley, who smiles. "If it's okay, I'd love to."

"Of course it's okay," I say quickly. While this is something I always do with Rose, I'm not going to complain that she's finding friendship with Ainsley.

Ainsley turns to Rose. "I'll meet you in there once you're ready."

Rose rushes into her room to get changed and then to the bathroom to brush her teeth. Ainsley comes close, nudging me with her hip. "Do you have any . . . plans for tonight?"

I lean in close. "For you?"

She nods.

"I think half of the fun is making you wait and wonder."

If she only knew the plans I had for her, she might decide to sleep somewhere else.

Ainsley grins. "Half the fun is watching you come up with a plan."

"You forget, I know how much you hate not knowing things."

There are perks to this arrangement. For one, I know her very well. We don't have many secrets from each other. Now we have even fewer.

One thing I'm sure of is that Ainsley does not like being left in the dark. She wants to make the plans—always has.

"I'm learning that there are some things worth the antic-ipation."

The water is still running, which means I have a few seconds ɪ show her just how much anticipation can heighten what's ɪming later. I move my hand behind her, where I can just barely ɪ my thumb along the small of her back. She shivers, and I lean face close to hers, where our lips could touch, but I don't seal ɪeal. "I promise tonight the only pain will be from how long ɪait before I make you come."

ɪ addy! Ainsley! I'm ready!" Rose yells as she runs out of the

"Can Ainsley do it?"

"Do what?" I ask.

"Can she read me the story tonight?"

I glance over at Ainsley, who smiles. "If it's okay, I'd love to."

"Of course it's okay," I say quickly. While this is something I always do with Rose, I'm not going to complain that she's finding friendship with Ainsley.

Ainsley turns to Rose. "I'll meet you in there once you're ready."

Rose rushes into her room to get changed and then to the bathroom to brush her teeth. Ainsley comes close, nudging me with her hip. "Do you have any . . . plans for tonight?"

I lean in close. "For you?"

She nods.

"I think half of the fun is making you wait and wonder."

If she only knew the plans I had for her, she might decide to sleep somewhere else.

Ainsley grins. "Half the fun is watching you come up with a plan."

"You forget, I know how much you hate not knowing things."

There are perks to this arrangement. For one, I know her very well. We don't have many secrets from each other. Now we have even fewer.

One thing I'm sure of is that Ainsley does not like being left in the dark. She wants to make the plans—always has.

"I'm learning that there are some things worth the anticipation."

The water is still running, which means I have a few seconds to show her just how much anticipation can heighten what's coming later. I move my hand behind her, where I can just barely run my thumb along the small of her back. She shivers, and I lean my face close to hers, where our lips could touch, but I don't seal the deal. "I promise tonight the only pain will be from how long you wait before I make you come."

"Daddy! Ainsley! I'm ready!" Rose yells as she runs out of the

twenty
Lachlan

"Can I please stay up late?" Rose whines as I have my finger pointed toward her room.

"Nope."

"But—"

I cut her off before she can try any bullshit reasoning. "No. You were up late last night after a long cheer practice, and tomorrow we're going to the Strawberry Festival, and then your competition." Much to my dismay.

Ainsley was explaining to Rose why she was going to miss her cheer competition, and my daughter decided that if we all went together, no one had to miss anything. This way, Ainsley can help the Admiral after the festival, and then we can go to the competition first thing in the morning.

Protesting would've worked if Ainsley didn't team up with her and then send me a text promising that tonight I could do whatever I wanted to her if I agreed.

Of course I agreed.

Like a fool. But a fool who is going to be very happy in an hour or two.

"Okay," she says with her lower lip jutted out.

"Come on, let's brush your teeth, and I'll read you a book."

bathroom, and we break apart so fast it's like we weren't even together.

Ainsley moves quickly, walking toward her. "I'm so excited. What should we read? Do you have a favorite? Your pajamas are so cute." She fires the questions off in one breath.

Rose smiles up at her, taking her hand. "I'll show you everything."

"Hey, pip-squeak," I say with a wide grin. Rose turns around, her brown hair spiraling like rays of the sun. "Do I get a good night hug? Since I've been relieved of duty tonight."

She releases Ainsley's hand and rushes over to me. I pull her into my arms, squeezing her and kissing the side of her head. "I love you, Daddy."

"I love you the most of anyone."

Rose giggles and hugs me tighter. "Is it too tight?"

I make a gasping noise, feigning that I can't breathe. "No."

She releases me and takes my face in her hands. "Daddy, you have to breathe."

"Oh, sorry, you're just so strong."

"Because I'm like you."

I grin. "Don't snore so loud you wake the bears."

She sighs dramatically. "I won't."

I made up a story about a little girl who snored so loudly she woke all the animals in the forest. They came to make sure she was okay, and the bear liked her so much he moved in. It was silly, but Rose loved all the sound effects of the animals I acted out.

"Good night, my little Rosebud."

"Good night, Daddy. Come home safe if there's a fire," she says as she heads back toward Ainsley.

"I always try."

She grins. "Try the hardest."

I wink and Rose laughs before taking Ainsley's hand. "Come on, Ainsley, we have books to read!"

"Books? How many do you want to read?"

Rose's laugh is deep, and warmth grows in my chest. "Until I fall asleep."

An hour later Ainsley emerges from Rose's bedroom. I'm on the couch, watching the game, when she plops down next to me. "We read eighty-two books, and she would've had me keep going."

I chuckle. "Eighty-two, huh? You're a speed reader."

Ainsley smiles. "Okay, maybe it was less than that."

"You never were good at math. Is she asleep?"

"I don't think so, but she's fading fast."

I lift my arm up. "Come here."

Ainsley nestles in next to me, head resting in the crook of my shoulder. Her body fits so damn perfectly with mine, and I wish we were other people. Ones who could have a future instead of this short blip in time.

"How many rounds of this do you have left?" she asks, looking at the baseball game.

"Rounds?"

"Yeah, like the ups and downs."

"Innings?" I ask, trying not to laugh.

"Whatever, I get my sports mixed up."

I laugh softly but pull her tighter. "There are four innings left, but we're not going to have time to watch them."

"No?"

"No, sweetheart, we're not."

Ainsley's brown eyes meet mine as her lips turn up. "What will we be doing?"

"Each other."

"I like that plan."

"I hoped you might." I grin. "The sitter will be here in two minutes."

She sits up. "Sitter?"

"I want to take you somewhere."

"Where?"

Once again her curiosity is going to make this so much more fun. Delaney knocks once and then enters.

"Sup?" she says, dropping her bag.

"Thanks for coming over. We'll be gone a few hours," I explain.

Delaney shrugs and then heads to the couch. "It's fine. I'll be here in case Rose wakes up."

"Thanks again." She gives me the peace sign, and Ainsley follows me into the kitchen. "Grab a blanket."

"Okay," she says apprehensively.

She comes back out a few minutes later, and I take her hand as we head out the back door.

"Where are we going?" she asks with a giggle as I pull her along.

"Just follow me."

Ainsley lets out a long sigh but does as I ask. We walk through the main field and then down the path that I know by heart. When I moved into this house, I had no idea there was a secret path. Rose and I were doing some exploring, found it, and then realized it took us to the falls.

I help her over the log and then down the steep hill before she gasps.

"Oh my God."

I smile because the falls are beautiful anytime, but at night, when the moon is bright and the stars are everywhere, it's breathtaking.

"Welcome to Ember Falls."

Ainsley's eyes are wide as she looks around. There is one large waterfall off to the left, and to the side of it are five small ones. The big one has a pool at the bottom where we love to swim.

"This is incredible."

"It's my favorite part of the property."

I lay out the blanket and extend my arm to indicate she should sit. She does, leaning back on her elbows, staring at the falls.

"I honestly didn't know you guys had a waterfall. I thought I heard something at Killian's, but I figured it was in my head."

"Why did you think the town was named this then?"

"I don't know. I thought maybe someone fell in a pile of ashes or something and thus the town was named."

I snort. "It would be plausible, but no, these are the falls."

"How have I been here this long and no one ever talks about it?"

I move toward her with a grin. "That's part of the town rules."

"Town rules? To not talk about the fact you actually have a waterfall in the town?" She sits up, crossing her legs.

"We take an oath."

She rolls her eyes. "Yes, and we all know how well people keep their vows on anything these days."

That much is true. Still, there are some things that people will honor, and this is one. "There is a legend about these falls."

Now she looks incredibly interested. "Do go on."

"The story is that over two hundred years ago, the settlers of Ember Falls wanted this place to remain a secret. The waterfalls were said to have healing powers, but they were a greedy bunch and worried the magic would run out if too many people knew." She shifts closer. "The falls are on two private properties, and those two farmers wanted to keep people off their lands, so they told no one. It wasn't until the first farmer got sick—he was told there was no hope and he couldn't survive the illness, but his wife believed in the power of the falls. She had her sons carry him down to the falls and bring him in. Two weeks later he was back on the fields, plowing and farming."

"No!" Ainsley gasps. "He was healed?"

I nod slowly. "Also, the two sons who went in the water had their scabies clear."

She makes a face. "Umm, eww."

"After that, the town made a vow that they'd protect the falls and its magic."

Ainsley leans forward. "And what exactly is the vow? Because I'm pretty sure you're breaking the rules by telling me. A journalist."

"Are we on the record?"

"Absolutely not."

"Then I think my secret is safe. The vow is that we let no outsiders know, and you, sweetheart, are definitely one."

"Thank you for bringing me here," she says softly. "For trusting me with the town secret. I promise I won't betray the trust you've bestowed upon me."

I trust her more than I've trusted any other woman. I honestly don't remember a time before she was in my life. I remember all the moving, not having friends, my mother being sad and alone, but not people. Not life, just as though it's fragments of time I tried to forget.

Then I met the MacKinleys. Things were never the same after that. Caspian was like a brother to me, always there when I needed him, and Ainsley was . . . well, Ainsley. She was always around, always driving us crazy and tattling anytime we left her out.

She followed us, did things she definitely shouldn't, and we'd get punished after we were caught.

Then we got older, and I went off to college. When I came back, she wasn't a little girl anymore. She was stunning, and I did everything I could to shut my feelings down, but I couldn't.

And once again I'm unable to resist her.

"I want to make love to you in these falls, Ainsley. I want to strip you down and take you while the water rushes around us. I'm going to show you magic in every way."

Ainsley and I move toward each other at the same time, my hand cupping her cheek and hers grabbing onto my shoulder. Our lips touch, and she moans when our tongues slide together. I kiss her deeper, holding her tighter, wanting to make good on that promise.

She pulls at my shirt, lifting it over my head, and I do the same.

"Lachlan." She breathes my name when I kiss down her neck.

"Lie down," I command.

Ainsley does and I slide her shorts off, ever grateful the woman doesn't believe in underwear.

"Look at you, naked in the moonlight." She's a goddamn nymph lying here, open to me and the sky.

She moves to cover herself, but I grab her wrist. "Don't. I want to look at you."

Her eyes dart around the clearing. "We're sort of in public."

I shake my head. "No one is coming. I would never let anyone see you like this. This is for me only. You laid out like a meal, ready for me, wanting me."

Ainsley sighs, her head looking to the water. "I want to swim with you."

"Not yet."

She looks to me. "Why?"

I push her legs apart and kiss the inside of her knees. "Because first I want to lick your cunt until I drown in you."

twenty-one
Ainsley

Yeah, umm, I'm going to die right here.

He seriously just said that.

Yup. He did.

My fingertips grip the blanket, pretty sure I'm going to orgasm just from that. At least I think that could be until I feel his tongue on my clit.

The one thing about Lachlan I've learned is that he's not much for preamble. Not that he isn't all about the foreplay, or maybe it was that the other guy just didn't know what he was doing. Either way, Lachlan is able to immediately find exactly what I need.

His tongue pushes in circles, harder and then lighter, the pressure making it impossible to think about anything else.

All I feel is him.

All I know is that I want this—him—far more than I should.

Lachlan is the dream and I never want to wake up.

"More," I pant, growing so close to my orgasm.

The wind blows softly, and between that and the heat of his mouth, I swear I'm barely holding on.

He lifts his head, moving his fingers in and out. "You're so close, aren't you?"

"Yes."

"I can feel you tightening around me. You want something to grip, something bigger, don't you?"

I want him. "You."

"My poor Ainsley, needing my cock to make her come."

I moan, my back arching when he pushes deeper. I close my eyes, focusing on the sensations that are building. "Please."

"Please, what?"

"Please, I need you."

I feel him at my entrance and my eyelids lift.

"Hmm, how much of me do you need?"

"All!" I nearly scream, but the word dies at the end as I feel him push a little deeper.

But not enough.

Not nearly enough.

He pulls out completely. "I'm not sure you can handle all," he taunts.

"Lachlan," I groan.

Again he enters me, just a little.

I want to scream, claw, find a way to take what I want—what I need. I arch my back, whimpering when he stills, not allowing me more of him. "I want you to come here, right like this, with my cock just deep enough to feel that throbbing, the way your pussy is contracting, begging for more." His thumb presses against my clit, and I tighten around him more. "That's it, squeeze around me." Lachlan slides in another inch. "Do you want more, baby?"

"Yes!" My body is so damn tight, it's desperate for release. "Give me you. Give me everything."

He rubs my clit harder, sliding a little deeper. "Come, Ainsley. Let go and I'll fuck you so hard another orgasm comes on its heel. Then, when that happens, I'm going to take you into the water and let you ride me as your perfect tits bounce in the waves we make. Come on, baby, let's see if I can make you see stars."

I glance up at the sky, the stars so bright, and he continues to put more pressure on my clit, rubbing in circles. The orgasm comes so fast I don't even have time to breathe. I grip his arms, my nails digging into the flesh as he thrusts so deep I scream, and my orgasm carries on longer than any I've ever had.

Lachlan doesn't let up or slow down. He just fucks me through it all, and I'm not sure whether it's one long orgasm or that he made good on his promise and this is back to back, but I don't care.

It's heaven and hell and everything in between.

I hold on to him and let him take control through it all.

He grunts loudly and pulls out just in time to cover my stomach with his cum. He collapses on me, and I rub his back as he works to catch his breath.

Lachlan lifts up and stares down at me. "I'm so sorry, Ainsley."

I blink at that. "Sorry?"

"I got carried away. I forgot a condom."

"It's fine. I have an IUD."

The relief in his eyes is instant. "I . . . it still shouldn't have happened."

I give him a soft smile. "I appreciate you saying it, and it wasn't the smartest thing either of us have done, but I didn't think about it either. I promise, I'm fine and not mad. Have you . . . been . . ." God, this is so uncomfortable. "Tested?"

"Yes, I get regular testing because of my job."

"Okay, well, I did as well after the one time, and everything came back normal."

He kisses my nose. "Good thing I planned for us to swim. Come on."

Lachlan gets to his feet, pulling me up with him, and we walk to the water. When we get to the edge, I tuck myself behind him.

"What are you doing?" he asks.

"I'm naked!"

"Yes, as am I."

I sigh. "Yes, but guys being naked isn't the same for girls."

He turns his head. "Do women have some naked cloak we aren't aware of?"

"Usually, but mine is in the wash."

Instead of saying anything, he walks into the water, leaving me buck naked and now alone by the edge. "Lachlan!"

"Get in and you can be naked in the water."

I'm not sure that's better. "Are there . . . fish and stuff?"

"Are you worried about the fish seeing you naked?"

"Well, I wasn't until you said it."

Seriously, I do not want to be in the water—at night—when I can't see what's lurking around.

Lachlan grins and comes closer to me. "I'll protect you, Berry. Now, get in the water." When I don't move, he raises one brow. "Or stand there and see if an animal comes by."

That does it. I move quickly, splashing my way into the water. "Lachlan!" I scream because dear Lord is it cold. "What the hell?"

"Oh, it's not that bad. I got in."

I was hoping for more of a bathwater-type experience, but I guess that's not happening.

I force myself to get in and make my way to him, wrapping my arms and legs around him. I'm seeking out available warmth, and since this was his brilliant idea, he can accept the consequences.

"Do you feel the magic yet?" he asks.

I feel something inside, but it doesn't feel like magic. It feels like love. It's been there for a long time, growing and then fading when it bubbled too close for comfort.

Sometimes, like four years ago, it surfaced fast and unyielding, only to be beaten back into its box.

Now that box is torn to shreds, and I can't put this back.

I have to hope I can just survive knowing this love won't go anywhere further.

Tears well in my eyes, and I'm grateful for the darkness and water so it can hide any tears that may leak out.

"Not yet," I admit, whispering to hide the emotion there.

"It'll happen."

It won't. It never was in the cards for us.

Lachlan has walls so high that I couldn't climb them if I tried.

The loss of his mother and the other women in his life have taught him to reinforce them and scale them higher.

I pull myself tighter, burying my face in the crook of his neck. His hand moves to my back. "Hey, are you that cold?"

Yes, the cold, that's what it is. "No, I'm fine."

"Then what's wrong?"

"Nothing," I say into his neck.

If I don't look at him, I can just pretend.

"Ainsley, I know you better than that. We agreed to be honest."

I really hate that stupid agreement. I won't lie, but I'm not going to tell him that I'm in love with him and wish this could be my life.

That will put an end to this real quick.

I lift my head and force a smile. "I'm just thinking about the past."

He pushes my wet hair back. "What about it?"

How do I even explain this? I'm not sure I can, but I exhale and do my best to tell him the truth, but not send him running back to his house to pack my shit.

"When I was younger, I used to dream about this moment."

"Naked and floating in the sacred waterfalls?"

"Of course."

He chuckles. "Now I know you're lying."

"I mean you, you big asshole."

Even in the darkness his smile lightens the space. "Again I'm hoping these dreams turn dirty."

"Not these," I confess.

"Too bad."

He's such a pain in the ass. I don't know why my nickname is Painsley when he's the one who embodies it.

I huff. "Do you want to know the story, or would you rather I regale you with the tales of my dirty dreams?"

"Is that really a choice? If so, I choose option B."

I walked into that one.

"I take it back. There is no option other than what I want to say." He's the one who wanted to know what my thoughts were. Well, I'm ready to spill.

"Typical," Lachlan jokes.

"Anyway," I say dramatically. "As I was saying, I daydreamed about moments like this. That you'd kiss me, we'd have sex, and then you'd hold me in some way after. I didn't exactly envision us floating in the magical water, but you get my drift."

Lachlan's quiet, and I wonder if I did exactly what I was trying to avoid and scared him away. Especially because he moves his arms to pull my embrace off his neck, which forces me to try to stand. However, he just adjusts me so that I'm not cradled against his chest.

Slowly his lips touch mine, and I take his face in my hands, kissing him slowly.

This kiss is different. It's slow and sweet. It's filled with regret and hope, a mix of happiness and melancholy and desire.

He pulls back, and then his lips press against my nose. "If there was anyone in the world who could make me want more, it would be you."

I close my eyes, resting my hand on his chest. The steady strum of his heart pulses beneath my fingers. There are so many things I can say to that. So many questions, but I came into this with eyes wide open.

Lachlan is not for forever.

No matter how much I wish it could be different.

"If there was anyone I would hope for more with, it's you."

"I can't, Ainsley."

"I know," I say softly.

He sighs heavily. "This is a mistake. I'm giving you false hope."

I glance up into his eyes while shaking my head. "No, this isn't a mistake. I refuse to let you call this that again. No matter how fleeting or short this time is, I'll never regret this. Will you?"

"No, God, no, but . . . you deserve more. You should have someone who is willing to lay down their life just to be near you."

"You went into a possible burning building for me."

Lachlan lets out a throaty laugh. "Not the sentiment I was going for, but this is you."

"I'm not a little girl, Lach. I know what I walked into with you. I'm completely fine with the arrangement. You have your life here and I'm in New York, getting ready to take the world by storm with my awesome sports story."

"Yes, all the sports you're so well versed in."

The heaviness has dissipated, and I'm going to just live in denial and pretend this is all going to be fine. It's better for me, and when I have to leave, I'll cry, eat a pint of ice cream, sing heartbreaking ballads, and write about it. Like mature, heartbroken women do.

I rub my fingertip along his collarbone. "You know, when I was in college and had to study, I was very motivated by the possibility of a reward."

"Why does that not surprise me?"

"I don't know. By all accounts I'm a mysterious woman."

Lachlan grins. "Maybe I cracked the code."

"Sure you did, Sparky."

"Sparky?"

I rather like this nickname. It's fitting on so many levels. "I was thinking, it's really unfair that you have a name for me, one I hate, I might add, and there's nothing I can call you."

"Do you not remember what you called us when we were little?"

I roll my eyes. "Please, that was child's play. I called one dumb and the other stupid. Sparky is more . . . adult."

"It is?" I can hear the disbelief in his voice.

Therefore, I must edify him on my reasoning. I'm sure he'll love this.

"You're a fireman."

"Obviously."

"And annoying."

"Takes one to know one," he tosses back.

"I'm going to just pretend you're not cutting me off at every turn."

Lachlan's smile grows. "I expected nothing less."

"Right. So. You're annoying and a fireman, but you're also incredibly hot."

"I like the turn of this one now. Please go on."

I swear he's the most annoying man ever. "I planned to without your permission." I mean, really, does he think I care either way if he wanted me to stop or start? No. I need to lay it out again because *someone* keeps cutting me off. "My point is, you're a fireman, you're hot, you're annoying, so when you combine them, you're a spark. No one knows if you're going to start a flame, and you're like that lighter that keeps clicking, so you try over and over and over to get it to light."

"Maybe it's out of fluid," he suggests.

"I think it's more that you're just annoying."

Lachlan laughs, pulling me to his chest tighter. "I'm pretty sure I know how to start a fire in you."

Yes, he does. I just worry about when I have to put it out, because I'm pretty sure I'm going to get burned.

twenty-two
Lachlan

"I want to get a whole bunch of strawberries!" Rose exclaims as we're in my truck on the way to Virginia Beach.

Ainsley twists in her seat so she can see her. "Did you know that your dad and I went to this festival every year when we were kids?"

Rose grins. "You did?"

"We did. It was my favorite thing to go to. I would eat so many berries that I would have the worst stomachache, then they'd make me ride rides and get sick."

I shake my head. "I think you have that a little backward."

"I remember it perfectly."

"You do?"

She nods. "Yup."

"Well, as I recall, you wouldn't *listen* to any of us when we warned you about eating from the containers as we walked. You'd just pick and refill, pretending like no one saw you tossing the tops of the strawberries on the path—which was a crime since you were stealing," I say with a hint of smugness.

"Please, arrest me."

"If I could, I would." I continue telling Rose the rest of the story. "Then we'd walk around the festival, where you'd spend the

entire time feeling like shit, and we'd have to skip going to all the
fun events because you would cry that your stomach hurt so
much and you needed to lie down."

She crosses her arms over her chest. "Lies. You and Caspian
would keep filling my containers as we walked, and then you
made me ride that horrible spinning and twisting ride." She drops
her voice to mirror mine. "'Come on, Ainsley, all the big kids ride
the ride.'"

Okay, maybe we did that once or twice, but only because she
was always talking and telling us how we should take her on the
rides. At least if she was gnawing on the berries, she was quiet and
we could plan how we were going to ditch her.

It wasn't my finest hour, but I was twelve, so . . . I give myself
a pass.

"And you kept eating them," I remind her.

"You were mean and—I say this *again*—annoying."

"Yes, and you're just . . ."

"A delight," she finishes.

"You keep saying that, and I keep wondering if you know the
definition of the word."

Ainsley sticks her tongue out at me and Rose giggles.

"Daddy, I don't want to get sick."

"No, baby, I won't make you eat them. We'll make Ainsley eat
them again, so she can remember how much she loves strawberries."

"Or . . ." Ainsley draws out the word. "We can make your dad
eat them all and see if he gets sick. What do you think?"

Rose taps her lips and I inhale. "Hey! I thought you were on
my side?"

She giggles. "How about no one gets sick? And we ride the
rides? And we eat the cake and strawberries?"

Both Ainsley and I glance at each other. "That sounds
perfect."

We drive the next two hours, having to make three stops
because Ainsley needed a soda, then to pee. The last time was
because she thought she left her wallet at the previous stop—she

didn't. Since then Rose has been chattering nonstop to a very attentive Ainsley.

"And then Rickie told Veronica who told Maddy that she didn't really like me. I liked her, but she was mean to me, so now I don't like her. But I love Maddy, she's my friend." Rose is moving on to her next topic.

"Wow, but maybe, just maybe, Rickie didn't say that. Did you ask her?"

Rose sighs heavily. "No."

"I understand that it hurt your feelings, but what if she said she didn't like roses, not Rose West?"

My daughter seems to ponder that and then shrugs. "I'll talk to her."

Ainsley looks to me with a smile. "And you said I was a menace. Ha!"

"You are a menace. Both of you."

Ainsley and Rose fist-bump.

We head over the bridge-tunnel, which fascinates Rose more than anything. "Are those ships, Daddy?"

"They are."

"Did you know my daddy and your grandpa were on those ships?" Ainsley asks.

"They were?" Rose's voice rises. "I didn't know that!"

Ainsley looks to me for a second, disappointment flashing in her eyes before it's gone, and she turns back to Rose. "When we were little, we'd get to come on board and see the ship. One time I got to ride on the ship."

Yes, the tiger cruise, which was literal hell for me. I hate the ocean, and for three days I was trapped on the metal can, floating aimlessly.

Maybe *aimlessly* is a stretch, but it felt like it to me.

The only bright spot was that Ainsley and Caspian came too. Her father wanted to start a program where navy families were able to see and experience what their sailors did. Since her dad was the Admiral, my father fell in line and was the captain of the ship that piloted the program. Which meant my family had no choice but to go, because we were taught to lead from the front.

We ate in the galley, we worked various jobs with sailors who sure as hell didn't want to be there, and we drove the ship.

"Daddy, can we tell Grandpa I want to ride on the ship?"

The muscles in my chest constrict at the thought of talking to my father. He calls, sends gifts for Rose, and leaves long-winded messages asking for me to hear him out.

I don't need to hear anything. He is the reason my mother chose to leave this world. She didn't have it in her to fight, and it was because he left her long before she got sick.

Which means she left me and Rose.

So, no, I don't need to listen to any bullshit.

Ainsley cuts in. "You know what? We can ask my daddy. He still has lots of friends here."

"We're not going to see the Admiral, just you."

There's no way with the surprise that's coming that we're going to her father's house.

She shrugs. "If you're in town, it would be rude not to stop by. He wants to see you both."

I clench my jaw because if I don't, I might ruin the surprise.

Besides, the absolute last thing I want to do is go by our old homes. My father will probably be there, and then I'll have no choice but to talk to him.

"No, we don't have time. We need to get to the strawberries before they're all gone. Maybe you should call him and have him meet us there," I suggest.

She snorts. "Considering I'm staying there tonight, that doesn't make a lot of sense. Besides, I indicated we'd be there for dinner."

"Did you?"

"I want to go see the Admiral," Rose says, crossing her arms over her chest. "I want to go on the boats."

"Ships." We both correct her at the same time and then laugh.

We're going to talk about all of this later. "Why don't you tell Ainsley about your teacher," I suggest, letting it drop for now.

Rose obliges, telling her stories about her friends, her class, and that Briggs is now her friend and he isn't being stupid anymore.

We enter the town limits of Pungo, and it's like being torn back in time. Nothing has changed. There are strawberry fields everywhere and people walking around, picking berries and heading to where the festival is.

"Okay, let's make a plan," Ainsley says. "I say we do the rides first, then pick, then eat."

"Absolutely not. We have a short amount of time, and we're here for the strawberries. If you remember these people line up early and always get the good ones. We need to pick first, for several reasons."

She purses her lips. "This is a ploy. I can smell it."

"I promise it's not."

It really is. She's got a big surprise coming in about two minutes.

I follow the line to the lot we're parking in and lowkey send a text while she's putting sunscreen on Rose.

We're here, meet you at the front entrance.

I slide my phone into my pocket, not waiting for a reply, and walk to the front. We're standing here, Ainsley is holding Rose's hand, and for a moment I can see what life would be like for the three of us.

Ainsley writing on the back porch, Rose playing outside while I work on the yard. Then we'd eat, put Rose to bed, and I'd make Ainsley very happy at night.

A baritone voice breaks me from my stupid fantasy.

"Excuse me, do you have a barf bag? My sister is prone to puking at these events."

Ainsley turns around, eyes wide. "Caspian!"

"Hey, Berry!"

She launches herself into her brother's arms, and he laughs, taking a few steps back from her assault.

"Easy, you maniac."

She laughs and then steps back. "What are you doing here?"

"I came to see my baby sister and . . ." Caspian looks down at Rose, who is bouncing. "I came to see this girl!"

He lifts her up into his arms, hugging her, and she giggles. "I missed you, Uncle Caspian!"

"I missed you more!"

I may not have had any siblings, but I got a brother anyway. He puts her down and we clasp hands and then hug like men do, banging our hands on each other's backs. "Good to see you, man."

"You too. I'm glad this worked out."

"Same."

Rose and Ainsley are standing there with huge smiles. Ainsley comes back, looping her hands around his arm. "I can't believe you're here."

"Lachlan thought it would be fun to get you sick again."

She shakes her head. "I bet he did."

Caspian chuckles. "It's been a really long time since we've all been together. I didn't realize just how much I've missed it."

It's been four years. Four years of me trying to pretend I didn't have feelings for Ainsley MacKinley. Four years of lying to myself and to everyone else. I lost more than just the girl I cared about. I lost my friend.

"Come on, Uncle Caspian! Let's go pick strawberries before they're all gone!" Rose, who appears to be done with this little reunion, exclaims.

There is no one, other than me, who compares to her uncle Caspian. He has been there, a constant in her life since she was born. When her mother decided that motherhood wasn't in her future, and I was given the choice to take Rose, it was Caspian and Ainsley who were by my side.

My mother and father were supportive. Disappointed at the

same time, but proud of the fact that I wanted to step up and raise my daughter.

When I needed to go to the fire academy, Caspian babysat Rose all the time. It definitely didn't go unnoticed, and the two of them have a special bond.

All of us enter the strawberry patch, and we find a row that doesn't look too picked over.

"Is this one good, Daddy?" Rose lifts one up.

"It is. You can put that in—" She eats it before I can finish. "Your mouth."

Ainsley laughs. "Don't eat a lot, silly. You remember the story about a bellyache?"

Rose drops the new one she picked.

I sigh. "Put them in your basket, Rose."

Caspian runs over, scooping her up, and she giggles. "Come on, Rosie Posey, let Uncle Cas show you how to do it. I bet we can pick more than Ainsley and your dad."

"Is that a challenge?" Ainsley asks, always taking the bait. "Because I will kick your butt!"

"We are going to beat you!" Rose taunts.

Ainsley crosses her arms over her chest. "You too? Well, I bet that we can fill our baskets before you can." Her eyes meet mine, and I'm just a pawn in this MacKinley war, just like it's always been.

Although usually I'm on Caspian's side. So this is a slight change.

Ainsley grins. "Three."

"Two." It's Caspian this time.

Rose claps her hands. "One!"

Caspian and Rose rush off, but the spot they picked to start at clearly doesn't have any. Ainsley and I head over a few rows and start filling our cartons.

"We have to let Rose win," Ainsley says, and I smile.

"Why?"

"Because you fuckers never let me win, and I know what it feels like to always be defeated."

Her statement stuns me. While she says it with a laugh and probably meant it as a joke, I hate that we did that to her.

"We should've let you win."

She shakes her head. "I didn't mean it like that, I swear. I'm just fine. In fact, I'm winning all the time now."

I take a step toward her, very aware that her brother and my daughter can easily see us, but this is important.

"We were cruel."

She shrugs. "You were teenage boys and I was . . . irritating."

"Still."

"Lachlan, seriously, I just meant that sometimes girls need a win and Rose will be happy. It's a good thing. Please don't let that offhand comment ruin today. So far it's been damn near perfect and . . ." Her hand rests on my chest, and I wonder whether she can feel it pounding at her nearness. "If we were staying together tonight, you'd so be getting a blow job."

"Really?"

"A long one," she says with a grin and then takes a slow bite from the strawberry in her hand.

What I wouldn't give to be that piece of fruit right now.

"Maybe you should sneak over to my hotel tonight. I can convince Caspian to keep Rose in his room."

She runs her tongue over her seductive, sweet lips. "Maybe I will."

Ainsley is like a siren, and I'm going to answer her call, even if it's the worst idea in the world.

twenty-three
Ainsley

"You know that the Admiral will go ballistic if he finds out you're in town," I tell my brother as he vehemently refuses to come with me back home.

"He can fuck right off."

I laugh once. "I dare you to say that to him."

We're standing outside of Lachlan's truck, Lachlan behind the wheel and Rose asleep in the back passenger area. Rose is totally exhausted. We walked, ate, went on the rides, and then took her to the animal auction and rodeo at the end.

She absolutely loved it. Now she needs to sleep, and I need to get as much as I can done for my father.

Caspian leans on the quarter panel, refusing to budge on anything. "What are you going there for anyway?"

"To help clean out some of Mom's things."

It was a big ask for my father to even consider this. Honestly, I was shocked when he called me the day after his surprise visit to ask me to do it. He's lived in the fantasy of her coming back to him, even though she moved to Florida and is dating someone.

Not that I've ever hinted at that last part. I think he'd lose his shit.

"Wow." Caspian's eyes widen.

Lachlan rolls down the window. "Are you two ready?"

I turn to him. "Almost. I need to work my magic."

"Oh, Lord."

I ignore that and return to my brother.

"It would be a huge help if you were there. This isn't going to be easy for the Admiral."

My brother shakes his head. "Why? So he can use me as a punching bag instead of you or the fact that Mom left him? No, thanks. I had enough of that when he drove to Tennessee to let me know what a disgrace I am to the MacKinley name. I have no real job, according to him, and I'm wasting my life away and will never make it in music."

I hate that my father doesn't support him. He's just a very narrow-minded, his-way-or-the-highway type of person. It's what made him a great leader, but a terrible father at times.

He never hit us. Never punished us in the extreme, because his words were more damaging than a belt ever could've been.

Especially for my brother.

"It's not true, Cas."

"I know."

"Do you?" I ask, resting my hand on his arm. "Do you know that he's wrong? Because he is. You're already doing amazing. You're playing more frequently, getting new gigs and rebookings. All of that is proving him and anyone else who doubted you wrong."

My brother gives me a half smile. "Anyone ever tell you that you're the bright spot in this world?"

"No, but I'm open to hearing it more often. I keep telling Lachlan that I'm a delight."

Lachlan laughs from inside the cab. "I keep telling her that she needs a dictionary because that's not the word I'd use."

"Neither would I," Caspian agrees.

I huff and shake my head. "We should go. I hope you'll change your mind and come by."

"Don't hold your breath."

I lean in and kiss his cheek. "One day I'm going to fix you boys and your fathers."

"You have way too much faith in the men in your life," Caspian says with a hint of sadness.

Maybe I do, but I won't give up hope.

I get in the truck, and Lachlan gives him a two-finger salute before we head off. I turn back to check on Rose, who is passed out in the back.

"She had a long day," I say softly.

"She did. We all did. I don't know how you're going to spend a few hours working with your dad."

I shrug. "He needs me, and I don't know how to say no to anyone I love."

"I'm proof of that," Lachlan says offhand, and my stomach drops.

I thought I was doing a good job hiding how I feel. Shit. He knows I love him. The pounding of my heart grows, and I force a smile, hoping I'm wrong.

"What?"

He glances over. "You know we're friends."

Thank God. He thinks it's a friendly kind of love. Sure, we'll go with that.

I do love him that way and in the marry-me-and-I'll-make-you-happy kind of way too.

"We definitely are. I would do anything for you, Rose, Caspian, and even the Frisbee guys now. I'm taking them into my inner circle."

Lachlan laughs once. "Well, they're halfway in love with you anyway."

"Only half?" I tease.

"Maybe three-quarters."

"Oh, well, I need to up my game then. Time for cookies and muffins."

He grins and then taps his thumb on the wheel. The closer we get to our childhood homes, the more anxious it appears he's growing. Lachlan grips the wheel a little tighter, his knuckles going white as we turn two streets down. There's a tension in his frame that wasn't there before.

I hate this.

I reach over, rubbing his shoulder, and then he starts to relax. "You can drop me off at the end of the street," I suggest.

"What? Absolutely not. The chances that he's home, let alone outside, are very low."

"You're obviously anxious about the possibility."

"I just don't want to see him."

"You don't have to. If he's outside, by some horrible coincidence, I'll talk to him and you can leave."

Lachlan places his hand on my thigh. "It'll be fine, Ainsley."

We turn onto the street we grew up on and pass Mrs. Langley's house, which my brother and Lachlan toilet-papered after she got them grounded, which then got them grounded for longer. Then on the right is Mr. Rapanotti, who always left candy in the mailbox for us when he saw us riding our bikes.

This street is filled with memories, and anytime I come home, it feels like a part of me is settling back into place.

We stop in front of my house, and Lachlan glances back at what was his house. The front light is on in the living room, where his father is probably sitting and reading.

I glance back at Rose, who is sound asleep, emitting a soft snore, and I smile. "If we weren't in front of my father's house, I'd lean over and kiss you," I whisper.

"If we weren't in front of your father's house, I'd do a lot more than that."

I grin. "You'll have to make it up to me another time."

"Yes, because I was promised a very long present, and I'm going to claim that."

"Long, you say?"

Lachlan chuckles. "Very long."

"I look forward to that then."

"Me too. Go get inside before I drive away with you."

The idea of it makes my heart flutter. I wish we could do

exactly that, but that threat is empty because of Rose and Caspian. "If only it were possible . . . I'd let you."

He leans forward, taking my hand in his and lacing our fingers together. "In some cultures, palms touching is equivalent to a kiss."

The way he does it makes me believe it could be. Something so simple, so innocuous, and yet it causes the butterflies in my belly to stir.

"Again, sir, you test the boundaries of propriety. If we were in Regency times, we'd be on our way to the altar."

"I won't tell if you don't." He reaches for my other hand, mimicking our palms kissing. "I'll see you in the morning."

I pull my hands from him, the tingling traveling up my arms and through my body. Jesus, I need to get a grip. This is madness.

"See you tomorrow."

"Text me when the coast is clear."

Meaning when his father isn't here. "I will."

On wobbly legs I exit the truck and walk up the steps of my childhood home, wishing the boy next door was there so he could climb through my window.

———

"How is the story coming along?" Caroline asks on our video call.

"I think good. The guys have been forthcoming and helpful in explaining their stories. Lachlan's interview was key to it, I just haven't really figured out what I want to do with the story. I have a call with three admissions advisers from various schools for some background info."

I'm sitting on my old twin bed, going through my notes since I can't sleep. Thankfully, my friend is also nocturnal during our deadline times.

"So what has you stuck?"

She knows me so well. "Other than the fact that I don't know dick about sports? Well, I slept with Lachlan."

Caroline's eyes widen, jaw dropping before she recovers.

"Okay then. Not what I was expecting since you're one step away from being a nun."

"Shut up."

She laughs. "Does he know you've been writing his name on your notebooks since you were a kid?"

"Yes and no. He knows I've lusted for him, but not that I'm in love with him."

"I imagine that would scare him off."

"You imagine correct," I say, getting up and walking over to the window.

My room faces the West house. The garden that his mother loved so dearly looks exactly the same. Four years and his father has done everything to maintain it. He told my father once that it's the only way to keep her alive with him.

I wish Lachlan could see it.

"Is it because of his kid?" she asks.

"I don't think it's that. I guess partially it's because of Rose, but not in the way you might think. His father was always gone when he was a kid."

"So was yours."

I laugh once. "Yeah, and that fucks you up. We were always good at pretending it didn't matter, but I would cry for weeks when the Admiral left. My mother would do everything she could to keep me from falling apart, but it took me a good month before I would settle into the new normal. Then he'd come back and screw it all up again."

Caroline falls silent for a moment. "Being a military kid isn't easy."

"No, it's not, but for Lachlan it was worse. He was an only child, and his mother would go into a deep depression when his father deployed. He almost had to become an adult. My mother would bring dinner to them every night. I remember one time Lachlan had the flu, he was so sick and Mom had to care for him. Every time his dad left, his mother did in a way too. He was on his own."

I was younger and didn't recognize that, but as I grew up, it was hard to watch. Lachlan acted out anytime his father's ship was deploying. He had an open invitation at our house, and he stayed here often.

"That's rough," Caroline says sympathetically.

"It was, and then Rose's mother got pregnant and she gave her up, which was really hard on him because it felt very reminiscent of his childhood."

Caroline nods. "I can imagine."

"When his mother died, that was the nail in his coffin. She got diagnosed with cancer when his father was deployed and didn't tell anyone."

"What?"

"Yeah, she kept it all a secret until about six months later and refused any treatment. No matter how much he or his father begged, she wouldn't do it."

It broke him.

I'll never forget one of their heated talks when I was in the garden, reading. He was begging her to fight. To just try to beat it for him. For Rose.

She placed her hand on his cheek and told him that sometimes letting go is the only way to go forward.

He stormed out of the house, and I could hear the tires screeching down the road.

"I don't understand it."

"I don't either. She had her son, who she loved, and her granddaughter. Rose was only two."

"You know that my mother had severe depression, right?"

"Yes."

Caroline and I spent hours talking about childhoods, and hers is semi similar to Lachlan's. The difference was that Caroline's mother sought help. In her home there was no stigma around mental health, and it was treated like any other illness.

"My mother would often have us go to therapy sessions with her. My brother and I fucking hated it. We were young and we really didn't understand any of it. Our parents shielded us from the really dark times. I had to live with my grandparents in New

Jersey for a few weeks. We just thought it was a vacation, but I learned later on that my dad had to take her to a specialty treatment facility and he wouldn't leave her there."

I smile just barely at the last part, and Caroline smiles bigger. "It's sweet, isn't it?"

"It really is."

"He loved her in sickness and in health. There were plenty of really great times. Once she was on the right medication and was in therapy regularly. My point is, Mom tried to explain to us what it felt like in her head. Depression is a liar and thief. It robs you of joy and makes you believe that the despair is deserved, she said. It takes one bad thought and feeds itself until it's so large you have no choice but to believe it."

I sit back on my bed, letting the weight of that settle around me. "It has to be such a burden living in that sadness every day."

Caroline sighs heavily. "My mother was able to get the help she needed and had the support of her family. If his mom didn't . . ."

"No, she did, in a way, but I understand what you mean. His father wasn't given the choice to stay home. He had to deploy."

"All I'm trying to explain is that the perspective that Lachlan has is different than yours. He lived it, watched it, felt everything, and then she chose—in his mind—to leave him. Doesn't matter that he was a grown man with his own child, because Rose's mother chose to leave her. It's just . . . messy."

It is, and I've put myself smack-dab in the middle of it.

"I would never do that to him."

Caroline gives me a sad smile. "But you will when this assignment is over."

"That's not a choice! I live in New York. I have a job."

"And his father didn't have a choice, but he still blames him . . ."

twenty-four
Lachlan

"I'll see you in a few weeks. I'll come visit you and Rose," Caspian says as he's loading his car.

"Sounds good."

"How are you and Ainsley getting on?"

My eyes widen for a second. "What?"

"You know, you guys hate each other."

"We don't."

We absolutely do not, and that's the rub. I love her. I have for a long time, and I know the way it will end. In a week or two, she'll head back to her life, and I'll continue doing what's best for Rose. Giving her a stable home, with a father who doesn't leave and where she is comfortable.

He laughs once at that. "Look, if you don't hate her, then you are deeply in love with that girl."

I chuckle and lace sarcasm in my tone. "I'm sure you'd love that."

Caspian closes the trunk and leans against it. "You and Ainsley?"

"Yeah, you and the Admiral with your overprotectiveness. No guy stands a chance."

"I wouldn't hate it."

What? Did he just . . .

"You wouldn't?"

"No, first of all, Ainsley is a grown woman and makes her own choices. If I ever tried to tell her she couldn't date someone, I think she'd marry him just to spite me. More than that, you're like a brother to me. I trust you with my life, and I definitely would trust that you'd never hurt her. I'm not saying I'm advocating for it, because I'm pretty sure she'd kill you. She's a scary one."

I force a laugh. "She's something."

His eyes narrow and he looks as though he can see right through me. "Do you . . . have a thing for my sister?"

I don't know that I've ever lied to him in all our years of being friends. I'm not going to start now. "I've had feelings for her for a long time."

His jaw drops. "I'm sorry, what the fuck universe did I wake up in? You do?"

"Look, Cas, it's complicated, but know that I would never hurt her. Ever. If something changes between us, you'll be the first to know."

There's no way I'm telling him about our current arrangement, and since there will never be anything more than this, it'll stay right here.

"You know she loves you, right?"

"She might think she does, but she's learning what an ass I am."

He runs his fingers through his hair and sighs. "If she hasn't figured it out in almost twenty years, I doubt she's going to start now."

I laugh once. "Like I said, I won't hurt her."

"Has something happened between you two?" When I go to open my mouth, he lifts his hand. "Forget I asked that. I don't want to know anything. Just know that if you do hurt her, which I know you said you won't, I'll beat the shit out of you and I'll take her side."

"As you should, and if I hurt her, I'll let you punch me until you're done," I vow.

"Okay then."

"Okay then."

He lets out a heavy breath. "Well, I better get on the road, and you need to pick up Ainsley."

"We're good?" I ask, needing to make sure before he leaves.

"Of course. I just . . . I'm a little shocked, but maybe I shouldn't be."

"What does that mean?"

Caspian laughs once. "Just that I have a feeling the signs have been there all along, and I just didn't want to see them. I don't know, you guys have always had this weird thing between you. When you stopped talking for the last four years, I was afraid to ask why. Now I'm really afraid."

I remember back to that night, when she came out like a goddamn angel who was going to take me from the hell I was in, and then I broke her wings.

I knew that Ainsley was the only person who could offer me solace, but then I took and took because I was just so beyond angry.

Every damn dream I had was falling apart.

I wanted to play professional football—that didn't work.

I wanted a family—the mother of my child walked away.

I planned to stay in Virginia Beach, lean on my parents—my mother chose to die instead of fight.

Plan after plan was just gone.

Then she walked out.

And every want, hope, dream, and desire were in front of me.

I look to my best friend, unsure of what to say. "Do you really want to know?"

"Am I going to want to punch you in the face?"

"Most definitely."

He glances in the truck and sees Rose there, smiling at him. "I'll add it to your tab."

"Sounds like a plan."

Rose rolls the window down. "Daddy, can we please go get Ainsley now? I want to see the Admiral and get on a ship."

Caspian chokes on a laugh. "What crazy stories are you feeding that kid?"

"Your sister told her about the tiger cruise where we went to sea with the ship."

"Ahh." Caspian grins, and I've seen that look before. He's totally going to make me pay for this previous conversation. "You know, Rose, you should tell the Admiral that you want to see the ship *today*."

"Today?" Her hazel eyes brighten.

"He'll take you, I bet."

I groan. "We don't have time to do that today because of your cheer competition, sweetheart."

"But, Daddy! I want to see the big boat!"

"Ship," I correct, as does Caspian.

"Okay, can I please ask the Admiral to take us?"

Caspian, the asshole, cuts in. "Of course you can. Your daddy would never deprive you of something so special."

I glare at him and he smirks. "I'll be deducting one punch."

"It was worth it."

"Go before I put a tally on yours."

He leans in and kisses his goddaughter's cheek and then flips me off as he gets in his car. As painful as that was, it's going to pale in comparison to what's next.

———

"Come in," Ainsley says at the door.

"We just have a minute. We need to get on the road soon."

Rose ignores that and walks in, taking Ainsley's hand. "I need to see the Admiral."

I sigh in resignation. No way is Ainsley going to let that pass.

"You do?"

"I have to ask him to take me to see the boat—ship. Right away."

Ainsley looks to me and then back to Rose. "Why right away?"

"Uncle Caspian said I needed to do it *today*."

At least she attempts to stifle her laughter, but she fails. Her eyes meet mine, and that damn look her brother had minutes ago is now in her eyes.

Why do I keep these people around? I swear the MacKinleys are nothing but pains in my ass.

"If Caspian said it, then we should go see the Admiral. Come on, he'll be so happy to see you."

And just like that, my quick pickup is going to become a freaking all-day thing.

Rose reaches for my hand and then pulls me with her. We head to the back of the house, where the sunroom, which is also his office, sits.

It's the same as it was when we were kids. Like time stood still here. The wood paneling is the same dark-oak color with photos of his naval career tacked up and shadowboxes with challenge coins. The desk that seemed bigger than life still sits facing the door with windows behind him, and out back is the pool.

He stands when we enter, and the tough man melts when he sees Rose.

Ainsley speaks. "Daddy, Rose is requesting to see the Admiral. She has something very important to ask."

His posture shifts, shoulders back, and he stands tall. "All right, what can I do for you, sailor?"

She looks to me and I jut my chin. I'm not helping in this.

Ainsley leans down and pulls Rose to her side. "Go ahead, sweetheart. Ask him."

Rose looks to the Admiral. "Mr. Admiral, would you take me to the ship? The big one."

He clears his throat. "The big one?"

She nods. "I've never seen a ship like that. Can you take me?"

The Admiral comes around his desk and smiles at her. "I'd love to take you, Rose. Do you have time to go today? Ainsley said you had a cheerleading competition."

"What time do we have to be there, Daddy?"

"In two hours," I remind her.

She looks crestfallen, but there's nothing I can do about this, other than kill Caspian for putting this in her head.

"Oh, well, that definitely won't work. What about after? Can you stay another night, and we can go tomorrow?" Ainsley's dad suggests, and I think I might hate him more than the other two combined right now.

"I don't . . ."

"Please, Daddy. Please. I need to go on the ship. Please. Please," Rose begs, and I work incredibly hard to come up with a reason we can't, but there's really none. Other than I hate this freaking town.

"Let's see how the competition goes and then we can let the Admiral know," I concede.

Rose basically launches herself at me, wrapping her arms around my middle.

He sighs. "The things we do for our daughters."

————

"You know you're so going to owe me for this," I tell Ainsley as we're sitting at the bar.

Rose's team lost the competition by three points, and while the girls were sad, all my daughter could do was ask about visiting the ship and how happy it would make her.

Amazing that at six she's already figured out the things to say to get me to cave.

Not that I've ever had much resistance with her.

"Owe you?" Ainsley asks with a laugh. "For what?"

"How about making me stay in this fucking town another night? Or worse, having us stay at your damn house."

That is really the one I could kill her for. Her suggestion was that we all stay at her home, save money on the hotel, and let the Admiral babysit so we could go out for some fun.

My idea of fun was getting a hotel and gagging her while I fucked her brains out.

Apparently we didn't have the same ideas.

"Well, your dad is gone for the weekend, so I didn't think there was a reason to deny Rose." She grins before taking a sip. "Plus, I have reasons."

"And they are?"

Ainsley leans forward. "You can sneak into my room tonight and find out."

"That was happening regardless," I inform her. "I've imagined that scenario a few times."

"Me too."

She drains her drink and orders another. "How did last night go? Did you guys have fun after you dropped me off?"

"We did."

"Good. I wish I could've said goodbye to Caspian this morning. I hoped he was going to come by, but I understand why he won't."

Yeah, this would be a good time to tell her about the conversation I had with him.

"So, speaking of Caspian and understanding . . ." I take a deep pull from my beer, hoping for some liquid courage. "I told him . . . sort of."

Her eyes widen. "About us?"

"Sort of."

"Sort of how? Sort of like you told him we were sleeping together or that you took me to a magical pond because you're a weirdo?"

"Neither of those, but I'm sure he's assuming we've slept together now." I shrug. Honestly, who can tell with this group?

Ainsley sinks back in her seat. "You told him? *Why?* Why would you say anything? Now we have to tell him why it didn't work out. He's going to punch you, you know this?"

"I do. He informed me of the same, but it was more that if I hurt you, not if this didn't work out. Which, again, I didn't tell him we were together, just that I had feelings for you. To which he told me you're in love with me." I wink.

"He did *what*?" Her increase in volume causes a bunch of heads to turn. Ainsley doesn't care, though. She soldiers on, slamming her hand on the bar. "I am not in love with you. I think you're hot. I like what we're doing. I'm going to kill him. I'm going to dismember him and leave him in pieces in the woods. I bet the bear would like that, little snack-sized bites. Ugh. I hate him."

I wait her out because even if I did try to speak right now, she'd cut me off.

"Do you know what my life was like with him and my dad? It was hell. I couldn't date. Who the hell wanted to be with the Admiral's daughter? No one. Then, to top it off, Caspian scared the shit out of any guy who came near me."

I lift the beer bottle up toward the bartender. I have a feeling I'm going to be here a while as she rants.

"I can imagine."

"No, you can't, you stupid idiot, because you were just as bad as him!"

"You liked losers," I inform her. "Really, if they were good enough for you, they would've fought for you."

"Like you should talk? You were with Ava Holtz, who is a raging bitch and was dating you because she wanted a ride everywhere."

I chuckle. "I got to ride too."

Her nose crinkles. "Gross."

"I was seventeen. Cut me some slack."

"No. You are trying to shame me for my dating, when I didn't even date!"

"I'm just informing you that if Caspian should ask, I told him that I had feelings for you, and he told me you love me, which I'm pretty lovable, so . . ."

She glares. "I'd love to hurt you right now."

"I'd rather you kiss me."

"I bet you would." Ainsley turns in her chair, letting out a heavy sigh. "Did you tell him we were sleeping together?"

"No."

"I guess there's that miracle. So what exactly did you tell him?"

I launch into the conversation, recalling what I can remember, and she seems mollified. At least for now.

I reach over, resting my hand on her thigh. "Forgive me?"

Ainsley tilts her head to lie on my shoulder. "I guess."

Sometimes her inability to hold grudges works in my favor. She's always found a way to just let things go, unlike me. I hold on to shit forever. I pretty much have learned that people are who they show you they are.

If you allow people to walk all over you, they will.

I've found it's better to find the right friends than have many who aren't worth their salt.

A slow song comes on, and I push out my chair and stand. "Dance with me?"

"You want to dance?"

"I just asked you, so yes."

Ainsley smiles and places her hand in mine as I lead her to the dance floor.

Like two pieces of a puzzle, we fit together and then sway to the music. Ainsley's fingers brush the back of my neck, sending emotions through me I wish didn't exist. She makes me want more, want love, want a life that we can't have.

"I think this is the first time we've ever danced," she says wistfully.

"No, I'm sure we've danced before."

"Nope. I would've remembered. At prom you were with Valorie and there wasn't a chance in hell you were going to ask me."

"You were a freshman."

She rolls her eyes. "Yes, yes, the peon of the high school days."

"You didn't ask me either," I toss back.

"Oh, please, like I would've ever dared to. You were Mr. Popular and a football god. I was only cool enough to talk to when people weren't around."

I don't think that was the case at all. "I talked to you."

"No, not really."

Now she's being ridiculous. "Ainsley, we sat together in lunch. I made everyone make room for you."

While Caspian and I were popular, Ainsley really wasn't. She was pretty, smart, and likable, but she was super shy.

I'll never forget the first day of school her freshman year. I walked into the lunchroom, and she was sitting alone, with her book, at the edge of a table. I almost lost my shit. The need to protect her was so fierce I walked over, plucked the book out of her hand, grabbed her lunch, and just walked to my table. There wasn't room, so I kicked one of the football players out and let everyone know that she'd be sitting with us.

"Oh, I remember that. I hated you for doing it."

"Why?"

"Because I like to read. Lunch was my time where I could get lost in a story and not have to talk to people, but then you made me sit there where everyone was nonstop talking. Dear God, I would have a migraine every day. Not to mention, I couldn't follow half of what you guys were going on about. Plays and scoring and penalties. Who cared?"

I laugh and pull her to my chest. "We did, but in the end, it really didn't matter."

"I wish we could go back." She rests her chin on my shoulder.

"I would've done things different."

Ainsley leans back to look at me. "Like what?"

"I would've danced with you."

She smiles. "I would've liked that."

"I'm sorry I didn't."

"You're dancing with me now, and if I'm honest, this is much better."

"Why is that?"

She leans in, her lips nearing mine. "Because I never would've had the courage to do this before."

Then she kisses me, and I swear the entire world disappears except for the beautiful woman in my arms.

twenty-five
Ainsley

"Shh," I tell Lachlan as I pull him into my room.

Tonight was everything to me. We danced, kissed, laughed, and now he's in a place I dreamed of so many nights.

The Admiral's room is four doors down, but I swear he hears everything. So we will need to be exceptionally quiet.

When we make it without issue, I close the door ever so softly, and then he grabs me from behind, turning me into his arms.

I stifle a squeak before his lips are on mine.

I don't think there's anything better in this world than kissing Lachlan. His hands are in my hair, tilting my head to get better access as he walks me to the bed.

My shirt is pulled up and then tossed to the side.

I do the same to him.

"I'm going to take you hard, Ainsley. Do you want that?"

I nod. Do I ever.

He turns me around, hands moving to my breasts before sliding down my stomach. Then he slips into my pants, just barely touching my clit. His lips are at my ear, words barely a breath. "Good. But you need to stay very quiet. Can you do that for me?"

"Yes."

"If you make too much noise, someone could come in here, and I don't think you want that, do you, baby?"

"No."

Lachlan pulls my pants down, and then I feel his warm chest against my back. "Spread your legs for me, Ainsley. Put your hands on the wall."

I do as he says, and he kisses down my spine, and then bites the globes of my ass. I squeak and he shoves a finger into me so hard I gasp. "Stay quiet."

Right. Quiet.

"You're so wet already. How long have you thought about me between your legs?"

My head falls back. "Always."

"I think about being here, licking your sweet cunt, tasting you as you fall apart against my tongue. I love the taste of you. So sweet. So perfect."

"Lachlan," I whisper.

"Let's see if you're sweeter after all those strawberries."

I close my eyes, trying not to make a fool of myself. Lachlan is the only man who has ever done this to me. I was always so embarrassed, and the guy before him wasn't really into it. Which was fine. However, now that I know what I was missing, I will never be the same.

Lachlan knows exactly what to do and is very, very into it.

His tongue swipes over my clit, and I arch my back. The pleasure running through every vein in my body.

"Even sweeter," he says, and then his tongue is there again. "You're like honey and berries. I might stay here all night."

Lachlan licks, alternating the pressure, driving me insane. He moves in circles, then flicks, and then sucks as the climb to my orgasm moves faster than ever before. He alternates again, leaving my head swimming. My legs start to shake and there's a sheen of sweat forming on my face. My muscles contract as I try to stay upright.

"So close. So close. Oh God," I pant, gasping for air.

He does it again, increasing the pressure on my clit and

inserting a finger deep into my core. I can't stay upright. My legs give out as the orgasm crashes through me. Wave after wave of pleasure drags me out to sea.

Lachlan pulls me into his arms, keeping me from shattering, and then he lays me on my bed.

When I catch my breath, Lachlan is on his knees, pulling his pants down. I watch as his cock springs free, and he grins at me.

His body is so freaking perfect. I know he wants to take me hard, but I want to make him feel good too.

"I want to touch you," I tell him.

Lachlan grins and lies beside me, putting both hands behind his head. "I'm yours to do what you want with."

"Yes," I say with a smirk. "You are."

My mouth traces a line down his shoulder, then his arms. I kiss my way back up and over his chest, where there's a scar from when he was twelve. Lachlan fell off his bike and hit a branch. It was so traumatic because his mother was beside herself, and I was so afraid.

There was so much blood. "I was so afraid you were going to die."

"I was pretty scared too," he confesses.

"The ambulance felt like it took forever."

He brushes my hair back off my face. "Do you know that the only reason I didn't cry was because you were there?"

My eyes widen. "What?"

"I didn't want to look like a pansy in front of you."

I let out a snort of a laugh. "I never would've thought that. I thought you were perfect."

Lachlan's hand moves to the back of my neck, and he pulls me close. "I couldn't risk it."

I look up at him. "You take risks all the time, Lach. You walk into burning buildings, you fight for the people you love. You need to be careful. I don't want to feel that fear again."

"I'm always careful, baby."

I kiss his lips, pouring all my fear and love into him. He has no idea how many nights I've worried, and now it's different.

Now I know what it feels like to be loved by him, even if it's just like this.

I need him so much.

I shove him back down, and he resumes his relaxed position. Let's see how long he can stay like that.

My lips return to the place I last kissed, moving down his body. I don't wait or tease him. I want to make him lose his fucking mind. My tongue rings around the head of his cock before I take him deep.

"Remember we need to be quiet," I remind him.

"Ainsley." Lachlan grunts, his hands moving to my head. "Suck my dick."

I bob my head as I watch his thigh muscles tighten.

"That's it, baby. Yes, so fucking good. Take me deep."

I do as he says, moving at a pace I know will drive him wild. I want him to be out of his mind. I want to do for him what he did for me.

I play with his balls as my other hand pumps in time with my mouth. Lachlan's fingers tangle in my hair while his other hand grips the comforter.

Lachlan is close. His breathing is coming harder. "Ainsley, fuck. Stop, sweetheart, or I'm going to come in your beautiful mouth instead of that cunt."

I lift up, and Lachlan has me on my back before I can blink.

In his eyes, there's something different as he stares at me. As though he's telling me something, wishing to say words he can't, and in my heart, I know what it is, because I'm pretty sure it's the same thing I feel.

I rub my finger down his strong jawline. "Take me, Lachlan."

He moves his hips, and I feel the tip of him at my entrance. I moan as he slides in deeper, and it's almost too much. I'm falling apart and coming together at the same time. My heart is pounding so loud in my ears as he pushes all the way in. Tears fill my vision as I wrap my legs around his hips, hands clutching at his back. Lachlan pushes deeper again and again. Setting a relentless pace.

"You feel so good, Ainsley. So fucking good," he murmurs.

I look up through blurry vision and fight back the tears. "Give me all of you."

"You have it. Fuck, you have it," he whispers before kissing me again.

Then, as we're tangled together, he pushes harder, faster, and deeper than before. I fall apart again, Lachlan following seconds later, and I know that even though that was frantic, we just made love, and I don't know how I'm going to walk away from him.

———

"Come on," I tell Lachlan as I pull him in through the secret passageway that his mother had installed.

"What the hell?" he asks, and I grin.

"You truly didn't know about this?"

He laughs once. "She never told me."

We crouch down and have to crawl through a small cutout in the fence. When we emerge on the other side, we're in the backside of the garden.

"This is how I would magically appear in your backyard."

He laughs once, brushing the leaves off his pants. "And here I thought you just jumped the fence or had a key."

I grin and lace my hand in his. "Let's go to the swing."

We quietly walk down the lit stone pathway over to the little nook I would spend hours in.

Lachlan looks around, and I wonder whether he sees what I do. That in the last four years, not a single part of this place has changed. The flowers are here, alive and thriving. The walkway isn't covered with dirt or weeds. His father has taken care of his mother's garden exactly as she would've.

"Are you okay?" I ask.

He pulls me close to him. "A lot of memories here."

"Hopefully more good than bad."

I lean my head against his chest, looking up at him through my lashes. "It might be a tie if I'm being honest."

"Okay, name a good one."

"This is where I first kissed you."

I grin. "Yes, but that sort of leads into a bad, since things ended pretty terrible."

Lachlan lifts my chin and then kisses me tenderly. I roll so I'm on top of him, letting the kiss become more. His tongue slides against mine, and even though we just had sex, I want him again.

However, the two of us being here isn't about this. I wanted him to feel close to the people who love him, so I pull back.

"That should've been our first kiss," Lachlan says, tucking my hair behind my ear.

"We can pretend."

"I'd like that."

"See, good memory made," I say, feeling triumphant.

Then I nestle back against his chest, pulling his arm to drape around me. "What about you?"

"This place is filled with good memories for me," I tell him. "I would come over here all the time, through my little secret door, and read for hours. Your mom would leave cookies and milk sometimes on that stone there." I point to the ledge that was almost like a table. "I wouldn't even hear her come out."

I was so lost in a story that the world ceased to exist.

"She wouldn't let me come out if she knew you were back there."

"Really?"

He chuckles. "She said every girl needed a place to hide away."

"It's why she created it."

"Yes, and why she spent so much of her time out here. I think she tried to hide but could never fully escape her pain and sadness."

I stay quiet, not sure what to say to that. "Tell me about Rose's mom."

He stiffens beneath me. "Why?"

"I'm just curious. I've never met her. You came home with Rose and that was sort of it. How did you guys . . . get together?"

Lachlan stays quiet for a moment and then sighs. "It wasn't anything great. We met at a bar on campus. We'd just played in the national championship. We lost. I was in this weird place because I was still this top draft prospect and then also this top loser. Claire didn't know a damn thing about sports, but she knew who I was because my face was on posters. We talked, drank a lot, hooked up, and then a month later she found out she was pregnant."

"And she didn't want to be a mom?"

His arm tightens a little. "I mean, I don't think either of us wanted to be parents at that point, but she and I talked, and I was able to take Rose."

"And you just gave up football?"

"I feel like I gained everything and didn't lose a damn thing."

I turn again, resting my hand on his chest, staring into those brown eyes I love so much. "Your life could've been a million times different."

"Sure, but then we wouldn't be here now."

I grin. "This is true. I definitely wouldn't be writing an article on athletes."

He chuckles. "Yes, this is true."

"Lach, writing this article, it's something I want to get right. Not just for me, but for Rose and you. I won't let you down."

"It's why I'm glad it's you who came, for several reasons. The sex especially."

I laugh and then wrap myself tighter around him. "I could stay here with you forever."

Before he can say anything else, the back lights flip on, and his father's voice booms in the quiet.

"Who's out here?"

twenty-six
Lachlan

My entire body goes tight at the sound of my father's voice. Ainsley pushes up. "Hi, Mr. West. It's me, Ainsley."

"Ainsley? Oh, hi, dear."

"Sorry, I used the secret passage. I didn't know you were home," she admits.

My dad takes a few steps closer, the light brightening from behind him. "I got home about an hour ago. I didn't know you were visiting."

Another step. One more and I won't be able to stay hidden.

"Yeah, umm, I'll head back."

"No need, you know you're always welcome. Isabelle loved when you'd sneak over."

The way he says my mother's name makes me want to rage. How dare he talk about her as though he cared or knew what she loved. He would've had to be here, know her, give a shit about what she wanted to know that.

I move, coming out of the darkness.

His eyes widen. "Lachlan? Is that . . . ?"

"We'll be leaving now," I say, taking Ainsley's hand.

"Wait, please . . . you don't have to leave. Your mother would want you to visit."

Again with him talking about Mom like he has a clue about her wants. "I don't think so."

He looks around. "Is Rose here?"

Ainsley squeezes my hand and I meet her gaze. Her brown eyes are pleading. I turn to my dad. "She's next door."

"I would love to see her. I have some things that I'd like to give you. Things that were your mother's. You could give them to her." My father's voice cracks at the end, and I feel a break in my heart.

With the lighting, I can see the garden in all its glory. This is exactly like I remember. Only there's something over to the left that wasn't there.

My father steps closer again. "Your mother's ashes are back there. I hired the same landscape people she used and asked them to make an extension for her. Her own place so she can always be in her garden."

I look to Ainsley, who smiles softly. "It's really beautiful."

"I sent you an email about it. I did a ceremony for her, hoped you'd come, but I don't know if you got it."

He had a ceremony?

Instead of opening the emails, I just delete them because there is nothing my father can say that will change how I feel. It was better to not open them instead of getting angrier than I was.

"I didn't."

"I delayed it a few times, but I wanted her to rest where I thought she'd be happiest."

I nod once. "Right."

"Lachlan, I . . ."

No, we're not doing this now. "I'd like to see it and then we're going back. Ainsley can bring Rose over tomorrow."

Ainsley's head snaps up. "Lachlan . . ."

I sigh heavily. "We'll talk and come up with something, but yes, either way, you'll see Rose."

"Thank you. I'll leave you both alone now," my father says as he takes a step back. "I hope you like her special area back there."

When he's gone, Ainsley rests her other hand on my back. "I didn't know he was here."

"I know."

"I'm sorry."

I shake my head. "It's not your fault. You knew about the memorial for her?"

"Yes, I was here the day it was dedicated."

"And no one told me."

Ainsley releases a heavy breath. "Well, we weren't talking, so I didn't think reaching out was a good idea. Caspian said he tried to bring it up to you, but you shut him down, and he wasn't going to push."

I run my hand through my hair and pace. "I should've been here."

"You're here now." Her voice is soft and there's no judgment there. "Go see it. It's really beautiful."

I turn to her. "Come with me."

I don't think I can be alone right now.

Ainsley takes my hand, and we make our way into a small clearing. I can't remember what was here before, but now it's perfect. There's a small water fountain in the center of a round area. The stone benches curve around it, and there are bushes and flowers everywhere.

"She would've loved this," I say absently.

"I think so too."

"When did he do this?"

"About six months after she died. I think he started the planning for it the day after. He told the Admiral he wanted something for her to live forever in. He didn't want to sprinkle her ashes. He wanted her close. When he had the fountain made, he had her ashes put in the concrete up here." She points to the top layer.

I lift my hand, allowing the water to rush over my knuckles. With my eyes closed, I try to remember her face, how she smiled, the way her tears would fall as she apologized for not being stronger.

I thought she was the strongest woman on the planet, even at her weakest.

She tried. I know she tried. I was there and watched her get up each time she fell, desperate to be the mother she thought I needed.

Little did she know she already was.

Ainsley's hand slides up my back and rests on my shoulder. "I would come here to talk to her," she confesses. "It feels like she's here. Your dad slept on that bench for a solid two weeks after this was built."

I turn to her, my heart pounding. "It doesn't change the past."

"No, it doesn't, but it doesn't mean that we can't find a way forward. Otherwise we're just stuck."

It feels as though I've been stuck for a long time, unable to let go of the past and unsure of how to handle the future.

All I know is that I want to do better. I want to give Rose stability, which is something I never had. At the same time, I don't know that I'm doing any better than my parents did.

She has no one, really, but me.

She wanted me to marry Ainsley after the first day because she doesn't have a mother.

I just can't handle watching another person walk out of my fucking life because things are hard.

Life is hard.

Staying is harder.

Leaving should be hardest.

"I've been trying to do that for years."

Her hand rests on my face, brushing the stubble on my chin. "Maybe you just need someone to give you their hand."

"I'd pull you down, Ainsley."

"I've got pretty good footing."

I wish that was true. The fact remains that Ainsley leaves and I will stay. We'd be building a house on unstable ground, hoping the foundation doesn't crack.

I remove her hand from my face, entwining our fingers.

"Come on, let's get to bed before your father wakes up and I have to answer those questions."

Sadness flashes in her eyes, but she recovers quickly. "All right. Let's get some sleep."

––––––

"And the ship was so big and I got to climb into a bed and see everything!" Rose exclaims as she jumps out of the truck.

Today was a day she'll never forget.

The Admiral was true to his word and got her a tour of the ship. She was in heaven. Her smile never wavered, and as much as this detour was not exactly what I wanted, Rose is happy.

"I'm glad you had fun," I tell her.

"I want to be in the navy like the Admiral and Grandpa were."

I crouch down in front of her. "You can do whatever you want when you grow up."

"I'm going to tell Becky all about the big ship!" she yells and then dashes into the house.

Ainsley comes up behind me. "She had a great time."

"Your dad came through."

"When it comes to this stuff, he's pretty good, and it was great you let Rose see your dad," she notes.

When we got back to her father's house, my dad was outside. There was really no way around it. I brought her over to the house, and he had a small box with some of my mother's things. Then I made an excuse about leaving, and we were on our way.

I look at the door my daughter went through just a moment ago, questioning so many of my choices. "She has so little family. I question if I'm doing the right thing some days."

"Rose has no shortage of people who love her. Don't for one second think you haven't given her all she needs. All I'm saying is that your dad does love her too. He loves you as well. He loved your mother and I think the guilt is eating him alive. You both have so much of the same feelings, and if you'd just talk to him, I think you'd see that."

I'm not saying she's wrong, but right now, I'm not sure I'm ready. "I'll consider it."

"Good. Now I have to get to work. I have another week here, and then I need to give my final draft to my boss."

While I knew that our time was limited, when she says it, my stomach drops.

One week.

Seven days and then she'll go back to New York and I'll be here.

Six nights where I can have her to myself before I have to let her go.

twenty-seven
Ainsley

It's just past ten and Lachlan and I are curled up on the couch together. So many things about this simple moment cause an ache in my heart.

The first one being that we could have this. Nights like this, days like we've had already, could be our normal. The second being I would do it for him.

I would walk away from the career I've worked for and figure it out. I just don't know how to tell him that without him fighting me on it.

Which is exactly what he'll do.

"Are you ready for bed?" he asks.

I nod. "Bed sounds good."

We both get to our feet and head back into his room. After our nightly routines are done, we climb into bed, and he's staring at me.

"What?"

"You're beautiful."

I smile. "Well, thank you. You're not so bad yourself, Sparky."

He rolls his eyes. "If you ever call me that around anyone, I'll have to kill you."

"I don't think you have it in you."

"Try me."

I grin. "You do know I have all your friends' phone numbers. I can very easily create my own group chat without you in it."

"Don't even think about it," Lachlan warns, and I laugh. "And why do you have their numbers?"

"Jealous?" I tease.

"Maybe."

I like him jealous. "I interviewed them, remember?"

He rolls to his side, and we lie here looking at each other. "Yes, hard work you do."

I scoff. "It is."

"You talk to people."

"I investigate, thank you very much. Please, I could so easily be a fireman, but what I do takes finesse and a writing skill that you, my friend, do not possess."

"Are you saying firemen are stupid?"

I gasp. "No! I would never. In all honesty, I could never do it. To run into a building that's literally on fire, no thank you. I run away from that."

Lachlan pushes my hair off my face, his knuckles brushing my skin. "I'd like to take a stab at your job."

"Oh?"

"Yes, you'll be my first try."

This should be good. "Proceed, please."

Lachlan clears his throat. "Tell me about New York."

Instantly my heart sinks. Of all the things I don't want to talk about, it's New York. I don't want to think of the life I have there and the ticking clock in the background of my life that's telling me time is moving way too fast and this will be over too soon.

So I decide to play it off and respond the way he did when I tried to get him to cooperate.

"Large."

His brows knit. "What?"

"It's large."

"Isn't it actually relatively small in miles?"

"Sure."

"Okay, well, tell me about your life there."

"Fun."

He clicks his tongue. "I see what you're doing."

I grin. "Being difficult?"

He rolls to me, grabbing me and then moving us so I'm on top of him. "Seriously, I want to know what you do, where you go. Tell me about your friends or anything."

I place my hands on his chest and rest my chin atop them. "I love New York. I really do. It was overwhelming at first, but then you start to understand it, love it, and it gets inside of you. I have an amazing best friend, Caroline. We went to NYU together and then ended up getting a job at *Metro NY*."

"So you guys hang out a lot?"

I smile. "We do. We love the theater, so we try once a month to catch a show on or off Broadway. I've gotten to see some pretty amazing actors when they're testing a show."

"Okay, what do you love the most?"

You.

I don't say that. I at least have enough common sense not to blurt that out.

I sigh, trying to sum up in a few words what it is that calls to me. "It's funny because the Admiral asks me that all the time. He hates it, which makes sense, right? There's literal chaos everywhere. Lord knows that man runs a tight ship."

"That he does. Okay, so far you haven't answered the question."

"You're doing very good keeping this interview on track," I inform him.

"Yes, and you're trying to derail it again."

"It's only fair since you were literally the worst."

Lachlan grabs my arms and slides me close so we're nose to nose. "I was trying to avoid you so I didn't end up doing exactly this."

I kiss his nose. "I like this."

"I like this too. Now tell me, what is the thing you love most?"

He moves me back down to the spot I was before. I exhale and let go with the first thing that pops in my mind. "I love the food, the way the city is alive all the time. I love that any given day you can run into someone famous who you love. I love that there's always something to do or eat or see. I love that I've lived there for all these years, and I still feel like there's so much more to see. It's sort of an all-encompassing thing. What can I say, I fell in love with the city."

"Listening to you talk about it sounds like it's everything you want."

It's not. It doesn't have him.

"It has most of it. Some things are missing."

His eyes are on mine, and I can see the questions swirling. I want him to ask me what it is I'm longing for.

We can find a way, I know we can. Sure, it'll be a lot and probably more difficult than either of us are prepared for, but it can still happen for us.

"Tell me about Caroline. What does she write?"

Definitely not the topic I was hoping for, but maybe he just doesn't want to deal with my impending trip back home either.

"Caroline is the best. She's a brilliant writer who writes much better articles than I ever will, and actually does a lot of sports pieces."

"I doubt that. You're a great writer."

"How would you know?" I ask.

"I've read your stuff."

My eyes widen. "You have not!"

"You don't believe me?"

I shake my head. "No, I can't imagine you sit around and read about hats and color choices based on the season."

"I didn't say I took the advice, but I read your stories."

I'm not even sure what to say to that. "Why would you read them?"

Lachlan's lips form a soft smile. "Because I wanted to feel close to you in some way. So when your brother talked about you working for the paper up there, I started getting them."

My jaw drops. "You what?"

"You know, for an investigative journalist, you kind of suck. Shouldn't you know, Miss I-Know-Everything-about-You, that I subscribe to your paper?"

"I don't exactly go into that department, but can we just stay on this for a moment? You subscribe—for how long?"

"Since you started working there."

I roll off him, sitting with my legs crossed on the bed. "Lachlan!"

He moves over to the side of his table and pulls out the lower drawer, then hands me a small stack of newspaper clippings. "See for yourself."

With a shaking hand, I reach out and take them, already tearing up. He kept my articles in a drawer beside his bed.

The first tear falls as I flip through, looking at my first printed piece. It was terrible. Truly, the writing is just awful, but he has it and he cared.

"Why did you keep these?"

"Because you wrote them."

My heart is pounding, and when I open my mouth to tell him how much it means to me, "I love you" comes out instead.

He rolls me on my back and hovers over me, taking my face in his hands. "What did you say?"

"I said I love you. I've loved you my whole life."

"Sweetheart, you can't imagine how much I love you."

And if I thought I was stunned before, it's nothing compared to this moment. He said he loves me. I'm pretty sure those magical falls did something to us.

"You love me?" I ask, almost afraid that he's going to take it back.

"How could I not? You're everything to me, Ainsley. You're beautiful, smart, funny, a little maddening, but it only makes me love you more. You have invaded every part of my life, but that's because you live in my heart and soul. No one has ever made me feel like this."

I pull his head to me, kissing him softly. But then his words really penetrate and my heart breaks. I know I have only a few days to convince him that we could at least try, because I don't want to lose him.

———

I woke up with swollen eyes and a heaviness in my chest after seeing the text from Lachlan saying that he and Rose had gone for the day.

LACHLAN

Good morning, sweetheart. You were sleeping and I didn't want to wake you. Rose is at Becky's for the day while I'm working. I'll be home around six and Rose would like us to do dinner out tonight.

Dinners. I love dinners with them. They're filled with laughter and talking about what we did for the day. I only have a few left.

All of this sucks.

I need to get a grip, because no matter what happens, I'm going to find a way to make all of this work. I'm going to talk to my boss. Maybe I can work remotely, or I'll find another job. Either way, I'm not giving up so easily.

As I'm about to reply to Lachlan, an email comes through from Mr. Krispen.

Ainsley,

Why the hell are you still in Ember Falls? I read the first draft, you have plenty of notes and information, there's no need for you to remain there. We need you back in the office by Monday.

The breath in my lungs expels and I gasp. No. I had days. Days. Not a day. I don't want to go back to New York now. I wanted to spend the next week with him. I quickly send off a reply.

Mr. Krispen,

While I understand that you believe I have everything I need, I've decided to take the story in a different direction. I think it's best I stay in Ember Falls until the previously agreed upon time to ensure the information I have is adequate. Mr. West and the other interviewees live in a more remote area of the valley, and cell service is often unreliable, as well as they are extremely busy. It's best, since publication is coming up, that I remain here.

Best,

Ainsley

Of course the reply from him is immediate and with one word.

No.

I mean, why would anything go my way? I climb out of bed and call Caroline.

"Hey, I hear you're coming back soon," she says as she picks up.

"No."

"No? But Mr. K said . . ." She's quiet for a second. "Ohh, you're like . . . quitting?"

I sigh heavily. "No, I can't afford to quit. I have a lease and a car payment, and it's not like he asked me to marry him and move in, so even if I did quit, I'd be homeless and broke. So, yeah, that's not the plan."

"Then what is the plan?"

"I don't have one yet."

She laughs softly. "Oh, Ainsley, you went and fell head over heels for the man, didn't you?"

I flop back on the bed and groan. "I don't remember a time when I wasn't in love with him."

"Does he feel the same?"

"He told me he loves me."

"And?"

The stupid tears are starting to pool. "And he told me he wouldn't let me give up my dreams."

"Dreams change," she says, always pragmatic. "Maybe there's a new dream for you both. You know, life is a ride."

I laugh once at that. "A fucking roller coaster or a free fall is more like it. I was doing okay before having to come interview him, you know? Like, I'd learned to live without him as a part of my life, and while it wasn't great, it wasn't terrible. There was an ignorance to it all."

She snorts. "Ignorance is bliss, but it's still ignorance."

"Well, now I don't even have that."

No, instead I have the knowledge of what it's like to love him and to be loved by him.

It all sucks.

"So, tomorrow?"

"I guess . . . I guess I have tonight to figure out if I'm getting in a car and heading to New York, or if I'm going to upend my life and live off my paltry savings account."

"I look forward to either holding you as you cry and we drink red wine floats *or* helping you pack."

Yeah, I just don't know which one it's going to be.

twenty-eight
Lachlan

"I think we should get her that one, Daddy." Rose points to the bouquet that Janelle, the town florist, is holding up.

"You think Ainsley will like it?"

She nods. "Or that one! She likes pink." Then she walks to the other side of the store. "Oh, I like this one too!"

So far there hasn't been a bouquet that Rose hasn't liked for Ainsley. "We're going to need to narrow it down, Rosebud."

Janelle puts the last bouquet down and comes to stand beside me as Rose continues her quest. "I could help her find one if you could give me a little about what you're looking for."

"Flowers."

She smiles. "You're in the right spot for that, but I think flowers are really about an occasion or the person who is receiving them. There's an art to selection, and I happen to be a professional in this area."

I clear my throat. "Right, well, I need flowers for a girl."

"For Ainsley?"

"Yes, she's a friend, who is not a girlfriend or anything. She's writing an article about me. That's what brought her here, at least. She's not just a journalist, though, because we grew up

together, and, you know, we've . . . got a complicated relationship."

Janelle nods slowly. "I see, so she's not a girlfriend, but she's
not *not* a girlfriend?"

"Exactly."

"Well, how much of the not not is she?"

"Well, she's not a not because I really care about her."

"Hmm, that does make it difficult," Janelle says as she looks
around.

"Yeah, it's very difficult."

Mostly because I'm in love with her, and in a few days she's
going to leave, and I'm going to have to let her.

No matter what she says, I've seen what happens to
women who give up their dreams. I've watched it eat
someone away until they had nothing left and just gave up.
It's why when Claire said she didn't want to keep Rose, I was
willing to take the pain of giving up mine and living a new
dream.

One where I can show Rose what it looks like to always have
someone there to put you first.

"Might I suggest that you look around and just select a flower.
One that makes you think of her the second you see it. It can be
color that draws you or just the way you feel. We'll start with that
and build off it."

"I'm not really . . ."

"Just humor me, Lachlan." Janelle nudges me to do as she
asks. "Rose, would you be able to help me with an order? I'm all
alone today, and it would just be the best day if you could."

Rose appears within seconds. "I can help!"

"Great." She turns to me. "Go for your walk and we'll be in
the back."

Unable to tell her no, I start to walk around. Nothing jumps
out at me. Nothing feels special or close to Ainsley. Some are too
delicate, which is definitely not like her. She's strong, beautiful,
and soft in certain ways, but still able to stand her ground and
hold up against the storms.

This is stupid. It's a damn flower. What the hell am I supposed to see in it that reminds me of . . .

Just as I was about to curse Janelle for making me walk around, I see one.

It's different from anything I've seen in the store. It's beautiful, but more than that, it's tightly wound, yet the outside layers look as though they're open and welcoming.

The petals are delicate, but not as though they can't handle whatever comes their way. It's truly stunning.

"Ahh, the Juliet rose," Janelle says softly behind me. "I just got those in today. They're very rare, but I have a bride who read about them and asked me to get some to see it in person. They took ten years to get to be this way."

"It doesn't look like a rose," I say.

"I think that roses are a lot like people. They don't all look the same, smell the same, or grow the same. They're unique and beautiful. They start as a bud that doesn't look like it can open because it's so tight, but then, as time goes, it gains its strength and opens layer by layer, until it shows you every glorious part of itself. It has thorns to protect itself when someone tries to steal it."

I chuckle once. "I feel like you're trying to teach me more than just roses."

"Remember I said I know this type of art?" she asks, but she doesn't seem to want an answer. "I've seen this canvas before. A man in love, knowing he's going to lose, but doesn't know where to go from here."

Sounds about right. "And what would you advise that man?"

She turns, grabs a flower from another rack, and hands it to me. "Buy her the Juliet rose when you're willing to give her your heart. Until then, give her the carnation."

———

"Ainsley?" I call her name as I open the door.

"She's going to love the flowers," Rose whispers as she holds them.

"I'm back here!" Ainsley replies from the rear of the house. We make our way to her, and she comes out of her room, pulling the door shut. "Hey."

Rose, who has zero patience, extends her hands with the bouquet of flowers. "We got you these!"

Ainsley drops down, squatting in front of her. "Oh, wow. Rose! These are so pretty."

They're your basic bouquet with a stupid carnation in the middle because Janelle had to make her point. The rest of the flowers Rose picked out, which means it's like a box of Skittles.

"I made it with Ms. Janelle. She let me go in the back and put them all together!" Rose explains.

"Well, you just did the best job I've ever seen. These flowers are the most stunning. Can I have a hug?" Ainsley asks.

Rose launches herself into her arms. "I love you, Ainsley! I wish you could stay forever."

"Aww, I love you too, Rose." Ainsley smiles up at me as she hugs Rose tighter.

Seeing the two of them like this makes me hate this all the more. There's this tightness in my chest that won't go away.

I place my hand on Rose's shoulder. "Why don't you go change for dinner?"

Rose releases Ainsley and rushes off.

I help Ainsley back up, and she looks down at the flowers. "They really are beautiful."

"Not as beautiful as you are."

Her cheeks redden, and she shakes her head before leaning in to kiss me quickly. "Thank you."

"You're welcome."

She sighs heavily. "Look, I . . . I don't know how to say this, so I'm going to just blurt it out before I get too nervous and ramble. Which I tend to do. I don't really know why I do it because when I write it doesn't really go in circles, at least not when I'm in the zone, you know? It drives everyone crazy, so I try really hard not to ramble."

"Ainsley, you're doing it now," I say, cutting her off.

"Oh. Right." Her nervous laugh makes me brace myself for something I'm not going to like. "When we get back from dinner, I'm going to need to finish up."

"Finish what?"

Her story? I thought she had another week or two to do that.

"Packing. I got an email from my boss, and he's being incredibly rigid about it. I have to go back to New York for a meeting tomorrow."

Relief hits me hard for a minute. I thought she was leaving for good. "So when will you be back?"

She blinks and then shifts her weight. "That kind of depends on a few things."

"Work stuff?"

"Or you stuff."

"Me stuff?" I ask.

"Yes, because he wants me back at work. He doesn't think I need to be here anymore."

"I see." The relief I felt dissipates as though someone just dumped water on smoldering embers. "So you're leaving tonight?"

"Tomorrow morning, I was planning. I wanted to spend time with you and Rose and . . . talk."

That ache now is a knifing sensation.

"Talk?"

It seems all I'm capable of doing is asking more questions.

"Yes, talk. I think we both have a lot to discuss, don't you?"

Rose runs back in, wearing a dress and a smile so wide it breaks my damn heart. She's going to be devastated when Ainsley leaves. The two of them have had their nightly story time, and Ainsley gets up with her in the mornings. They've become friends, and this is exactly the kind of shit I wanted to avoid.

"Rose, what do you think about staying in instead?"

Ainsley reaches her hand out. "No, please. I want to do our fancy dinner. You got these beautiful flowers, and Rose is already in her very pretty dress. I just need to change. Do I have enough time before we have to go?"

Rose looks to me and then to Ainsley, and nods. "I think so."

Ainsley's brown eyes meet mine. "Lach?"

Even though I want to rail at the world for bringing me Ainsley only to take her again, I force a smile because I need to protect my daughter. "Yes, of course."

She kisses Rose's cheek and then heads into her room. I don't even remember walking away from her door, but I'm standing in the middle of my bedroom, the sheets still a mess from where we slept, and on her side table the lotion that she has to put on before bed. All of it there. All of it will be gone.

Fuck.

I sink onto the edge, my head in my hands. How did I let this happen? How did I let myself get so deep with this woman? I knew the ending. I saw the interception before the ball was even thrown.

However, I didn't pivot. No, I stayed on course, knowing that I would be the one to tear myself apart, because it's what I always do.

I did it with my mother.

I did it for Rose's mother.

I'll do it again for Ainsley.

———

Dinner is like being put through a twelve-hour-long play in another language. You sit there, hearing the things around you but comprehending none of it. You just . . . endure.

Ainsley is her normal, perky self. She laughs, talks to Rose, they have their little inside jokes, and I sit here watching it all while completely numb.

Our meal is at no charge, thanks to some Good Samaritan who probably saw the story about the fire. We climb into my truck and make it back to the house.

Rose falls asleep in the back seat, and Ainsley reaches out, resting her hand on my forearm. "Are you going to talk to me at all?"

"We talked."

She sighs through her nose. "If that's what you want to call it. I know I blindsided you, and I'm so sorry, Lach. I didn't know. I tried to fight my boss, to convince him I needed to stay here, but he's adamant I return to the office."

"I understand it. I'm not mad or anything. I just hate it, and I know she's going to hate it more. Rose loves you. She's going to be crushed when we tell her."

Ainsley turns her head to look out the window. "I know and I hate myself for that, but I don't want to spring it on her in the morning. I'd like to talk to her when we get back."

"If that's what you want."

It's definitely the better plan. At least then Rose can have a little time to be sad, but hopefully see it more like when Caspian comes to visit.

I pull up to the house after we finish the last part in silence. I'm fully aware that I'm being standoffish, but I know what has to happen here.

"And what about you? Are you crushed for yourself?"

"You know how I feel about you."

I fucking love her.

Ainsley pushes her long brown hair back. "I don't know how I'm going to get in that car and leave you willingly."

I don't know how I'm going to survive her doing it.

I force a smile. "We have tonight. Let's not even think about tomorrow."

Because if I do, I might fucking scream.

"Can we go to the falls?"

"What?"

"I'd like to go back, if Delaney can watch Rose, or I can ask Hazel."

At this point, all I can hope for is some magic to make all this work out. "Sure, I'll text Delaney, and if not, we can ask Hazel or any of the guys. They owe me."

"Okay."

"Okay."

twenty-nine
Ainsley

"I don't want you to leave," Rose says with an ache in her voice that has me wanting to cry.

"I don't want to go, either, but maybe we can make some plans? Like, I'll come to your competition, and maybe I can visit when Uncle Caspian comes?" I suggest, hoping her father will allow it.

She nods, that promise slightly mollifying her. "Do you think you can come to the carnival?"

I glance up at Lachlan. "There's a carnival?"

"Yes, we have a big Founder's Day carnival with rides, games, food, the whole thing in two weeks. You should come. We'd both love it."

It's the first time he's talked about any kind of a future for seeing each other after this is over. I knew we weren't going to completely cut each other off, but it's nice to hear that he wants to see me again.

"I'd love that." I smile at Rose. "I'll put it in my calendar."

She smiles and then wraps her arms around my neck. "I'm going to miss you, Ainsley."

"Oh, sweet girl, you have no idea how much I'm going to miss you. But as long as your daddy says it's okay, you can call me and tell me all about what's new, and I'll be here for the carnival."

"All right, Rose, off to bed. You're up way past your bedtime."

"But I want to stay with Ainsley."

I didn't know it was possible for a heart to shatter, but here it is. Breaking off into tiny shards, cutting the inside of my chest open.

"I promise I'll wake up early tomorrow and we can make pancakes and a surprise for your daddy," I tell her.

She bobs her head and then walks off toward her room. Lachlan calls after her. "We'll come in to say good night in a few minutes."

"That was hard," I admit.

"You did great. She isn't wailing, so that's something." He pulls me close, kissing my nose. "I think I'll be a bigger baby tonight and tomorrow."

I wrap my arms around his middle. "You will, huh?"

"Probably."

"You'll miss me that much?"

"More than I'll care to admit."

I smile at that and nip his chin. "I'll have to be extra nice tonight, then, so you'll be a sobbing mess thinking about how much you wish I was still in your bed."

Not that I won't be sobbing every night I'm away from him, but hopefully we can talk and find a way around this.

He kisses me softly and then heads to Rose's room, and I start to form a plan on how to make this work.

We walk hand in hand down to the falls. Hazel came over at my request, and there was sadness in her eyes when I explained I had to leave tomorrow.

I'm going to miss this place. I'm going to miss the people—and most of all Lachlan.

When we reach the water, he turns to me, his lips finding

mine almost immediately. There's a hunger, passion, and urgency that steals my breath. After one of the most frantic kisses I've ever had, he pulls me close, resting his forehead against mine. "Give me tonight, Ainsley. Don't try to find a way or get in your head, just give me tonight. Please."

"I'd give you forever."

His mouth is on mine in a heartbeat. I lean back, tilting my head to allow him better entry. He kisses me deeply, pouring all his emotions into this moment. Lachlan's hand moves to my back, guiding me down to the blanket laid out at our feet.

I use all my strength to shut my thoughts off. I want tonight to be all about us and this moment, because I don't know whether I'll ever find a love like this again. So I'll give him tonight and pray that when I get in that car tomorrow, I still have a heart left to mend.

His mouth moves with mine languidly and ardently. All I want is more. I want aggression and roughness, because the tenderness is breaking me. I want to forget the fact that tomorrow I'll drive away. I need to get lost in him, in us, in this moment.

His lips leave mine as he kisses from my neck to my collarbone. "I want you more than the air I breathe." Lachlan pulls my shirt over my head, bringing his lips to my shoulder. "I'm going to memorize every inch of you so I can recall you anytime I need you."

"You don't have to remember. I'd come to you if you needed me."

Lachlan turns me to him, cups my cheeks, and waits for me to look at him. "I need you, Ainsley. I need you to give me all of you tonight and don't think about tomorrow."

My heart pounds. "You have me. You've always had me."

He pushes my pants down and I kick them off.

"God, you take my breath away," he says as he tears off his shirt.

"Let me," I say, moving toward him.

My fingers go to the button on his jeans, undoing it. Our eyes stay on each other as I move the zipper down, feeling like I'm exposing myself more than him in this moment.

I love him.

Slide.

I need him.

Slide.

I'm so afraid of losing him.

He stops my hand from going farther. "Don't focus on anything else but right now."

I nod and then push the material over his hips. "Don't let me think, Lachlan. Take it away from me."

His lips crush mine and he lays me down. I relish the way his tongue dances with mine, volleying for control. When his hands softly graze my stomach, I shiver. He pushes me to the ground, and his body weight anchors me.

He never breaks eye contact, forcing me to stay in the moment and not retreat into my head.

"You're mine," he whispers against my lips.

"Yours."

Slowly his tongue slides down my neck, and he kisses the hollow there. "I love you," he says as he moves to my chest, swirling his tongue around my nipple.

But love isn't enough, is it?

Not when you have four states and eight hours to combat just to see each other. It's too much, and despite the fact that I knew this going in, it still hurts.

"Please make love to me," I request, hoping he'll stop talking and causing my heart to break.

"Oh, I plan to. First, I need to taste this sweet cunt." His fingers brush against my clit, and my back bows off the ground.

I sigh as he spreads my legs apart and I feel the scruff of his cheek against my inner thigh. "Yours," I say as more of an afterthought.

My fingers slide into his dark hair, gripping the locks as his tongue moves against my clit. I close my eyes, letting the sensations wash over me. Each movement brings me closer, and the way he moans has my heart racing. I'm moving with him, my hips swaying, desperate for more.

"Lachlan." I pant his name as the pleasure starts to crest. I'm so close. Everything feels distant and as though I'm in a haze. All I feel, see, sense, is him. He inserts a finger and holds my hips, fucking me with his mouth. "Oh God. I can't. I can't take it!"

But he doesn't stop.

He pushes me over the cliff, holding me as I fall.

When I come back from a glorious orgasm, he moves up my body, pushing my hair back. "Tonight I'm going to love you as though we have all the time in the world."

"If only that were possible."

"It can be. Just be with me. Only me, Ainsley."

My fingers cup his scruffy cheek and I force a smile. "It's only ever been you, Lach."

As we hold each other's gaze, Lachlan enters me. All of it is overwhelming. We come together like magnets, the pull too great to resist.

When he's fully seated, I think my heart might explode. Everything feels so intense, so freaking perfect. He's inside me, loving me, and I wish this could go on forever.

"I need you," he says as he slides in and out. "I hate that you made me need you!" Lachlan slams into me harder.

It's as though a part of him has broken and he can't control himself. His fingers dig into my hips as he bucks, going so deep I can feel it everywhere. "Yes!"

"Take me. Take it."

I do. I let him have everything I am because without him, I feel like a part of me is missing.

"I love you. I love you. I hate that I love you," I confess.

My life was just freaking fine before, but now all I've ever wanted is going to end.

Pleasure and pain mix in my veins, and his finger moves to my clit. I moan and close my eyes, wanting the pain that will become my constant companion in this world.

"Open your eyes," he says through gritted teeth. "I want you to see me as you come."

His dark-brown eyes stare back at me while he continues to hit the spot that's driving me to orgasm. "I can't stop it," I gasp between thrusts. I grip Lachlan's face, pulling him to me, and kiss him deeply.

The orgasm crashes through me so fast I break away, crying out his name as I come.

Lachlan continues to thrust his hips, a sleek sheen of sweat across his face. He comes hard before collapsing onto me. My fingers move up and down his spine as I fight back tears.

We lie here, spent both emotionally and physically.

After a minute, he rolls to his side, taking me with him so I'm tucked against him.

We don't say anything for a long while, just wrapped in each other's arms, staring up at the vast sky.

The stars seem to multiply, and I make a million wishes on them. Each one I ask for the same.

Please don't let me lose him. Please let him not fight me on this.

"We should get back," he says after a while. "It's getting late."

I pull myself tighter around him, refusing to go. Once we get back to the house, we'll be one step closer to the end. "I don't want to leave," I confess, my heart in my throat.

"I don't want you to."

"And what if I didn't have to?" I toss the possibility out there. I have nothing left to lose. I'm already destined to give him up.

"I'm not sure how you think that's possible."

I sit up, crossing my legs. "There are a hundred different ways to make this work, Lachlan."

"Until there's not."

Okay, that hurt.

"You're giving up without even trying?"

Lachlan sighs heavily. "Fine. Let's hear your hundred ways."

"I could come here on the weekends. You could come visit me. Rose would love New York—there's so much to do and see."

"And when she has cheer? Or soccer? Or she has a birthday party that weekend and we're unable to make it work?"

I shrug. "Then we figure it out."

"Ainsley, you make it sound easy. New York is like eight hours from here."

"It can be easy! I love you. I've loved you my whole damn life, Lachlan. Now I know what it's like to have you, and I don't want to give it up. Why are you so okay with this?"

"Okay with this? You think I'm okay with this? God, you can't be more wrong. I'm not okay. I'm fucking dying inside at the idea of you leaving tomorrow. Of not holding you, kissing you, taking you to these goddamn falls, which you've ruined for me now. I'll never be able to come here without thinking of you."

"You've ruined me, so we're even!" He pinches the bridge of his nose, and I continue. "You love me and yet you'll let me go?"

Lachlan's sigh is weighted with a heaviness I can feel around me. "I've seen what happens when you hold on to a woman who is meant to fly."

I shake my head. "I'm not every other woman in your life."

"You forget that it was you who walked away four years ago. Not even walked, you ran. You got in your car without a word and then wouldn't talk to me. I called you and not even a text back. So, no, you're not every other woman. They hurt me— you'd destroy me."

It's as though he's punched a hole in my chest. "I never meant to hurt you. I couldn't . . ." I let out a shaky breath. "When you said it was a mistake, when you looked at me like I was the last thing in the world you wanted, I couldn't handle it."

"That wasn't what happened."

"In my eyes it was. I was young and stupid and embarrassed more than anything. In the beginning, it was self-preservation to stay away from you, because I didn't know what to say or even if you wanted to talk to me. Then it became feeling stupid for staying away and cutting you off."

When I say it aloud now, it all seems so freaking stupid. I

should've answered his calls or messages, but I didn't think I could say anything to make the pain in my heart disappear. I never wanted us to be a mistake. I never even thought there would be a Lachlan and me, let alone have it happen that night, in that way.

"I was drunk, Ainsley."

"I know that, which made it even worse for me."

"Why?" he asks with a tinge of frustration in his voice.

I sigh, hating that we have to talk about this, but knowing it's long overdue. "I wasn't even sure if you'd remember it."

"I remember every single second of that kiss, of how you felt in my arms, of your scent, your touch, your warmth." He takes my hand in his. "Then you left."

I hate myself for hurting him. I hate that I did exactly the same thing he has had happen to him repeatedly.

"I did," I say softly. "I didn't even think about anything else. I'm sorry."

"Look, I know we're not the same people. I can understand what happened, get past it, but I have a life here with Rose. She loves her home, her friends, and the life we've built here. I can't make her give that up. Just the same as I can't ask you to give your life up. It's why I said we needed rules around this."

Tears form and my heart is breaking into a million pieces. Yes, I knew this was going to be the outcome, but God, I hoped for something more.

"I would never ask you to leave here."

"And you're going to move? You're going to walk away from your job?"

"I don't know. I could. I would for you."

He smiles and wipes away the tear that trickles down my face. "Oh, sweetheart, I wouldn't let you. Loving you means wanting you to be happy, giving you more than you give up. I know all about letting go of dreams. I know what it feels like when you walk away, always looking over your shoulder."

"You said you were happy that you left football." I turn my face and wipe away another tear.

Maybe he didn't say he was happy, but he didn't regret it. I could do the same. I can write from anywhere. Even if I have to burn through my savings, at least I'd have Lachlan.

"I was never happy. I loved the game. I was good at the game. I could've made it in that league. I know it. When I walked away, I did it because I knew I had to for my daughter. It wasn't because I was done with football. It still lives in me like a dull ache. It's why I found Frisbee, which may sound ridiculous, but I'm on that field. No, I don't have cleats on. No, I'm not lining up with a football in my hand, feeling the rush of the play that's coming. I still touch the grass, though. I still line up with my team as we start a play. It's all there, in a different way. So I don't regret it, but I miss it. Every day. That doesn't go away when you love something. I can't watch you feel the same. Not for me. I'm a grown-ass man. I'm not a child who needs a choice to be made for them."

I want to argue with him, but the finality in his tone tells me that he won't be persuaded. I've spent most of my life wanting him, this, and now I've had a small sample and have to walk away.

This is a heartbreak that I will never recover from.

I stare down at our entwined hands, tears falling as the ensuing pain starts to bubble. It's like knowing you're going to be in a crash and bracing for impact.

"You don't get to decide that for me. I'm not a child either."

He sits up, rubbing his face before looking at me. "I do, though. Do you know why?" he asks but answers before I can. "Because I watched what happens to women who give up their dreams. I've lived through it. I've seen my mother go from this vibrant woman to a shell of a human."

"I'm not your mother," I remind him. "I'm not giving up a dream, I'm gaining one."

"I'm not your dreams, sweetheart. I was there throughout your entire life as you talked about writing and telling people's stories. I know what your dreams are, Ainsley, better than I know my own."

But he is. He's part of it. "So what? I give you up for a *job*? For something that is going to leave me broken anyway? What about what I want, Lachlan? What about the fact that I choose you, damn it!" I press my hand to his chest. "I choose you. I choose to walk away from a job that doesn't fulfill me even a part of the way that these last few weeks have."

He gets to his feet, grabbing for his pants. "You want this life, Ainsley? You want to be a fireman's wife? Raising Rose, dealing with small-town meetings and carnivals? You're going to be okay giving up the glamour of the city? What happens when the people you work with start covering national headlines? What about all the money, time, and energy you've put into becoming a reporter? Have you thought about all of that?"

He's now dressed, and I'm still sitting on the blanket, naked. Never have I felt more exposed before.

I hesitate because I've thought about it, but not fully reconciled it.

"It's my decision to make," I tell him.

A deep sigh falls from his lips. "You'll regret it. Every day I'll have to look into your eyes and watch that fire dim." He moves to me, taking my face tenderly in his hands. "It'll kill me. It'll make me the man I've spent my entire life working not to be. I'll be my father. Putting my wants and needs before the woman I love. I'll have to see this incredible woman wither away until she just gives up."

My jaw trembles as a tear trickles down my face. Nothing I say here will change the way he thinks. It's going to take me leaving and coming back to prove to him how I feel. "Why don't you trust me?"

That causes him to jerk back. "I do trust you."

"No, if you did, you'd hear what I'm saying."

"Ainsley . . ."

I let out a heavy breath, not wanting to waste tonight. "Let's just go back and spend tonight together, okay?"

He nods. "If that's what you want."

I want to bite back with "Now you care about what I want?"

But I don't. I've known him practically my whole life, and he's a stubborn ass.

If he thinks this is the only way, well, I'll just have to prove there's always another option. And if he still doesn't want to hear it, I'll just call Caspian, and he'll kick his ass.

thirty
Lachlan

Rose went to Becky's so I could say goodbye to Ainsley alone. I didn't want Rose to see the aftermath.

The two girls hugged and promised they'd see each other soon, while I worked on packing Ainsley's car.

Now Ainsley and I are standing outside her driver's door.

Ainsley speaks first. "Before you say anything stupid, I want to say something."

"Okay."

"I love you. I've loved you my entire life, or at least it feels that way. I know you think I have big dreams, and I do. I won't lie and say I haven't worked toward those, but love is a dream for me too. To have a man who would do anything for me, love me the way I want and need in my life, is also something I've hoped for."

I'm that man.

I love her so much that I'm willing to let her go. For her.

She inhales and then speaks again. "I'm going to New York today because it's my job and I need to take care of things, but I'm coming back." Ainsley steps closer, placing her hand on my chest. "I'm coming back to you. I chose you, Lachlan. You've always said that no one ever chose you, well, I'm going to show that changed the day you let me fall in love with you."

I wish that I believed that.

I would give anything to be a different man. One who hasn't seen the truth of the world and how things change.

"I will never be the reason someone gives up what they want," I tell her. "I can't be that person."

"And you're not asking. You're not encouraging me to give it all up for you, are you?"

"No."

"Exactly." She leans in and kisses me. "I have to go. I'll be back, so if you could, don't fall in love with any random reporters who might show up."

Then the beautiful woman gets in her car, waves, and drives off, taking my heart with her.

———

It's been two days, and already the smell of her shampoo is fading from the pillow. All her little hair ties are gone, and I miss them. I miss her.

We've spoken every night, she's read to Rose on video calls, and I've hung up, feeling so fucking alone.

Today she has a big meeting where she'll see whether her story made the print edition, and she promised she'd call afterward.

I hear the ping of a text and I look down, but it's not her.

EVERETT

So, you let her go?

MILES

What do you think he did?

KILLIAN

And they wonder why women think we're stupid.

MILES

Oh, he's stupid for sure.

> Fuck off. All of you. She has a life and it's not here.

EVERETT

> They have these new things called planes. They go up in the air, really high, and then come down in a new place. I hear they even go to New York City.

KILLIAN

> I've been on one. They're very fast and efficient.

EVERETT

> That's right! You go to Boston.

I exhale through my nose, trying to remember why I like my friends.

> And what about Rose? Do I leave her? Make her quit cheer so we can travel to New York so I can be with her? Did any of you think about my daughter?

MILES

> Did you ask her? Rose is a smart kid who loves her father, and she loves Ainsley. I think we often forget they have wants too. I'm not saying you leave it up to her, but I'm pretty sure she misses Ainsley as well.

I know she does. She's had no issue expressing how much she wishes Ainsley was here, and she loves her.

> This isn't cut and dry.

KILLIAN

> Nothing in life is. It hasn't been easy
> reconnecting with my son who hates my guts,
> but I'm out here, making the hard decisions.

EVERETT

> None of us think it's easy, we just think it's
> right.

> Advice heard. See you at practice tonight.

I go back over the paperwork on my desk and try to figure out why the town denied my request for new gear. I'll never understand these denials, and I also get why the previous chief told me I would regret leaving my truck.

This is all politics, and while the pay is much better, the headache is much greater. I miss the jokes in the barracks, the nights we played cards.

My phone rings, and I'm like a goddamn teenager frantically reaching for it on my desk.

Although it's the wrong MacKinley's name on the screen.

"Hey, Cas."

"What's wrong with you?"

Okay, I see he talked to his sister.

"Not sure what you mean."

"Not sure what I . . . you're a fucking idiot."

I sigh. "I can only imagine what you heard."

"Heard? About what?" The surprise in his voice catches me off guard. Maybe he hasn't spoken to Ainsley.

"Nothing. Clue me in on what I'm an idiot about."

"Your dad."

I'm a little shocked at that one, since he's no freaking better when it comes to parental relationships, but I'll bite.

"What about my dad?"

"You saw him. You saw the garden and you're still pissed at him?"

One of the things about my friendship with Caspian that I've always respected is the ability to call each other out on our shit. Today, I'm not admiring that. I'd like to punch him in the face for it.

"And how are things with the Admiral? Did you stop by after Ainsley and I left?"

"Fuck off. We're talking about you."

"I'd rather we talk about you, since you brought it up."

"I bet you would. How about we talk about the fact that you ended it with my sister?" he offers.

"Let's focus on my father instead."

He snorts. "I see. You know, I think we'll talk about Ainsley instead. See, I've always respected you. I thought, that guy has his shit together. You walked away from football for Rose. You bought that house, have a great job, got promoted over and over again. You've lived smart and always put Rose first. So I'm curious, when the fuck are you going to do that for yourself?"

"I am doing that."

"Really? Because I talked to Ainsley. She told me all about her brilliant plan, which I'm one hundred percent sure you're not worthy of."

"I would agree. I'm not."

"Right, well, she's on her own path to proving her love for you, as though anyone with eyes could miss it, and my thinking is that you're going to push her away. Since that's what you always do when you're worried someone might get hurt."

If he was in front of me, he'd be on the ground for that one. "If you were anyone else who said that . . ."

"Yeah, but I'm not. I'm not going to lie and tell you some lame shit you want to hear. You're the one who pushed me to go to Nashville. To put myself out there, try, work hard, fight for what I want. I swear all those words came out of your mouth."

I did. Caspian is talented as fuck, and he can make it in music. He just would've never done it if people hadn't pushed him. He lived under the Admiral's thumb, always doing what he was told and never stepping out of the box he was made to sit in.

When we got to college, he was fucking miserable.

I loved every damn second of it, while Cas just wanted to hang at the bars with the musicians.

"This isn't the same thing."

"No shit. This time it's about you."

I grumble. "Did you call to yell at me?"

"Pretty much."

"Are you done?"

"Not even a little bit. You and Ainsley will figure your shit out. I have faith in her to fix your ass, but . . . I've let this shit with your dad go because I get it. Fathers and sons are complicated. Lord knows my relationship with the Admiral is fucked, but your dad cares, dude. He's tried and wants a relationship that isn't about making you into the son he always wanted. You already are that. Also, he loved your mother, and I know that you went through absolute hell, but what if you're missing something? What if you don't know the whole truth, Lachlan? What would happen if your entire foundation has been built on sand instead of concrete?"

"Thank you, Dr. Phil, for your unsolicited advice. I appreciate what you're saying, but I have a tractor trailer's worth of issues regarding my father."

"Then it's time to unload, Lachlan, because you're carrying too much weight."

The fucker hangs up before I can say another word.

———

I'm sitting in my truck outside my father's house, not even sure what the hell possessed me to get my keys, call Delaney to stay with Rose, and head here.

I take that back. I know what possessed me—Caspian.

However, after we hung up, I cursed him to hell. I thought

about the absolute shit he said to me. I'm not a fucking kid. I was there. I saw her spiral and waste away.

Then I thought about the possibility that he was right. What if I don't know everything?

What if with everything I've done my entire fucking adult life, I was missing something, and now I might miss everything?

I kept circling the fact that I assumed Ainsley would be like my mother if she gave up anything for me. That she'd be unhappy, in a place she doesn't want to be, wishing she'd chosen another life.

The only person who can answer any of this is sitting in the living room, reading in his chair.

I knock twice, and my father opens the door, stepping back with wide eyes when he sees me.

"Lachlan. Is everything okay?"

"Why did Mom give up and choose not to fight the cancer?" I spit the words out before we can talk about the weather or Rose or anything else.

My dad's hand is gripping the edge of the door. "Is that really the question you're asking?"

"I need to know why she gave up. I need to know how she could just think her life was worthless and the people around her weren't going to suffer because of it."

His hand drops and he steps back, opening the door more. "Come in."

I haven't been in this house since the day she died.

I look at the wood floors that I walked on for most of my life. The fifth floorboard on the right will creak if you step on it. All the memories, the way she'd laugh and chase me around with whipped cream on her spoon, the stain still there from the spot we missed.

My feet cross the threshold, and I follow Dad into the kitchen.

"Do you want something to drink?"

"I'm good."

He nods once, and then we both sit at the table.

"Before we get into things, I wanted to thank you for bringing Rose over. It meant a lot to me."

"She liked talking about the ships."

He smiles and laughs a little. "You used to like talking about them too. She's a lot like you, at least in the short time I got to spend with her. There were similarities."

"She reminds me of Mom."

Dad's eyes mist over a little. "As do you. Remind me of your mother, that is."

I sigh, looking away, feeling uncomfortable. "I need to know the truth, Dad. Caspian seems to think there's some missing information that I wasn't privy to."

My father shifts and then laces his fingers on the table in front of him. "Your mother, despite all her struggles, didn't just choose to give up. I know you saw it that way, and, honestly, I did, too, for a long time. She didn't want to be sick, and I thought she had a real simple solution to it—fight."

"That was the damn solution!"

"Yes, but not to her," he says, leaning back. "I pleaded with her. I offered her a million things if she'd just try it. She'd touch my face, tell me she loved me, but that she wasn't going to prolong a life that was not going to be anything like she lived."

"But she'd live."

"Would she?" he tosses back. "Your mother who loved to bake cakes, dance around this kitchen with her horrible music blaring, spend hours in that garden trimming? Because she wouldn't have that life anymore. She'd be tired all the time, be stuck in her room, be afraid of getting sick because it could be what ended her instead of the cancer. That's how she saw it."

I push back, anger starting to fill me. "She lived that life too, Dad. Because of you."

"Yes. I know that I did that to her."

My head snaps to meet his gaze. "What?"

"She did. She went into her horrible depressions where life

wasn't worth getting out of bed some days. Before a deployment I'd watch her day by day start to sink. No matter what medication we tried, therapy, or anything else we could do wouldn't stop it. I had to get on that ship, knowing that my wife and son were going to fall apart. Sure, I would ask the Admiral and Ms. MacKinley to check on you both. I even hired someone to come help her when you were young, but she fired her and sent me an email cursing me out." He smiles at that. "She didn't like anyone telling her what to do. I don't know if you remember when I decided to leave the military?"

I shake my head.

"You were maybe thirteen. We'd just moved here a few years before, and I was on shore duty, so things were good, but then they explained I'd need to go back to a ship again. I'd gotten special permission to stay on an extended shore duty because your mother was struggling. When I told her, I explained that I was done. I wasn't going to leave her again. She lost it."

I lean back. "What do you mean?"

"She lost it, Lachlan. I'm talking full-blown freak-out. I'd never seen her so angry at me. I had several years left before I could retire, and she told me she'd divorce me if I didn't finish out my time."

"So you stayed?"

My father sighs heavily and nods. "I couldn't lose her. If you think I didn't love your mother, you know nothing. That woman was the reason I breathed, and when she found out she was pregnant..."

I can't explain it, but something feels strange. "When she found out she was pregnant, what?"

"We knew your mother's mental state when we married. I loved her, and I didn't care that she struggled. We were going to struggle together. We grew up in nowhere Nebraska, and I wanted a better life for us. So we discussed it and decided to join the navy. She, well, she just didn't ever want to be a bad mother. It was a huge surprise when she got pregnant."

I sit back, feeling the breath leave my lungs. "But she was the best."

"She was, but she was terrified. She didn't think she should ever have a child, and leading up to your birth were some of the worst times in her life. She had to come off her medication, and it was hard, but she loved you. Before she met you, she loved you, wanted you, was willing to fight every battle to have you, even though we both agreed we never should've gotten pregnant. At your birth she had her tubes tied because she knew she couldn't endure another pregnancy."

My father's eyes are distant, and I can see the weight of this on him.

My mother never once made me feel like she regretted having me, nor did she ever say she didn't want to have kids. She loved my father and me. I knew that, but I don't understand why she wouldn't let him retire early. Why did she always have to put herself in pain to help others?

And when I ask myself that simple question, it's as though someone just turned the lights on inside me.

It's the same shit I do.

I look at my father, feeling for the first time in four years a sympathy for what he must've felt on the other side of her decisions.

"She wouldn't let you give up your career for her. She wouldn't let you protect her because she was so damn busy doing it for everyone else."

My father nods. "When she got sick, she lied for months. Months and months she told me the doctors didn't find anything. It wasn't until she collapsed that she confessed. I only had a year left until I was fully retired, and she knew I'd go AWOL if that was what I had to do to be there for her."

And here my father was willing to do the same for her.

"Why didn't you push back?"

He chuckles and sighs. "I pushed with all I had, but she was tired. She wanted to live out the rest of her days in the garden, pulling weeds or watching us do it for her. She wanted to see Rose, you, and everyone else without tubes and wires everywhere. When she told me that this was her choice, I felt as though someone ripped my heart out. It wasn't my choice, Lachlan. I would've chosen one more day, one more hour, one more minute with her. There is nothing in this world I wouldn't have done to keep her with us. I know you blame me. I know you think it was my fault that she gave up, and while some of it might have been the exhaustion from battling her mental illness, it was her choice to live out the rest of her days how she wanted."

All this time I've assumed that it was because my father didn't ask her or show her how he could finally be there. The years that he left her alone, I thought was his decision because of his career choices.

I saw my mother suffer time and time again as he'd leave.

A tear falls from my eye, and I swipe it away.

"You made leaving look easy," I say, my throat growing tight.

"Easy?" Dad huffs. "It was never easy, son. Leaving you and your mother was horrible. Even if she wasn't sick and I didn't know how things were going to happen, I would've hated it. However, knowing that she was going to suffer and I couldn't stop it was absolute agony. I spent six months out to sea, sick to my stomach. I'd call every chance I could. I emailed ten times a day. I sent things so that she'd have to get out of bed and had Denise come check on you both. There was no joy in my deployments. I didn't go sightseeing when we were in a port. Instead, I found somewhere quiet to video chat. Every single time, I asked her to please just let me leave the service and I'd figure it out. Her answer was always the same . . . do it and I'm gone."

It's funny how I'm basically doing the same thing, only in reverse.

"I think I fucked up, Dad."

"With?"

"Ainsley."

He leans back with a smile. "Let me guess, you told her she couldn't leave her job for you?"

I nod.

"Do you love her?"

"Yes."

"Then don't take her choice to love you away. Don't make her choose, Lachlan. Just be her choice."

thirty-one
Ainsley

"Yes, Mr. Krispen, I'm sure."

"I don't understand. You got the exact position you wanted," he says, pacing the room. "You wrote one of the most evocative pieces this company has seen, we gave you carte blanche to write about politics, and you want to quit?" he asks, clearly mystified.

I'm sure to anyone else this looks like a mistake, but . . . it's not. It's Lachlan.

It's the man I love, and he's a dumbass, but there's no one else in the world for me.

So I'm going out on a high note and searching for jobs.

"It's truly what I want."

"To be unemployed in New York City?"

I smile. "I'm moving to Ember Falls."

He groans and tosses his hands up. "For the love of God. You fell in love, didn't you?"

"I did," I answer honestly.

"Of course you did. That's why this article reads like a love letter."

I shrug because that's exactly what it is, and when it prints in three days, he'll see exactly how I feel as I'm standing at his door.

"I think it was you who said writers who speak from their soul tell more than an article. They tell a story that's rich and engaging…"

"I was drunk."

A laugh escapes from my lips. "I don't think so."

"No, I wasn't, but … I may have been hard on you, Ainsley, but it's because I saw true talent. You were able to take a mundane topic that would be black and white and paint it in Technicolor. You're gifted and I hate the idea of you leaving."

I hate the idea of it, but not the reality. I want to continue doing what I love, especially now that I have free rein to write what I want, but at the same time, it's not what I need.

I need Lachlan.

I don't want to go back to a life without him.

"Would you give up everything for your wife?"

Mr. Krispen sighs. "I'm assuming there's no way to change your mind on it?"

I shake my head.

His buzzer cuts off any chance at a reply. "Mr. Krispen, umm, a Mr. Knight is here. I'm sending him in."

My boss's eyes go wide as saucers. "The owner is here. Shit."

A moment later there's a knock on the door and Mr. Krispen nearly hurdles over the desk to get there quickly.

"Mr. Knight, hello."

A very handsome man with light-blue eyes nods and smiles. "Charles, good to see you." Then he looks to me. "Hello, I'm Carson Knight."

I take his extended hand. "Ainsley MacKinley."

"Well, this works out great," Carson says. "I actually came here to meet you."

Mr. Krispen clears his throat. "I apologize if I missed an email."

He shakes his head. "You didn't."

Watching my boss nearly crap himself is pretty entertaining, but as intimidating as this man is, and he is, he pales in comparison to the Admiral.

"You wanted to meet me?" I ask.

Carson turns his attention to me. "Yes, I received an advance copy of the paper, as usual, and read your article. I wanted to tell you that it was outstanding, and my wife agreed as well. She said I was an idiot who should pay closer attention to *Metro NY*, since the talent is underappreciated."

I smile at that, sounding like something I would say. "It's an honor to meet you, and I wouldn't say we're underappreciated, but happy for you to see how great we are."

He chuckles. "So tell me, Ainsley MacKinley, how long have you been a member of the team here?"

"About six months."

"Six months and this is the first article I've read?" He turns to Mr. Krispen. "How is that?"

"She's actually had quite a few articles printed, but this was the first time we gave her a human-interest piece."

Mr. Knight nods. "Impressive. Well, now that I know what great staff I have, I plan to have you write more of these."

Of course I get noticed when I'm leaving.

I smile warmly. "You do have great staff, Mr. Knight, and I will deeply miss being a part of *Metro NY*. It's been both my honor and privilege to work here."

"That sounds like you're leaving."

"I am," I say with sorrow.

"Where are you going?" Carson asks, coming farther into the room. "Surely after writing an article like that you're not being fired?" He looks to Mr. Krispen, who is shaking his head.

"Absolutely not, Mr. Knight."

"Please, call me Carson, Charles. We've had this conversation."

Mr. Krispen looks like he might be sick. "Of course, sir."

Carson grins and turns to me. "If you're not being fired, then why would you be quitting?"

"Can I be honest?"

"I'd hope you would be."

I smile. "I fell in love with the man in the article—more than I already did before I went there."

He laughs once. "Did you?"

"Yes, we grew up together—it was a thing—but I'd rather give up everything than live my life without him."

"My wife would love you," Carson says with a grin as he sits on the couch and motions for me to do the same. "And I'm assuming this man in the article feels the same?"

"I think so."

Carson leans back. "You think? You're taking a pretty big chance on love."

"I am."

That seems to impress him in some way. "In business and in life, sometimes that's what we have to do. Buying this paper, for instance, was a bit of both."

The purchase of our paper was a huge thing. One day we were owned by a different company, and then *Metro NY* was bought by Carson Knight. No one knew why or how, but the staff who didn't agree to his rules were let go, and everyone else stayed. We didn't print for about a month, though.

"I think, sometimes, the biggest risks bring the greatest rewards," I explain.

"I'd agree. Let me ask you, what would it take to get you to stay?"

I shake my head. "I don't think . . ."

"Don't answer too fast. Is there a dollar value? A promotion?" Carson asks.

"No."

He nods once. "I see. So it's Ember Falls or bust?"

I grin at that. "Pretty much. I think, if I stayed, I'd be unhappy and then leave anyway. It's better that I take the leap now."

He gets to his feet and starts to pace. "I don't think that's going to work for me."

I blink. "I'm sorry. What?"

Carson turns to me. "I don't like letting competent people go. Let's negotiate."

"Mr. Knight, I have nothing to negotiate."

"Bullshit. There's always a compromise."

"Okay," I say, knowing there really isn't. "Move the paper to Ember Falls."

He chuckles. "Starting at a pretty lofty place, I see."

I shrug. "I'm giving you my terms."

"Okay, then. Stay here and I'll give you a large raise where you'll be able to travel there easily."

I shake my head. "I'm afraid that won't work. I spent years away from him. I don't want to endure another few years."

His light-blue eyes turn soft. "I understand that more than you would think. Okay, how about this? You don't quit and you get to keep the man you love?"

"I don't see how that would work," I say, feeling defeated.

He sits back down on the couch, and then steeples his fingers. "I believe in keeping good people in my company. When I purchased this paper, my thought was to just shut it down, but my wife encouraged me to keep it running and not have anyone willing to agree to the new company terms lose their jobs. Since then, I've just sort of let it do its thing, checking each circulation, not getting overly involved, but then I got this publication." He leans forward. "And I read your article and wanted to come here, see more, learn about the talent we have that clearly is being underutilized."

"I'm not sure what to say," I admit. "I was only doing this article to be able to write the stories I was passionate about."

"And what stories are those?"

I smile, imagining the things I would want to tackle. "World issues, politics, national issues where we could actually make a difference. I want to write about things people care about or should care about. Thought-provoking stories that make us want to be better, do better."

Carson gets to his feet. "Here's what I propose, you write those stories for this paper—from wherever it is that you were going to move to. You can work remotely and come up once a month for the major meetings."

All the oxygen is sucked out of the room and I gasp. "What? Mr. Knight—"

"Carson."

"Carson, that's an extremely generous offer, but how? The paper is here."

He tilts his head slightly. "Do they have the internet wherever this man lives?"

"Of course, but . . ."

"But?"

I don't even know what I was going to say. Clearly, I'm a dummy because he just offered me everything I want and I'm arguing.

"I don't know, I just . . . I came in here and gave my notice, and now you're telling me I can keep my job and move to Ember Falls."

Carson grins. "I'm just happy I came in before you left then."

"Me too."

"So you'll stay at *Metro NY*?"

I stand, tug on my shirt to straighten it, and nod. "It'll be my pleasure."

Now to go home and pack and prove that he's my choice.

———

"I'm going to miss you so much. Who else is going to window-shop with me and ride out to Brooklyn so we can go to that book-store for only romance books or go get pizza at midnight?" Caroline slumps in my desk chair.

"I'll miss you, too, but now you have a reason to leave the city," I say, knowing that's not exactly a good thing.

If Caroline could, she'd never leave Manhattan. It has every-thing she needs, and she feels it's far superior to anywhere else.

While I've loved every minute I've spent in this city, I'm ready to go where it feels like home.

"I'm not sure about that."

I grin. "Well, it gives me a reason to come back."

"So what exactly is the full agreement?" she asks as I'm cleaning off my desk, putting things in a box.

"I'm going to remain a reporter for *Metro NY* but write what I want, kind of. I can cover politics or anything that I've pitched since I started here."

"That's amazing."

"I just have to convince Lachlan that we can actually be a couple and ask if I can move in." I let out a nervous giggle.

That's the only kink in my plans. There's not a lot of real estate or rental options in Ember Falls. I have, like, three choices. The cabin in the woods, Lachlan's house, or sleeping in my car. So, really, I have one option.

"That's going to go over well."

"Yeah, this plan is flawed."

Caroline pushes back, tossing her legs up on my desk. "You'll be so much closer to DC too."

"Yeah, that'll be the good thing. I can get there in a few hours to cover anything big."

Although I really want to focus on smaller-level government issues to start. I want to talk about what will give immediate help to others.

"I know that politics and all that is what you really wanted to write about, but this article about Lachlan is really good. You should consider more human-interest pieces, just maybe not athletes."

I laugh and lean against the edge. "I think I did okay."

"Look, most people didn't even know Ultimate Frisbee was a thing, so you could've written anything about the rules and no one would know."

"I'm pretty sure I could do the sports reporting."

"No."

I laugh and then let out a long sigh. "I'm going to miss you."

Caroline was the first friend I made here. I was this sheltered military brat from Virginia Beach who felt as though I was dropped off in another world. Caroline was in the room across the hall, and we instantly clicked.

She was from Jersey and spent most of her teenage years taking the train into the city, so I had a tour guide.

"I always thought you and I would be like Carrie and Charlotte, always living here, but you'd marry well, and I'd still be writing in my apartment."

I thought the same. "I'm not sure I'm Charlotte. I feel like I'm more Samantha."

She laughs at that. "You're not tough enough."

"Whatever. I can be tough."

"You can be, but you're not jaded yet. The city only gave you a few scratches. You haven't felt the deep cuts." Caroline stands, helping put more things in the box. "I'm proud of you, Ainsley."

"What? Why?"

"Because you're going after what you want, no matter what obstacles are in your way."

"Well, it's one large obstacle that I may not be able to get around."

Especially if he remains his normal stubborn self.

"You'll get around it or over it or on top of it." We both laugh and she nudges me. "Seriously, if he doesn't see how amazing you are, then he doesn't deserve you, and you come back here."

"I think he knows. I just think he's scared."

The sky opened up when I was three blocks from my apartment, soaking my cardboard box with the contents of my desk, and I look like a drowned rat.

Seriously, today went from being sort of amazing to ending in a crazy mess.

Lachlan didn't answer my calls or texts, and I want to at least tell him about meeting my boss. I plan to just show up tomorrow with a suitcase and be like, *I'm not leaving until you stop being stupid.*

That's the best plan I've got.

My bad luck changes a little when a neighbor is holding the door open.

"Thank you."

He smiles. "No problem. It's really coming down out there."

I nod. "It is."

I make my way up the stairs, my hair and clothes sticking to me, and I do thank God I wore black and not a white shirt today. When I get to the top of the stairs, I put the soaked box down, brush my soppy wet hair back, and fish for my keys.

"Do you need help with that?"

The voice causes my breath to catch. I lift my eyes and see Lachlan crouching beside me with a smile on his face and flowers in his hands.

"Lachlan? What are you doing here?"

"Let me help you and I'll explain."

My heart is pounding, and I'm one of those stupid people on television who look dumbstruck and can't speak. "Here, these are for you."

I take the most gorgeous bouquet of roses I've ever seen. "Wow."

"They're called Juliet roses."

"Well, they're stunning. You came here to bring me flowers?" I ask. I'm hoping that he came here to bring me home, but I tamper that hope down.

"Come on, we'll talk inside." He grabs my box of stuff from the office, and we head to my apartment. My nerves are going bananas, and it takes me three tries to get the key in the lock.

Lachlan brings the box inside after I open the door. He looks around, taking in my mismatch of an apartment. Nothing goes together, and yet somehow it seems like it all belongs. One of the articles I wrote about was how fun antique shopping can be, which required me to spend a lot of time doing it.

In the end, I learned it actually was fun.

However, he's not here about antiquing or my apartment.

I go to speak, my mouth open, and he steps forward, talking first. "I need to say something."

I close my mouth and nod.

Lachlan steps toward me. "I was stupid."

This is off to a good start. "Yes, you were, but what exactly are you talking about?"

"I thought that if I made the hard decision for you, that it would hurt us both less. You wouldn't regret leaving a job, a city, and a life you love. I thought if I took away the choice, and I bore the brunt of it, then you'd be happy, and you wouldn't hate me. In my head, it made perfect sense, but then I spent the last few days without you, wishing I wasn't so stupid and didn't push you away."

I cross my arms over my soaking-wet chest and nod. "I guess that's not working out so well?"

He laughs and comes closer. "It's not. You see, I love you, Ainsley MacKinley. I love you more than I have ever thought possible. I'm not asking you to choose me, because I choose you. If that means I have to move to this city to have you, then so be it. If it means I'm on a flight every weekend or taking a train or driving. No matter what, I'll do it."

My eyes widen. "But Rose."

She was his biggest worry, and I understand that he needs to put her first.

"Rose loves you too. We both do, and I think that love is what matters, don't you?" His right hand cups my cheek. "I think that you matter, we matter, and I choose you, however I can have you. If it means we fly back and forth until we figure out what's next, then that's what we do, but we make that decision together. I'm not making choices for you, and you're not for me. I never want to take things from you, sweetheart. I just want to give you the world, whatever I can. I want to make plans, build a life together. I want you. No, I need you, Ainsley."

A tear falls down my cheek. "That's good, because I quit my job."

"You what?"

"I quit today. That's why I have that box. See, I wasn't going to let you choose to be done with me. I'm not done. We're not done. I love you, and I do not want to be in this city if it means I can't have you."

Lachlan pulls me into his arms, kissing the top of my head. "Call them and get your job back. I'll move. I'll find a way to make this work. Please, baby. I need you to have all your dreams."

I shake my head. "That's the thing. They wouldn't let me quit."

"No?"

"No. The owner came because he read my article, and he told me I shouldn't have to choose between them when there's internet in Ember Falls. I'm going to be able to keep my job and move."

He smiles, cupping my face. "You're serious?"

"Yes, I know we're extremely new to dating, but I'd like to move to Ember Falls. I can look for a place close by—"

He cuts me off by sealing his mouth to mine. "Ainsley MacKinley, you'll live with me."

I hoped he'd say that. "You're sure? It's really quick and . . . Rose."

"Rose is the one who told me I better come get you and bring you home."

I smile. "She did?"

"We talked. I told her that I loved you and wanted you to come back. She was very happy when I told her I was coming here to win you over."

My hand rests on his chest, and I stare up into his beautiful eyes. "We haven't been together long. I don't want it to feel too sudden."

"Is it? I feel like we've been dancing around a relationship for a really long time."

"I know I've been in love with you for most of my life, but this is different."

Lachlan closes his eyes and rests his forehead on mine. "Live with me. Please."

How the hell could I ever say no to that? "I would love to."

He lifts his head and kisses me softly. "You're going to be okay leaving this place?" he asks with a little shake in his voice.

"I know all too well what it feels like to live without you, Lachlan, and I don't want to ever do it again. I'll live in a cardboard box as long as it means I'm with you."

"Then let's go home."

But before we do, we kiss, and he makes love to me on the floor of the apartment.

thirty-two
Lachlan

"Ainsley!" Rose yells as she runs off the porch toward us. "Rose!"

The two of them hug, and Rose looks up at me. "Is she staying with us, Daddy?"

"She is."

"Yay!" my daughter says, and the two of them laugh. "I missed you!"

"I missed you too."

"I missed you both," I say, joining in.

However, neither of them pays me any attention. Typical.

"Are you going to live with us? Daddy said he was going to bring you back so you could stay here all the time, if you wanted."

Ainsley's face grows serious. "Are you sure you're okay with it?"

Rose nods. "I hope you stay forever."

Ainsley takes both of her hands and smiles. "I hope the same."

So do I.

We left New York early this morning with some of her things. There's a lot of stuff, and there was no way we were going to get it all figured out in a day. We're going to go back up a few times in the next month, which is what she has left on her lease anyway.

"Daddy, can Ainsley come to Becky's house with me? I have to tell her that she's back and is going to live with us."

"I think we have to get Ainsley settled, but she'll be here when you get home. Becky's mom won't be here for another hour, anyway."

Delaney comes out with her bag on her shoulder. "I'll send you a bill."

I laugh once. "Okay."

She turns to Rose. "I'll see you soon, kid."

"Are you coming to the carnival?"

Delaney shrugs and tosses up a peace sign as she leaves. I really don't know why my daughter loves her so much.

The three of us head inside, carrying what we can. Ainsley stops at the door where her room was and starts to enter, but I stop her. "Where are you going?"

She looks back to me. "Umm . . ."

"You're not moving in and staying in the guest room."

"Lach . . ."

"You'll be with me."

Her eyes move to Rose, who is beaming, clearly over the moon about Ainsley and me dating. Before I went to get Ainsley, Rose and I talked. I explained that I loved her, the way a man loves a woman and wants to be with her. She asked if we were getting married so Ainsley could be her mom, to which I said not yet, but we were going to live together first.

My daughter couldn't have smiled any bigger. It's clear that they formed a very strong bond and she's very happy to have Ainsley here.

"Okay, then."

All of us cram into the space, Rose jumps on the bed, and Ainsley flops beside her. The two of them giggle, and I swear my heart grows from this scene.

"What are you girls doing? We still have boxes to move."

Ainsley rolls onto her stomach, and Rose mimics it. "The boxes can wait. Come lie here with us."

"Yeah, Daddy, come lie with us."

I'm in so much damn trouble with these two.

I turn and flop between them on the bed. "Now what?"

"I think we should tickle him," Ainsley suggests.

"He's not ticklish," Rose informs her.

I smile and Ainsley makes a humming noise. "Are you sure?"

Rose nods. "I tried."

I chuckle. "Nope, not ticklish."

Ainsley leans over and whispers to Rose. Great, this is definitely not going to go my way. The two of them come to each side of me, and both kiss my cheek.

In this single moment, my entire life changes.

Call it stupid.

Call it cheesy.

Call it whatever you want, but it does.

I have the two women I love the most on each side of me.

They break apart and both laugh. I push up and make a large show of chasing them, and the three of us laugh, running around, forgetting about the boxes in the car.

―――――

"Well, it seems someone isn't so stupid after all," Miles says as we walk up Main Street toward the carnival.

Ainsley grins up at me. "Aww, did your friends think you were stupid?"

"Maybe."

"I agree, Miles, he totally got smart."

"I hear an official welcome to Ember Falls is in order?"

I roll my eyes. "You already know she moved in and we're together."

"Yes, but did she get a welcome basket?"

Ainsley gasps. "A basket? I get a basket?"

Miles cuts in. "You do, and you get to know the official town secret."

"Just how many town secrets does this place have?" she asks, since she already knows about the falls.

"You told her about the falls?" he asks.

"Oh, please, don't even. They're on my land." I turn to Ainsley. "Way to sell me out."

"Listen, I'm not good with authority, and he's a principal and former military. It's just kind of the way I am. Blame the Admiral."

"Speaking of your dad, when are you planning to tell him about your move? Maybe we should call him now," I suggest, pulling my phone out.

She grabs it and puts it in her bra. "Not today, Satan."

I chuckle and pull her to my side. "Tomorrow then." I kiss her temple, and she stares up at me with so much love in her eyes it's almost overwhelming.

"Tomorrow."

The last two weeks have been so easy, as though we've been together for years.

We've settled into a great routine, and Ainsley's former bedroom is now her office. We moved the rest of her things down last weekend, and we'll probably need one more before she's fully out of the apartment.

Each morning I wake up with her breathing in my face, hair whipping me across the cheek when she flops over, and I've never been happier in my life.

"As much as it's been an absolute pleasure running into you, Miles, we have a lot of carnival to cover," I say, placing my hand on her back.

"Where's Rose?"

"She's with Rickie, Maddy, and Veronica's families," Ainsley says with a smug smile.

Turns out Rickie does like Rose, but she didn't think she liked her, or some other girl nonsense. I stopped listening after she said they were friends again.

"Well, I'll let you two lovebirds make the rounds. I'm sure the town will all want a piece of the new girls."

"Girls?" I ask.

"Yeah, Hazel just hired a new manager who moved into

town."

"Really? I hadn't heard."

Which is strange, since I swear the firehouse could double as a gossip mill most days.

"Yeah, her name is Penelope. She's a single mom, moved from somewhere in Illinois," Miles explains.

"Oh! Hazel mentioned it when I was in there the other day. Said she's super sweet, and her son is about Rose's age. Do you know where she's staying?" Ainsley asks. "Please tell me it's not that cabin I got stuck in."

Miles laughs once. "No, I asked. Hazel said she's renting one of the old ranchers' houses on the Mitchells' land."

"Not much better than the cabin," I note.

The ranchers' houses are tiny, but at least they're up to date with running water and electricity.

Ainsley looks to me. "Maybe it would be a good thing to meet her and introduce Rose to her son? I'm sure it's hard for him."

"I met her when she came to register him for school. He's a cute kid," says Miles.

"Okay, well, I'll . . . make a point to go get coffee, and we'll find a non-creepy way to introduce her to Rose. On that note"—I take Ainsley's hand in mine—"we're going to find my daughter."

"Have fun," Miles says as he walks off.

"This is really cute," Ainsley notes.

"You're really cute."

"We're ridiculous, you know that?" she asks while resting her head on my arm.

"Why? Because I love you?"

Ainsley glances up at me through her long lashes. "No, that's definitely not ridiculous. That's kind of perfect."

"So then what makes us ridiculous?"

"You know what? Nothing."

I stop, pulling her into my arms and staring down at her beautiful face. "If a man telling the woman he loves that she's cute or perfect or anything else is ridiculous, then prepare for me to be the most ridiculous man in the world. I never want you to question whether I love you or what I think or what I want. You're everything to me, Ainsley. Every fucking thing that matters."

She lifts her hand to my face, brushing the scruff there. "You're not ridiculous. You're sweet and caring, and I love you with all my heart. You can tell me anytime you want just how much you love me."

"Good."

I lean in and kiss her.

"You can do that too."

"Oh, I plan to."

She giggles. "Come on, Sparky, I have rides to ride."

"I have a ride you can get on anytime you want."

"Does it get hard?" she asks with a mischievous smile.

"Only for you."

"Well, then, when we get back home, I'll have to give it a spin and see if I'd like multiple turns."

That's it.

I grab her hand and start walking her back toward the car as she laughs and yanks me the other way.

"Lachlan!"

I turn and toss her over my shoulder, which of course causes several people to stare. Ainsley wiggles until I put her back down, her body against mine, and I work really fucking hard to not have a raging erection in the middle of the town.

"You're trying to kill me."

"Not even a little, just giving you something to look forward to."

Every single day she gives me that. When I'm at work, I can't wait to walk through that door and have the girls run to me. When she's at the coffee shop, I count down the minutes until she'll be back and I can watch her work. No matter what it is, I long for her.

"You're my something to look forward to, Ainsley."

"And you're mine."

I kiss her nose, and then I head back to the carnival with the most amazing woman on my arm.

"Why do I feel like I'm walking in to face a firing squad?" I ask Ainsley as we're outside her father's door.

"Because you basically are."

Right.

"Maybe we don't need to tell your dad until later."

She scoffs. "Are you nuts? The longer we wait, the worse it is."

Her logic is sound, but there's still a little dread pooling in my stomach. My father was obviously happy for us, since he was the catalyst for me to get my head out of my ass. Now it's time to tell the Admiral that we are not only dating, but living together.

Ainsley thinks that last part is going to be what pushes him over the edge.

"I'm rethinking leaving Rose at my father's house. That would've ensured he doesn't kill me."

Ainsley purses her lips. "We didn't consider that angle." She shrugs. "Oh, well. Too late now. Let's go."

Before I can say anything, she rings the doorbell and then enters. "Daddy," she calls out.

"Ainsley? Is that you?"

"It is. Lachlan and I are here."

Her father emerges from the back, where his office is. He smiles when he sees us. "I didn't know you were coming." He kisses her cheek and then extends his hand to me. "Lachlan."

"Admiral."

"Come in, I was just working on my coins."

Ainsley smiles. "Always working on those coins, Daddy. You know they don't change by moving them around."

Challenge coins in the military are really special. My father has maybe a hundred of them that he's exchanged over the years. It's a commemorative coin that is unique to either the person or the team. I have one for being a fire chief that I hand out to other chiefs or law enforcement agencies. Where I may have ten, the Admiral has probably a thousand. Everyone wants to trade coins with the Admiral.

"I like to remember where each one came from," he says with a hint of defensiveness.

Ainsley rubs his back as we walk into his office.

On the wall, where photos of Ainsley's mother used to hang, are now rows of shadowboxes with the coins proudly displayed.

"This is incredible," I say as I look at the first box.

"Those are the ones I got from Congress and the Senate."

It's impressive. "And these?"

"Those are deployment traded. I did my fair share of those and always left one coin with a sailor who went above and beyond the call of duty," he explains. "So what brings you both here, and where is Rose?"

"Rose is next door. She's spending some time with my father."

The Admiral's eyes widen, and then he smiles. "You spoke with him?"

"I did. A few weeks ago, I came here, and we discussed a lot of things that needed to be said."

"I'm proud of you, Lachlan. I know you're not my son, but it takes a strong man to face his demons and overcome them."

I nod. "Thank you, sir. I'm hoping he and I can find a new way forward."

"You will."

He says it as though he has no doubts about it. While my father and I have a lot of things to overcome, we both are making an effort to work through the past and focus on a future. He wants to be a part of our lives, and he's the only family I have left.

Ainsley looks over at me with a smile. "I'm proud of him too."

The Admiral looks to her and then to me. Well, here we go.

"Sir, I came with Ainsley because we wanted to talk to you."

He shakes his head. "I'm not sure I want to hear this."

This is going just about how I expected. "We don't want to lie to you, but I love Ainsley, and she and I are together."

Ainsley looks at her father, and with zero finesse she blurts out the rest. "We're living together also. I tried to quit my job, but they wouldn't let me. So I'm working for *Metro NY* still, but in Ember Falls, and living with Lachlan and Rose."

I swear I think she wants her father to kill me.

His gaze moves to her, then to me, then back to her. "You're living with him?"

"Yes. I love him, and since I was staying with him anyway, this was just the easiest way to move forward."

He sighs and leans back in his chair. "You couldn't just get your own place?"

"I'm sure I could, but again, this was easy, and as a grown adult, this was the choice I made," Ainsley explains.

The Admiral turns to me. "And what happens if this doesn't work out?"

"I have no intentions of that being the reality."

"You plan to marry her?"

This isn't exactly the way I planned this, but I should've expected as much. "I do, at some point. I'd like to marry her and become a family."

She reaches out, taking my hand. "I'm in no rush, Lach. We're a family without a ring."

Her father coughs.

"Like I said, my intentions are clear."

The Admiral gets to his feet, and the two of us do as well.

"Daddy, I don't want to fight with you or anything like that. Lachlan and I wanted to be honest with you because we respect you."

He lets out a heavy sigh. "I appreciate that. It's not how I would've liked things to go, but I realize that my wants aren't what matter here."

Okay, I didn't think that was going to be what he said.

He comes around the desk and extends his hand. "Thank you for being honest."

I shake his hand. "Of course."

"She's a lot of work."

"I know."

"She's a lot like her mother, which means you're going to need a lot of patience and tolerance."

"Tolerance?" Ainsley cuts in.

"I'm aware. She's very opinionated as well," I inform him.

"She gets that from me." He chuckles. "I want to warn you that she's also very expensive."

She scoffs. "Please. I'm so low maintenance."

Her father grins at her. "You forget I have been the one who paid your bills for years. There's nothing low maintenance about you."

"I've been paying my own way for the last how many years?" she reminds him.

"She's learning because those funds were cut off. A word of advice—always tell her you're broke. It helps."

I laugh. "Thanks, sir." I reach into my pocket and grab my challenge coin. Ainsley suggested I give it to him, since he appreciates it so much. I extend my palm. "I'd like to give you this. While you're giving me something much more valuable, this coin was made after I saved that girl and Ainsley came back into my life. It's important to me and holds a lot of meaning."

He takes it and looks it over. The coin is two-sided and acts as a bottle opener. On the one side it looks like a Frisbee and says "Disc Jocks," since that's what ultimately brought Ainsley to me. The other side is the fire chief part. It has EFFD for Ember Falls Fire Department and the axes.

He reaches across his desk. "While you may have one of the most valuable things I own, here." The Admiral gives me his coin. "Keep both of them safe, Lachlan."

"I will."

The Admiral walks back behind his desk.

Ainsley comes beside me, wrapping her hands around my arm. "Look at that, he didn't kill you."

Then he laughs. "I will if he breaks your heart."

And I don't doubt that for a single second.

epilogue
Ainsley

~Five Months Later~

"I really have no desire to learn Frisbee, you know this?" I say to Lachlan out at the field.

"I do, but your brother is over there and waiting for the Frisbee. You need to throw it to him."

Caspian came up for the weekend, which has been an interesting change of dynamics. The first time Lachlan kissed me in front of him, my brother gagged. The second time he made some noise that caused us both to look over to make sure he was all right. Now he just grumbles.

My father actually handled things like a champ, where my brother is being stupid.

"Can I hit him in the head with it? That sounds like more fun."

He shakes his head. "Flick it."

"I'm going to flick you," I grumble.

This is one sport that, no matter how much he loves it and has been trying to teach me, I just . . . don't get it.

Sure, the rules are simple, and I did a whole freaking article about it, but I have zero physical ability, nor the desire.

One would think that throwing, flicking, whatever-ing a Frisbee would be easy. I can attest—it is not.

I'm terrible.

"Stand like I showed you," Lachlan encourages.

"Stand like I showed you," I mimic like a child, but I do it.

He snorts. "Okay, now when you let it go, flick your wrist."

I do this every time, and do you know what happens? It hits the ground.

I let my arm fall and look at him. "Lachlan, you know I suck at this."

"I do."

"Gee, thanks."

He grins. "Just try, baby, I swear you'll get it. Just practice. Rose was able to get it down."

Yeah, that makes me feel better. Rose has some of her father's athletic abilities, but I do not. I'm the worst and I don't care. I just want to sit on the sidelines, cheer him and his friends on, and drink wine with Hazel and Penelope.

That's become our new favorite thing. We drink, laugh, and make fun of them.

"If I do this and make a fool of myself, can I go back to my friends?"

He looks over at the group of them on the sidelines. "Yes."

"Deal."

I take the stupid Frisbee from him, stand like he tells me, and what happens? The damn thing goes two feet and hits the ground.

"Ainsley," he moans, running his hand over his face.

"I did what you asked, babe. It's broken."

"Seriously, Ainsley!" Caspian yells from the other side of the field.

I flip him off. "See, I'm good at flipping, just not flicking your stupid Frisbee."

He laughs and then sends it across the field to Caspian. "Cas, check that out and make sure it's not defective."

I roll my eyes. "Clearly it's not. Now, I love you. I'm going back to my friends."

"Wait." He grabs my arm before I can get far. "Just give me one minute. Please?"

When he looks at me like that, it's hard to deny him anything. Which is why I think he uses it so much.

I stop and look at him with what I'm sure is a very petulant, very not-excited kind of look. "Why are you so adamant about this?"

"I thought maybe we could bring the girls on the team."

I laugh at that. "I'm not enrolling in college again."

"We're looking for a new league."

"Oh, I guess playing against the college kids is too easy?"

Lachlan shrugs. "Pretty much."

"So older people are going to be a challenge?"

"More like, I'm so busy with work and my pain-in-the-ass girl-friend that traveling to Frisbee tournaments in other states isn't working so well."

At that I feel a little bit of triumph. At least I'm able to do some good in regard to this league.

"I'm very sorry I put a kink in your plans of total Frisbee domination."

"You're forgiven—after you do this."

Seriously, he calls me a pain in his ass. "You promised I could go back."

"And you will."

"Lach!" Caspian calls, and the stupid thing comes back, but lands like halfway to where it should.

"See, maybe it's a MacKinley thing."

He smiles at me. "Stay put."

Lachlan jogs over to the disc and grabs it. "You know what, you might be right."

I like the sound of that. "I usually am, but what about this time?"

"There's something wrong with this Frisbee."

I look at it, not that I would have a single clue what the hell would be wrong with it since I don't know jack shit about sports.

"What's wrong with it?" I ask.

"Rose! Can you come bring me a new one?"

"You have more of them?" I whine.

Rose comes running out before I can tell her not to bother, and he hands me the new one. "See that?" he asks, flipping it over. "It's smooth and the air can move through it. There's something on this one."

Because I'm always one to want to look into things, even things I don't understand, I take the other one.

"There's tape on it," I say, confused. I don't remember seeing that when I "threw" it to my brother.

Lachlan tries to peel the tape off, but stops. "I can't get it, can you?"

I shake my head, exasperated by this entire thing, and pull it back with no issues. When I do, I see that stuck to the tape is a ring.

A very beautiful diamond ring.

My eyes dart up to where Lachlan is sinking to his knee. "Ainsley MacKinley, I have spent a long time dreaming of this moment. I've rehearsed, thought of the perfect thing to say—"

"Yes!" I yell.

"I didn't ask you yet."

I cover my mouth with my hand as the tears start to pool.

He grins. "I love you. My love for you is more than I knew love could be. Each day I thank God that I fell in love with the girl next door. Your smile soothes my bad days. Your love healed my broken parts. You make me a better man, and I want to spend the rest of my life with you. Will you marry me?"

I drop to my knees in front of him, tears now falling without a chance of stopping. "Yes, yes, yes, you wonderful man. Yes."

He cups my face and kisses me softly as cheers and clapping erupt behind us.

Lachlan breaks the kiss and slips the ring onto my shaking finger. "I love you."

"I love you."

"I love you too!" Rose yells, and we both laugh, pulling her into a huge hug.

This is family. This is love and life and everything that I've dreamed of.

I stand, and my brother is next to congratulate us, then our friends, and both my father and Lachlan's step to us.

I'm surrounded by everyone I love. I know that our lives have only begun, and I can't wait for the rest.

Next is Miles & Penelope!
Single Mom just moved to town and the hilarious school principal!
This one is going to steal your heart!

Preorder:
Here and Now
A Single Mom, Woman on the run, Small Town, Golden
Retriever x Black Cat romance!

I wasn't ready to let Lachlan & Ainsley go just yet. Swipe to the next page for access to an EXCLUSIVE Bonus Scene!

Have you met all the Whitlock Family?
Read them free in Kindle Unlimited!
Forbidden Hearts (Age Gap/Single Dad)
Broken Dreams (Fake Dating/Single Parents)
Tempting Promises (Enemies to Lovers/Forced Proximity)
Forgotten Desires (Billionaire/Single Dad)

Dear Reader,

I hope you enjoyed All Too Well! I had a hard time saying goodbye to Lachlan & Ainsley. I wanted to give just a little more of a glimpse into their lives, so ... I wrote a super fun scene.

Since giving you a link would be a pain in the ... you know what ... I have an easy QR code you can scan, sign up, and you'll get and email giving you access! Or you can always type in the URL!

https://geni.us/ATW_Signup

If you'd like to just keep up with my sales and new releases, you can follow me on BookBub!
BookBub: https://www.bookbub.com/authors/corinne-michaels

Join my Facebook group!
https://www.facebook.com/groups/corinnemichaelsbooks

books by corinne michaels

Want a downloadable reading order?

https://geni.us/CM_ReadingGuide

The Salvation Series

Beloved

Beholden

Consolation

Conviction

Defenseless

Evermore: A 1001 Dark Night Novella

Indefinite

Infinite

The Hennington Brothers

Say You'll Stay

Say You Want Me

Say I'm Yours

Say You Won't Let Go: A Return to Me/Masters and Mercenaries
Novella

Second Time Around Series

We Own Tonight

One Last Time

Not Until You

If I Only Knew

The Arrowood Brothers

Come Back for Me

Fight for Me

The One for Me

Stay for Me

Destined for Me: An Arrowood/Hennington Brothers Crossover
Novella

Willow Creek Valley Series

Return to Us

Could Have Been Us

A Moment for Us

A Chance for Us

Rose Canyon Series

Help Me Remember

Give Me Love

Keep This Promise

Whitlock Family Series

Forbidden Hearts

Broken Dreams

Tempting Promises

Forgotten Desires

Ember Falls Series

(Coming 2024-2025)

All Too Well

Here and Now

Against All Odds

Come What May

Co-Written with Melanie Harlow

Hold You Close

Imperfect Match

Standalone Novels

You Loved Me Once

acknowledgments

My husband and children. I love you all so much. Your love and support is why I get to even have an acknowledgment section.

My assistant, Christy Peckham, you always have my back and I can't imagine working with anyone else. I love your face.

Melanie Harlow, you have no idea how much I cherish our friendship. You are truly one of my best friends in the world and I don't know what I would do without you.

My publicist, Nina Grinstead, you're stuck with me forever at this point. You are more than a publicist, you're a friend, a cheerleader, a shoulder to lean on, and so much more.

The entire team at Valentine PR who support me, rally behind me, and keep me smiling.

James, my editor for taking such great care with my story. My cover designer who deals with my craziness, Sommer Stein. My proofreaders: Julia, and Michele.

Every influencer who picked this book up, made a post, video, phoned a friend ... whatever it was. Thank you for making the book world a better place.

acknowledgments

My husband and children, I love you all so much. Your love and support is why I get to even have an acknowledgment section.

My mentor, Christy Fletcham, you always have my back and I can't imagine working with anyone else. I love you too.

Melanie Fletcher, you have no idea how much... of a friendship, but are truly one of my best... life, and I don't know what I would do without you.

My publicist, Nina Grunstad, you're stuck with me forever at this point. You are more than a publicist, you're a friend, a cheerleader, a shoulder to lean on, and so much more.

The entire team at Whatever PR who support me, who... behind me, and keep me smiling.

Julie, the art and design... thank you will never. My court designer who deals with my craziness, Sonja... Steen, my proofreaders, Julie, and Michele.

Every influence who picked this book up, made a post, blog, phoned a friend... whatever it was, I thank you for making the book world a better place.

about the author

Corinne Michaels is a *New York Times, USA Today, and Wall Street Journal* bestselling author of romance novels. Her stories are chock full of emotion, humor, and unrelenting love, and she enjoys putting her characters through intense heartbreak before finding a way to heal them through their struggles.

Corinne is a former Navy wife and happily married to the man of her dreams. She began her writing career after spending months away from her husband while he was deployed—reading and writing were her escape from the loneliness. Corinne now lives in Virginia with her husband and is the emotional, witty, sarcastic, and fun-loving mom of two beautiful children.